Copyright © 2025 Jason Busboom
Published by Shrewsbury House

All rights reserved. This book or parts thereof may not be reproduced in any form, stored in any retrieval system, or transmitted in any form by any means—electronic, mechanical, photocopy, recording, or otherwise—without prior written permission of the publisher, except as provided by United States of America copyright law. For information regarding permission requests, write to *www.shrewsbury.house*.

ISBNs    eBook: 979-8-9929275-0-4
             Paperback: 979-8-9929275-1-1
             Hardcover: 979-8-9929275-2-8
             Library of Congress Control Number: 2025905462

First Edition
Book production and publishing by Brands Through Books
*brandsthroughbooks.com*

By reading this document, the reader agrees that under no circumstances is the author or the publisher responsible for any losses, direct or indirect, which are incurred as a result of the use of information contained within this document, including, but not limited to, errors, omissions, or inaccuracies.

LEGAL NOTICE:
This book is copyright-protected. Please note, the information contained within this document is for educational and personal use only. You cannot amend, distribute, sell, use, quote, or paraphrase any part of the content within this book without the consent of the author or publisher.

*www.jasonbusboom.com*

# SOWING DISCORD

AN **ERIC BUCHANAN** ESPIONAGE THRILLER

## JASON BUSBOOM

Shrewsbury
House

*To my bride, Christine.*

*I had so much fun creating this book*

*with you. Here's to many more!*

# CONTENTS

| | | |
|---|---|---:|
| Chapter 1. | Gray Zone Invasion | 1 |
| Chapter 2. | Lab Rats Feeding the World | 17 |
| Chapter 3. | Enemy of My Enemy | 27 |
| Chapter 4. | Small Town Living | 39 |
| Chapter 5. | Bellying Up | 51 |
| Chapter 6. | Playing the Long Game | 59 |
| Chapter 7. | Friday Night Lights | 71 |
| Chapter 8. | Duty to Party | 91 |
| Chapter 9. | Conspiracy or Reality | 105 |
| Chapter 10. | You've Been Warned | 123 |
| Chapter 11. | Duty to God | 133 |
| Chapter 12. | Labor Day on the Farm | 145 |
| Chapter 13. | Scorched Earth | 157 |
| Chapter 14. | A Woman's Intuition | 167 |
| Chapter 15. | Friend or Foe | 177 |
| Chapter 16. | The Red Line | 183 |
| Chapter 17. | No Help | 193 |
| Chapter 18. | Hail to the Chief! | 203 |
| Chapter 19. | Hide the Evidence | 213 |
| Chapter 20. | Duty to Country | 219 |
| Chapter 21. | Ignorance is Bliss | 229 |
| Chapter 22. | More Discord | 239 |
| Chapter 23. | Duty to Family | 247 |

| | |
|---|---:|
| Acknowledgments | 255 |
| About the Author | 257 |

**PRIVACY STATEMENT**

To respect the privacy of those family and friends who prefer not to be recognized, I have altered various names and personal details, but none of the details are really that accurate to anyone specifically anyway since this is a fictional book. But those included in this book are very important people to me, my family, and our lovely small town. You know who you are.

**NOTE TO READERS**

This book is sold with the understanding that neither the author nor the publisher is engaged in providing life lessons that may or may not be discussed. The reader should consult a competent person before adopting any of the suggestions in this book or drawing inferences from it.

No warranty is made with respect to the accuracy or completeness of the information or references contained herein, and both the author and the publisher specifically disclaim any responsibility for any liability, loss, or risk, personal or otherwise, that is incurred as a consequence, directly or indirectly, of the use and application of any of the contents of this book.

# CHAPTER 1
# GRAY ZONE INVASION

"Invading the United States should really be a lot more difficult," Chinese Communist Party (CCP) Director David Lee jokes in Mandarin to his three long-term Ministry of State Security (MSS) spies as they duck the razor wire separating Mexico and the California desert. Jacumba Hot Springs, California, is especially hot today for the uninvited guests returning to America.

David discreetly removes an envelope with one thousand dollars in cash from his back pocket and hands it to the border patrol agent, then mockingly says, "Thanks for your help as always." David is quickly reminded by the stench of the immigrant tent city, barely one hundred yards away, that most of these people don't fly a private jet into Tijuana, Mexico, only an hour away.

"Over there, sir," the pudgy agent lazily gestures to an aged gray minivan about two hundred yards away, past the line of the hundreds of migrants who also crossed into the US illegally that early spring morning.

David, always focused, walks ahead of his leadership team. He studies the minivan for dangers, then quickly glances back, summoning Ziqi, or "Z," his most trusted advisor and head of counterintelligence. Z, also keeping an eye out for potential threats, quickens his pace so he'll be within David's earshot should danger present itself.

David murmurs to Z, "It's amazing; even after *60 Minutes* did a special on this exact crossing location, the Americans still allow us to easily cross this border. Can you drive the first leg and get us into Texas? Someone else can drive the rest of the way to Illinois."

Z hustles to grab the keys inside the gas cap, left by the Mexican cartel. "I slept great on the flight into Tijuana, so no problem, boss. It would be nice to fly our jet directly into Illinois next time, but I understand we can't risk our identities. I'm good though."

Z unlocks the doors and throws the group's minimal luggage into the back of the minivan. The overwhelming smell of garbage and human waste causes Z to pull his shirt over his mouth and nose. "Man, that smell is awful. Let's get rolling, team."

Z, muscular yet agile from his time in the People's Liberation Army (PLA), effortlessly slips into the driver's seat and buckles his seat belt. He motions to his lanky and always well-dressed ex-girlfriend, Qiyun Yi, or Chinaloa as she is called. She is also head of infrastructure obstruction, and her pampered qualities don't reflect her sophisticated capabilities to be ruthless on behalf of the CCP.

"Chinaloa, you can take the front seat," Z says as he winks and gently pats the passenger seat next to him. "Then Tom can sit in the back with David and eat his Doritos. Oh, nice! The cartel guys even left waters in here for us. Such good guys," Z comments as he motions for Tom Liu, the portly head of espionage, to sit in the back seat with David.

"We're never dating again, Z, so just focus on driving this hideous minivan," Chinaloa quips as she slides into the passenger seat, carefully placing her designer handbag next to her feet. "I'm not doing jail time for you again."

"It was one time, and it was only for a year!" Z asserts as he turns the key to start the nondescript minivan. "And now we're making so much money you can keep buying your fancy handbags, and I can throw a Liberty Walk body kit on my Nissan GT-R." Z laughs a bit, trying to make Chinaloa mad.

"Just drive, Z. You can daydream about your tricked-out Supra when I'm napping," Chinaloa responds, quickly deflating Z. Then she turns to the left back seat. "David," she sweetly panders with a forced smile, "San Diego is just an hour west of here. Maybe we could make a quick detour before we are stuck in the Illinois cornfields?"

"Sorry, Chinaloa," David responds as he dusts off his tan, form-fitting chinos that highlight his athletic frame. "We're here on very real business. Maybe next time."

Z makes sure his hair is pulled back tight into a man bun and his beard is tidy, then he starts to drive down the winding, bumpy road past the border patrol buses loading the other illegal immigrants. He peers at David sitting behind him through the rearview mirror and sees the faded scar on his cheek, earned from a knife fight almost two decades ago. That scar motivated David to master martial arts to protect himself and his younger brothers while growing up in the rough hutong alleys of Beijing.

"Boss," Z says to David, "Let's get back to a little business before you sleep." Then he jokes, "I'm considering getting a new Ferrari, and want to build it out in my head while you all pass out on me during the car ride. Can you give me a quick update on our revenue projections for the year?"

David unclicks his seat belt and shifts forward, popping his head in between the two front seats and meeting Z's eyes in the rearview mirror. David emphasizes, "This past quarter, we cleared almost one hundred million dollars in revenue. I'm meeting with Diego in Illinois next week to discuss increasing to two hundred million per *month* by the beginning of next year."

Z whistles. "Wow! Chinaloa, we were clearing five million dollars a month just a few years ago and thought we were on top of the world."

David shakes his head as Chinaloa bristles in her seat, then he redirects. "Well, we learned a lot from your casino operation in Guatemala and how the DEA infiltrated us. Those were great lessons that have improved our processes significantly. Our black-market technology is much more advanced these days, including foreign exchange access. Also, the CCP is heavily supporting us behind the scenes since President Xi's direct associates and family are cut in on the business."

Tom finally works to get his seat belt comfortable under his pot belly and wrinkled button-down dress shirt. He asks sarcastically with a gloating smile, "How is that even possible? I didn't know we were doing that well."

Chinaloa spins around to look at Tom's ornery smile.

David knows Tom's love of American culture helped foster his extensive political relationships in Chicago. He smirks at his dear middle-aged friend. "He's joking, Chinaloa. Tom was instrumental in creating the money laundering program in China and here in the States. We all know his deep political connections and experience in espionage always play an important role. Granted, he has plenty of blackmail material from running up a huge bar tab to help politicians make terrible choices at 2 a.m. The reality is that we are much more involved in drug trafficking with the cartels now and just getting off the ground. Tom, can you pay attention to this explanation again?" David teases.

Tom opens a bag of Doritos and then confidently removes a bottle of water from the cup holder and swaps it for a Mountain Dew. "No problem, boss. Always here to serve. You have my undivided attention."

"I can't believe you took food off the plane, Tom," David says, patting his friend's belly. Then he faces front again, shifting forward further in his seat so that Z and Chinaloa can hear him over the blowing air conditioning. "Okay, we've made some great strides recently. Here's the current status of the program."

Z pumps his fist and says with excitement, "Excellent, boss, I've been waiting patiently for an update. We need a faster jet. That flight still takes too long for me. What's the latest?"

David ignores Z and continues, "When I was in Beijing, General Houbin and I set up black-market digital exchanges on our banking network. Now we can charge the Sinaloa Cartel a 1 percent laundering fee versus the Colombians charging them 15 percent, but they need to trust the program. We've proved the process works inside China, so Sinaloa is expected to funnel more business to us. That's what I'll discuss with Diego next week, but El Chapo's kids, "Los Chapitos," have already approved the program. Now we just need to sell it to their captains. We need to make sure we have enough runners for the cash. You're on top of that, Tom?"

"We have a network of a couple hundred drivers stationed in restaurants in Chicago and Central Illinois, mainly Champaign-Urbana, who are ready to drive cross-country within an hour," Tom says proudly. "Our directors in Chicago's Chinatown are ready to scale even more, if need be, but funding that manpower washing dishes in empty restaurants isn't cheap."

David puts his scarred hand on Tom's shoulder as the big man washes another Dorito down with his Mountain Dew. "Very good, Tom. Keep them all very low profile so we don't garner any more attention than is necessary. The revenue to support those extended operations is coming soon." David jabs Tom in the arm to make the point. "This is very unlike your social media tour when you were gaining access to American politicians."

"I know you're a black belt sir, but that really does hurt when you hit me like that." Tom rubs his arm. "And it was all part of the plan, David. Game knows game." Tom cleans his orange-stained hands on his baggy blue jeans. "I've adjusted now and am much lower profile."

"Ok, that's our money laundering program, everyone." David leans forward and taps Z on the shoulder. "Make sense?"

"I still don't get it," Z says rather apathetically as he drives along Interstate 8 on their way east toward Phoenix. "I do hate this road.

There's literally nothing out here."

"What's the issue now, Z?" David sits up further knowing that Z is going to push for a grander plan.

"We have tens of millions in profits each month, and that is going to grow, right, boss?" Z quickly turns to look at David in the back seat.

"Watch the road!" Chinaloa points ahead and rolls her eyes.

"Correct, Z. We expect about twenty million dollars in profits a month in the near future." David is getting agitated but wants to let Z have his say, for now, so he has more buy-in down the road.

"And currently, we have the capability to do real damage to the US infrastructure," Z says forcefully. "The Volt Typhoon malware op was such a tremendous success, and we have access to so much of the US infrastructure. We're able to knock out AT&T's network at will, as we demonstrated with Salt Typhoon. Why don't we shut down a few water treatment plants, take out the AT&T network, and let the Americans freak out? They'll be at each other's throats within twenty-four hours."

"All true, Z, but we have talked about this too much already. I'll humor you since it's a long car ride," David says calmly, patting Z on the shoulder. "We will stay inside our gray zone war for now and continue to cause smaller issues and test our other projects as directed by Beijing." David knows Chinaloa and Tom are also very curious about slow-playing these programs. "Think about it this way . . . you want someone dead, and you have the ability to create cancer inside their body."

"Okay, but I'm not sure how that relates to our programs at all," says Chinaloa as she looks out her window at a twelve-foot, mangled cactus along the side of the road. "I still can't believe how big those cactuses get," she says absently.

"They get enormous, Chinaloa. It's rather weird to me as well. But, of course, it relates," says David, shaking his head at Chinaloa's infatuation with the cactus. "'Cancers,'" David says with air quotes, "are created all the time, but let's imagine a longer time frame. Asians get diabetes from eating too much rice over the course of years, right? Chinese people get lung cancer from smoking cigarettes their whole lives, too, yes? They don't just pop up one day with cancer; it's been developing over years or probably decades."

"I guess that's all true," says Chinaloa as she turns up the AC to blow on her long neck. "It's so hot down here. Drive faster, Z."

"Drive only the speed limit, Z, and stay with me, Chinaloa." David reins in Chinaloa's focus. "Okay, so now consider our projects in the same light."

David finds he's getting more animated from his excitement about the significance of their current projects. "We are sowing discord, doubt, and anxiety directly into the American fabric of trust, their freedom of movement, and the integrity of their basic infrastructure: clean water, reliable power, and soon, their food supply. If Americans don't trust these things, they can't function at a higher level to stop *our* long-term goals."

"But if we have the ability to do most of those things right now, then why don't we do them?" Tom asks as he munches on another Dorito, followed by another sip of his Mountain Dew, and adjusts a vent to blow on his chubby face.

David strokes his jet-black hair in frustration from his team not fully understanding the plan but takes a deep breath and considers a new analogy. "Let's think again about the long-term causes of cancer—diet, smoking, alcohol, whatever—but also the treatments of cancer. If someone has cancer, and it is found early—stage 1— there is about a 95 percent chance of survival if the cancer is cured. Sound about right, Chinaloa?"

Chinaloa spins around in the passenger seat, looking a bit more intrigued. "That's about right, David. Cancer is basically curable if caught early enough."

David points at Chinaloa. "Exactly. If caught early enough. That's my *entire* point. We, this group and the CCP, do not want to get 'caught early enough.'" David uses air quotes to stress the point. "We want to be caught when there's nothing left for the Americans to do but to suffer defeat . . . or death," David says a bit whimsically. "And then we will have our leverage."

"I'm starting to understand a bit more here, boss," says Z as he points out a fifteen-foot cactus to Chinaloa, noticeably flirting. "But keep going for me, please?"

"You bet, Z, but let's agree that going forward, you remember that you all work for me. I'm not going to explain myself again. I'll just tell you what to do," David says a bit forcefully, his jaw tense, reinforcing the message to the group.

"Understood." Z sheepishly looks back toward the road with renewed focus.

"Ok." David pounds his large fist into his hand for emphasis. "We are spreading cancer inside America. We are the ones who are creating and improving the cancer that will be the demise of America so the CCP will again dominate the world order." David's dark eyes widen. "This is certain, but we need to be patient, intelligent, and oftentimes, cruel to accomplish these goals. The end always justifies the means."

Chinaloa seems focused on David's words, maybe even enthusiastic, until Tom chomps on his chips. Then she says, "I'm sold on the long game, David, but I need a separate office from Tom's eating habits in Illinois."

"Very good, Chinaloa. You can have your own office." As a man in command of the details, David focuses and then says slowly, "And we will spread our cancers—our corn seed project, our water contamination project, and our nuclear power destruction project—in a controlled manner over years. Not months. Not days. And probably over decades. These cancers will be throughout America at stage 4, the last stage of cancer, where death is almost guaranteed. At that point, not before, we will move from our gray zone tactics into full-scale war."

Tom taps David's leg, signaling to him that he would like a shot at explaining. David gently nods to say "go ahead" to his old friend, and Tom continues. "But by that time, the Americans will be sidetracked looking at Taiwan or Africa or even Japan, as we will have completed building our expansive military through the Belt and Road Initiative. The reality is that the foundation for the destruction of America was laid years ago . . . we just need to execute the final steps. America will have stage 4 cancer and won't have the capability, through sheer weakness, to challenge us anywhere in the world. It's like a subtle Pearl Harbor," Tom articulates rather well.

David sees that Tom is feeling rather confident in his explanation, so he encourages him to proceed with a slight wave of his hand.

"And here is where Americans will also help us. I saw this consistently during those years inside US politics. American journalists always come to the rescue of people doing terrible things to their fellow Americans. It could be enemy countries, like China or Mexico. It could be their own politicians or city leaders, like our friends in Chicago whom we buy off. Those guys mostly hide in the shadows under generic titles but control way more than the American public understands. Regardless, the American media will still do a lot of heavy lifting for us by explaining away reality."

David sees Z looking quite confused and interjects. "Z, does this make any sense?"

Z responds, "Yeah, boss. We used to buy off journalists in Mexico, but there were some who just thought we were helping Mexico. Those reporters believed that painting the cartels in a positive light was good, that it allowed the people to believe in positive, even patriotic, stories and in the idea that the cartels were still helping the locals. Same thing here?"

Tom jumps back in, as Z is a bit off track. "Not really, Z. Many of these journalists have a genuine dislike, even hatred, for their own country's businesses and people who work hard. These media types believe hardworking people are *mooching* off the system and that is the true source of their success. We, the CCP, know those types of Americans are the exact people we need to be attacking, as they have the skill and drive to destroy our plans. Luckily for us, the American media won't report the truth, so those folks just go on their merry way as the water gets hotter and hotter until the proverbial frog is cooked."

David reinforces Tom's comments. "It's true, Z. These journalists are so important because they help us hide our plans in plain sight by labeling truth as conspiracy theories, Marxist, misogynist—all the names they love to say. They will surely do the same for our projects until it's too late. But we don't need to do anything special. The majority just do it on their own by trying to make successful people look greedy."

David smiles proudly at Tom's comprehension, then continues, "Very nice job, Tom! I'm impressed. But here's an example: when you get cancer for real, the media will blame the Mountain Dews you keep drinking and not *you* for drinking them." David laughs.

"But Z and Chinaloa." David faces forward again. "Once America discovers that we have control over their food, water, and power," he says, counting them off with three fingers, "they will have to assume we've infiltrated every location and even other sectors of industry. The Americans' trust in their infrastructure and institutions will be completely lost. They will become paranoid about all areas of their lives. Simply put, can they even trust the water they are drinking? Can they trust the food they are giving to their children? The reality is they cannot trust *any* of it. But we will not reveal that part of the plan for a very long time."

Chinaloa's body withers in her seat, as she is ready to complain again. "I get all of that, David, but why do we need to drive all the way to the University of Illinois Urbana-Champaign? This thirty-hour drive is brutal, and we're heading to those stupid cornfields? And what does Urbana-Champaign even mean?"

"I know it's been a few months since we've been here, and you weren't with us last time, Chinaloa, but, Tom, want to explain why we're doing our work in Central Illinois?" David grabs Tom's Mountain Dew, looks over the vibrant green labeling, then steals a drink. "Huh, that's not bad at all, Tom."

"Yes, sir." Tom leans forward so Chinaloa can hear him better. "Do you remember when I infiltrated that presidential political campaign and even got a picture with the president of the United States?"

"Yes, Tom. Who could forget both of you having your stomachs and chins take up most of the picture?" Chinaloa keeps staring ahead.

"Anyway," Tom says. He won't miss an opportunity to tell this story. "I was directed to infiltrate American politics, so I initially went to Washington, DC. There are hundreds of thousands of people in DC who will do almost anything for campaign contributions. They don't have any party affiliations, lack morals that govern decision-making regarding right or wrong, and have proven they don't care about who is going to give them money. They just need the money to increase their ability to broker power around town."

Chinaloa relents a bit. "Tom, it was impressive the way you pulled off getting into those political circles, I'll give you that. Well, before you got caught bribing DEA agents to give you fake passports, that is. But what does this have to do with going to the U of I?"

"Oddly it's very similar, Chinaloa," Tom says calmly. "The University of Illinois is desperate for more money to stay competitive with other high-level institutions. They have opened their arms to our Chinese students and do almost no due diligence. Plus, anyone who questions the students' motives or a proper US customs vetting process is quickly labeled racist, so we use that to overcome more serious issues. We have also refined the F-1 visa program over the years, so US Customs doesn't stop many, if any, of our agents as they head to school."

"Okay, I understand that's how they get into Illinois without being questioned." Chinaloa is still trying to figure out why they need to be stuck in cornfields. "But what's the real draw to Champaign-Urbana?"

Tom sees this isn't all about the programs but also Chinaloa's disdain for rural living. "You can still have access to the Magnificent Mile for your shopping, Chinaloa. Chicago is only two hours away. But here's why we're in Illinois: Illinois's engineering, business, and even ag departments' willingness to take so many of our students gives us incredible access to labs, technology, security networks, and even chemicals that we can use to create serious damage. And we steal that knowledge and bring it back to China, then repeat that process. At this point, we have hundreds of agents around town—students, professors, restaurant workers, business owners, and even high-level executives in larger corporations. David was instrumental in creating our and it worked very well. So, we're doing the same in Central Illinois." Tom nods in deference to David.

David taps Tom on the shoulder as he reenters the conversation. "Chinaloa, did you know that the University of Illinois Business and Engineering Colleges have taken out insurance policies with Lloyd's of London in case there are admission changes—like to the visa program—that would make their Chinese student population decrease and cause them to lose revenue? I had no clue that was even an option, but it really shows how dependent the university is on foreign tuition."

"Classic. What's the policy?" Chinaloa turns around, waiting for the answer. "Was this because the state of Illinois is broke and cut back on funding?"

David is now sitting back in his seat, knowing his crew is losing interest. "That's exactly why Illinois is taking on so many of our students. But sixty million dollars is the insurance plan. It grows every year and costs hundreds of thousands of dollars, about five hundred thousand for three years. Our Chinese students make up about 10 percent of the business college. It's even higher for the engineering schools, with most paying full tuition, or even a premium, to attend. We simply fund dozens of our agents' tuition from our money laundering operations."

Tom jumps back in. "That's true, guys. As we all know, there's a fifty-thousand-dollar limit on US dollars sent from mainland China. But there's no limit on tuition if we send the money directly to the universities from the Bank of China or use the money to buy a home with cash," Tom says a bit nefariously. "And there's a little extra incentive for our new collegiate agents to cooperate because we know exactly where their families live, and we track their movements back home. They will do almost anything for us. And because of all the Chinese students, there are plenty of Chinese restaurants acting as front companies to launder money. Their workers are great for running cash across the country or doing other small errands, like running drugs for the cartel when needed."

"And there are plenty of Sinaloa Cartel members just up Interstate 57 in Chicago and down in Memphis," Chinaloa confirms.

David agrees. "Yes, that's right, Chinaloa. And you know the DEA can find you in Memphis too. You still got a bad beat on getting busted in Memphis, but I'm glad your jail time wasn't too long. Lots of street cred on that one . . . I still don't know your real name."

"Very funny, David. I am still grateful for your help to get me out of jail early. There, I said it." Chinaloa seems done with the conversation and is visibly perspiring, drinking water, and adjusting the air conditioning. "I'm so freaking hot."

"Okay, Z, you're good to make it to Amarillo, then Tom can take the final leg to Champaign?" David confirms as he reclines his seat.

"I've got it all the way, boss, but one last thing: I need to get one of our lab analysts, Helen Chan, to be more aggressive with our corn seed projects for Elevation Seeds and Shafer Chemicals. We're meeting with the CEO of those companies, Thao Te, in the next few days and need to coordinate with her."

"What's the concern, Z?" Tom is very serious about having only great talent. "Should we recruit another agent? We need to fully trust our agents, or we're all in trouble."

"Not yet, Tom. She's extremely bright and has proven she's very good with the research she's provided back to Beijing." Z speeds by another car on the desolate interstate. "No real problems so far, but we need to be on high alert to stay concealed in that biochemistry lab. She still needs more focus to keep the seed program moving forward."

Chinaloa seems concerned. "Helen just seems young and inexperienced for this level of a project. I can chat with her when we arrive to judge her potential while giving suggestions."

David leans forward again. "Yes, Helen is only twenty-five years old, but remember, her Uncle Houbin has been teaching her how to be an American agent since she was a child. I've known her myself since she was five years old. She graduated top of her biochemistry class from university, too. And if we need to apply any more pressure, we know where to find her immediate family.

"This program has been running for almost six years now with loyal students and professors at the U of I," David reminds his team. "This is where we need to be overly cautious to not tip off the local farmers. We have been very secretive about this program with very little suspicion."

"So, what is Thao thinking?" Z accelerates.

David settles back a bit more and crosses his burly arms to take a nap. "Thao has been running the front company for the corn seed treatment for many years. She has developed reliable political connections in Springfield and Chicago, like Tom. As everyone in Illinois knows, most politicians have a price, and typically, it's not a very high one."

"Thao has done such a great job of creating connections through political donations and public events," Tom chimes in. "And no local farmers are questioning why yields with Elevation Seeds are higher than our competitors' yields. Higher yields equal happy farmers . . . who don't ask too many questions."

"Keep driving the speed limit, Z, and be careful; we don't need to get pulled over with our fake passports. We're on enough of the same page now, so let's get some sleep for a few hours." David closes his eyes and says with heavy sarcasm, "And I can't wait to deal with the cartel this week."

# CHAPTER 2

# LAB RATS FEEDING THE WORLD

ERIC Buchanan, the director of the biochemistry lab in the School of Molecular and Cellular Biology at the University of Illinois, proudly calls the meeting to order in his state-of-the-art formal conference room. "Good Monday morning, everyone. First, as we kick off the baseball season with spring training coming to an end, I'd like to highlight that my Cubs won the NL Central last year, and the Cardinals did not. That is all, and please discuss."

After being director for a couple of years now, Eric has a friendly but professional relationship with his lab technicians: Helen Chan, Chris Lee, and Steve Smith. Keeping the lab's environment energetic but focused and highly effective is a high priority for Eric. Having fun is required but so is having incredible attention to detail. The group is aware they are not saving babies by any stretch, but they are playing an important role in improving the food supply for the entire world. Eric's team has been so productive that they have received numerous unprecedented grants under his leadership. This includes international grants that allow for hiring very high-achieving analysts, like Helen Chan, who support him and his full-time techs.

Steve, who has been in the lab for around two years, says in his high-pitched voice that matches his small stature, "Come on, man, the Cards had a ton of injuries, and the Cubs will choke again immediately this year." Steve looks down the table at Eric standing at the head. "You need to get settled in for another 108 years before a World Series comes your way."

"Chris, *The*," Eric stresses and pauses for effect, "Ohio State University fell apart again against Michigan in the Big Ten basketball tourney." Eric, taking a mock golf swing, pokes fun at his other lab technician's love for all things Ohio State Buckeyes.

Chris Lee, a seven-year veteran of the lab and Buckeye undergraduate alum, sulks in his chair, contemplating his basketball team's showing that weekend. He grabs his coffee. "So disappointing. I really thought we had it this year. I do hate to root against the Illini, but there's no way I'm getting onto the Illini *football* bandwagon this fall. It's impressive how you think they aren't terrible, Eric. I get that you played—and I use that term lightly—for a few years, but the fact that you played at all is a true testament to how bad football is here. No offense though, boss."

"None taken, Chris. The only time I wasn't the tackling dummy in college was during my ROTC training when I could pick on much smaller dudes. The good news is now *you'll* get to clean up our lab tests this afternoon, and I'll probably send you into a grain bin to get more samples, but you'll need to wait until it's 160 degrees inside the bin." Eric finally lowers his athletic frame into the office chair, sits back, and rubs the back of his short auburn hair, reveling in Ohio State's failure, although it was against Michigan and, well, everyone hates Michigan. "And you can't take Steve along with you while he knocks back Miller Lites."

"Well then, what's the point?" Steve shoots back at Eric. "I can only look at crops with a roadie."

"Boys . . . maybe you can wrestle later to really prove your masculinity, but I have things to do today if we feel like working." Helen Chan, the newest research analyst from China, works to get the meeting back on track. "These corn seeds are going to grow up faster than you three. But I will say, it was nice to finally see the Illini make their free throws at the end of the game and not give it away like usual."

"Whoooooaaaa!" Steve and Chris are blown away by Helen's Illini basketball acumen.

"What just happened, Helen?! Look at you!" Steve shakes his balding head in disbelief at Helen's knowledge and willingness to mix it up with the guys. Some guys have a face for radio, but Steve is truly built for the lab.

"I pay a little attention to sports; it's not just guys, you know. Now, let's get back to work before we drop the ball again." Helen drops her pen onto the table, acting out dropping a basketball.

"I have no idea what's going on here," Chris awkwardly high-fives the petite Helen sitting next to him, "but it's awesome. Good for you, Helen!"

"Okay, let's get into it." Eric redirects the group to their laptops and the corn yield data projected on the room's drop-down screen.

Eric sees Chris is focused again and gestures for him to proceed. "You look ready to go, Chris. Please kick us off."

Chris eagerly jumps up and walks to the screen at his turn to geek out. He points to his first data chart. "You're going to love this, boss! As we know, corn is optimally harvested at around 15.5 percent moisture and eighty-six degrees Fahrenheit here in Central Illinois, then adjusted based on 50 to 80 percent relative humidity and temperature. Areas in more arid and hotter climates can get as low as 30 percent relative humidity, but the vegetative, V, and reproductive, R, stages will vary. We have our control cases in increments of 5 percent relative humidity, and, wait for it . . . our 30 percent relative humidity level sample just sprouted!"

"No way!" Eric gives Chris a big thumbs up.

"Yup, Steve has been running the backup lab tests for me as well." Chris clicks the controller to show another data slide with pictures of the sprouted plant. He turns to Steve for verification while beaming with pride.

"It's true, gang." Steve points to the screen. "In theory, once these hybrids are perfected this year, we will have commercially viable seeds that can produce cornfields for almost 95 percent of the world in their own backyard. We're still focused on Africa and South America, but the implications are global."

"That's incredible, guys!" Helen studies the humidity and yield data on the screen, furrows her eyebrows a bit, and asks, "Any idea if that will grow in most of China?"

Chris looks at Helen with confusion. "Well, um, yeah, Helen. It would work almost everywhere in China except for the very high altitudes and extreme cold environments. Are you considering going back to China to farm?"

"No . . . I was just curious because it helps me to understand the applications as it continues to develop was all." Helen jots down some notes in her ever-present notebook.

"Helen, what do you have going on?" Eric continues to move the meeting forward with more purpose now. "You can pop your data onto the screen now."

"Well, Eric, as you know, our current seed treatment results are quite incredible regarding pantaphos and nematodes." Helen stands up and gently straightens out her chic blue dress, then she walks to the front of the room.

"Agreed, Helen, but can you spell that out a bit for the fellas before we lose them?" Eric points to Steve and Chris, who are both rubbing their temples and looking rather confused.

"We're solving world hunger over here, Helen, so feel free to use bullet points with us," jokes Steve. "I'm joking, Helen. I'm following. This is very interesting."

"Sure." Helen shares her computer screen to the overhead screen. "The simple explanation is that we have been working with Shafer Chemicals to create a seed treatment that removes pantaphos from adult corn and another application that removes nematodes."

Chris and Steve look at each other and say, "But . . . we're solving global hunger." They laugh.

"You're doing great too . . . I'll continue." Helen turns her small frame back to the screen, detailing her research on the microbe pantaphos, which causes rot in onions and corn. "We are very close to controlling and removing pantaphos to eliminate premature rotting inside the corn husk. It would add an average of ten to twelve bushels per acre on most normal harvests. It can also stop a complete loss if the corn rot becomes aggressive."

Eric sips his coffee, rubs his blue eyes to focus on the data, and pushes back his thick hair. "Seriously good stuff, Helen! I know the farmers will love an extra ten to twelve bushels. Assuming, say, five dollars per bushel, that's fifty thousand dollars in extra revenue per one thousand acres. That will buy some new combine tires. And what about the nematodes?"

"I'm getting there." Helen acknowledges Steve, engaged in her report. "As we know, nematodes are microscopic worms. Roundworm is another name for it. They are like the ghosts of corn and very hard to identify. You need advanced technology, like we have here," Helen points to a new confocal microscope just outside the conference room, "to even see them. However, they're very costly to farmers, as these worms reduce yields by up to ten bushels, which is equivalent to almost fifty dollars per acre in lost revenue."

Eric points to the half dozen examination tools just outside the conference room. "Very good, Helen. And you're about the only one who knows how to use that testing equipment out there. You'll have to show these guys how to do that at some point." Eric stands up and lightly pushes Steve's phone down onto the table so he'll pay attention.

Steve protests, "I'm taking notes, Eric. And I know how to work that thing."

Eric pats Steve on the back. "Okay, gang, let's get back to our stations. It's already March, and we need to make sure we have all of our dirt samples from the fields, tests are run, and we are prepared for detailed reporting for this fall's harvest."

Chris and Steve head off to the technician workspaces of this rather new and very advanced, especially for a university, lab. Each analyst has their own station with equipment funded by Jimmy John's, no less. "Who knew that a sandwich company would care so much about biochemistry, but I guess it makes sense given they need the best crops in the world to make their delicious number 4, Turkey Tom," Eric says. He then looks at Helen as she sits down again, curious as to why she's not heading to her station.

Eric consciously slides himself back into his chair, sensing there is something Helen needs to discuss. But first, he tries to make small talk. "I'm also glad that we still get extra funds to run our labs from CIEF, or the Chinese International Education Foundation . . . you know, the old Chinese Ministry of Education. If it weren't for those programs, you probably wouldn't be allowed here to help us. You truly are a huge asset to our team with your technical skills. Honestly, some of these international analysts seem a bit goofy to me; I'm glad you're so normal and fit right in with us," Eric says with a gentle smile.

Helen fidgets with her jet-black ponytail. "Yeah, that is true. CIEF was called the Confucius Institute a few years ago but got some negative press from Congress and changed its name. They still sponsored my studies and do magnificent work. CIEF provides students like me with incredible access to some of the most advanced lab technologies in the world. I'm so grateful for their support, but, like you said, I also do see some of the lab techs can't socialize because they are so focused on their work."

Helen begins to pack up her computer and notebook, then pauses. She isn't quite done with what is on her mind.

Helen takes a deep breath and sincerely says, "Eric, I do just want to say thank you again for how much autonomy you've given me to work and learn. When I was in Nanchang, my lab partners, and even my professors, were super controlling, especially to the women. I know I've only been here for about a year, but I am grateful for how much you and the team have embraced me. I'll keep working day and night this summer so these projects are successful in the fall. I just want you to know that."

Eric softens his clean-shaven face and says kindly, "My pleasure, Helen. Is everything okay? You are doing a great job, so please tell me if you need anything. I know from your lab access swipes that you are working a ton. Eighty hours a week is no joke. Please be sure to take a break from time to time. Being a local guy to Central Illinois and knowing this area like the back of my hand, I'm sure I overlook some of your struggles coming from China. Remind me, though, you're from outside Hong Kong?"

Helen looks out to the main lab area where Chris is focused on his work and Steve is looking at her. Chris walks to the locked refrigerator that holds the current inventory of enzymes, living microbes, and special testing mediums that he uses almost daily. The immaculate lab is about three thousand square feet and takes up the entire third floor of the rectangular building.

"That's right. I am from just outside of Hong Kong, but I attended Illinois's sister school, Jiangxi Normal University, in Nanchang, China. Then I moved here." Helen confirms. "Many of my fellow Chinese friends come from Shanghai Jiao Tong University in Shanghai, China, as well. That university has a larger relationship with the University of Michigan."

"More Michigan? Boo. Okay, I did remember it correctly." Eric feels some pride in his listening skills but had never heard of the other university. "And yes, that is quite a bit different than my little village of Royal, Illinois, and our three hundred people in the middle of cornfields twenty miles from here."

"True, but much less than you would think." Helen appears calmer. "Other than you being a giant over there in my hometown, many of the Chinese students who come to Illinois are really drawn here because they do not like the big cities. You're not a huge fan of Chicago, right?"

Eric sees from Helen's focused gaze that she is very curious about his answers. "Yeah, that's probably true. I love going to Cubbies games at Wrigley but usually take the Amtrak train so I can get up there and back home in one day. I used to love spending time up there in Wrigleyville, but it's just not that safe anymore to me. I don't go to the South Side of Chicago, and not just because the White Sox are terrible."

"I can see that. I don't know if I've mentioned this before, but I have gone to the South Side of Chicago a few times to see Chinatown. It has great food but gets a little dodgy there too. And there are plenty of Chinese restaurants here with great food and other students who help me when I feel homesick."

"What's your favorite restaurant here? Let's check it out," Eric says enthusiastically.

"I would say Shiquan Wonton, but there are plenty of good ones on Green Street," Helen quickly responds.

"Okay, I'll check it out. But again, I'm really glad you've gotten settled in over this past year and are doing such great work. Now get back to it and go be awesome!" Eric flashes his big smile and holds the door for Helen.

"Will do, boss. You enjoy your time in your 'bougie' office. I can't wait to have a door." Helen strolls through the doorway. Steve, who has been milling around outside, is seemingly waiting for Helen to leave Eric's office.

"Well, keep knocking it out of the park and you'll get the same clearance I have in no time. Then, you too can have a door that locks so you can nap in peace," Eric jokes as he heads to his glass-walled office. In the distance, he can hear Steve ask Helen, "Do you mind if we chat real quick about some of your lab work? It seems like I'm getting weird results."

Eric sits down at his desk and reads an updated report on cancer research from the Cancer Technology and Data Science program. The lab shares work under the same interdisciplinary grant as Eric's lab in order to find new cancer treatments. *I can't wait to let our team know their research is helping to cure cancer*, he thinks to himself. Eric pulls up his email and types:

*Dear Professor Wickard:*

*We have new lab results from our corn seed analyses that may benefit your Mustargen and pantaphos program for the treatment of various brain cancers. In addition to Mustargen's proven benefit for chemotherapy, the pantaphos chemical has proven to be significantly toxic to the glioblastoma (GBM) cells of brain cancer, per your most recent report. Our lab analysts have isolated several traits that may benefit GBM therapy.*

*At your convenience, I would like to share some recent results with you.*

*Sincerely,*
*Eric Buchanan*
*Director – Biochemistry Lab*
*Professor of Biochemistry*
*School of Molecular and Cellular Biology*
*College of Liberal Arts and Sciences*
*University of Illinois Urbana-Champaign*

## CHAPTER 3
# ENEMY OF MY ENEMY

Z DRIVES David onto the dilapidated and decommissioned Chanute Air Force Base in Rantoul, IL, just fifteen miles north of Champaign. "You know, Z, I was in Peru last year for a forward operating base that we're building there. It's just remarkable how we're building our military and America is shrinking theirs."

David has met Sinaloa Cartel's Midwest captain and relative equal in these drug trafficking dealings, Diego Pineda-Sanchez, at Chanute many times in the past. The aging base provides increased safety for these meetings due to its high visibility, allowing them to see danger coming (e.g., police, DEA, FBI, competing cartels, etc.), isolation from the public, and easy access to Interstate 57, which connects Chicago and Champaign.

Z is driving the blue Honda Accord too fast, as usual, along a makeshift road that used to be a busy runway for C-130s. The bright afternoon sun highlights the weeds growing in the cracks of the concrete.

"That's been my point, boss. I've studied a lot of Chinese history and some limited world history. I've never heard of a country being at war with another country when the other country doesn't know it. Granted, we dress to fit in, but we just move freely around here with no issues."

David scans the massive empty buildings as Z starts to slow down. "You need to read more then, Z. History is littered with those examples. Do you remember Britain's Chancellor Chamberlain and how he let the Germans get fully into position and believed they were to be trusted? Within a year, the Germans had taken over

France and were freely pounding London with bombs. I know our plan of patience is troubling for you, but there are plenty of lessons on how this gray zone invasion of the United States is steeped in the successes that history shows us. Remember one of the key principles that Sun Tzu taught us: 'The greatest victory is that which requires no war.' *That* is our ultimate goal."

Z sighs. "Okay, boss, I'll pick up another World War II book, but we're almost at the meeting point. It's inside that abandoned hangar over there. That's Diego's blacked-out Harley out front, and I'm assuming his guards are driving that green Land Rover. I scoped it out a few days ago, and it appears safe without any planned traps. We'll see a lot of old tractors and combines inside but just stay close to an exterior wall so we can't get outflanked as easily. I know they are friends of ours, but I don't trust them either."

"I really don't like these cartel guys very much, but I want to make sure we always come across as friendly to them as well. We're on their turf now and need to make sure they trust us," David coaches Z.

"Understood, but we need to be careful, David." Z pulls the car up to the hangar and points the car away from it so they can leave quickly if needed. "I will say, though, as long as our checks keep clearing, we're going to be just fine."

The men get out of the sedan and gently close their doors, then they walk through the forty-feet-tall by one-hundred-feet-wide hangar opening. They start to see the old farm equipment that is stored inside.

"Diego! ¿Cómo estás, mi amigo?" David and Diego give each other a warm hug as Diego's two bodyguards, Raul and Pedro, look on. The Mexicans on the security detail are about as tall as they are wide and have tattoos all over their arms and even a few on their bald heads. David finds it funny that they are both enamored with the very old tractors and combines.

"¡Muy bien! David," replies Diego. "How the hell have you been? Did the guys take care of you at the border last week?"

"No issues at all. It's getting easier and faster to cross that Southern Border these days," says David. "We used to have to cross in the middle of the night with the help of your coyotes. Not anymore, though. We just walk through the same hole that hasn't been fixed in years. I still wish we could take the jet straight into Champaign or Chicago and skip that twenty-hour drive. These Americans up here aren't as easy to buy off as those border patrol agents, though." David quickly glances at Z, who nods slightly to say that all is safe.

Diego agrees with David by rubbing his fingers together in the international sign for money. "You may be right; we have no issues at all trafficking our drugs and people across the border anymore. Just stay toward the California side of things, and it's no problem at all. We still have plenty of options for crossing the border, and fentanyl is a whole lot easier to transport than weed. And if any officials give us a hard time, plata o plomo, verdad?"

"Silver or lead, money or a bullet; that's been a great business plan for decades." David nods in agreement. "Same thing in Hong Kong; we have almost all the politicians on lockdown these days. That brings us to our business. How's everything working so far with cleaning your money?"

"It's working well enough, but I wouldn't mind a faster turnaround time for the deposit into our account." Diego glances at Raul to get him to stop looking at the huge tires on the combine. "These guys." Diego shakes his head at David, and then he continues. "It's better than it's been, but we still lose money from drivers losing the actual cash from time to time."

"What do you mean?" David leans in to listen better.

"You know . . . the busts from random DUIs. Very rarely does one of our guys get held up, but that obviously doesn't end well at all for the guys robbing from Sinaloa. We also have couriers who steal from us. We find them or their families quickly, but it's still a risky way to move a lot of cash."

"Well, Diego, you're going to love our new process then. We're shaving off two weeks, and it'll all be handled digitally," David says with some excitement.

"¿Verdad?" questions Diego with some hesitation. "Tell me all about it."

"For you, it'll be super easy with this process, and we'll guarantee the pesos clear your bank account within seventy-two hours of our couriers' exchanges. Just follow the same protocol of sending a picture of the correct serial number on the dollar bill, and we'll begin the transfer," says David.

"So, the normal three hundred fifty thousand US that fits into our suitcases will be in our bank accounts in Mexico and in pesos in seventy-two hours?" asks Diego.

"That's right! And we'll do it for 1 percent too, instead of the 15 percent we—and the others—take today," says David. "If something happens to the suitcases on our watch, you still get the money. It's on us to make sure the money is safe."

"How is that possible? That sounds too good to be true," questions Diego.

"Well, for you, it just may be too good to be true. Do you want the high-level version or the black-market foreign exchange via the Bank of China detailed version?" David jokes.

"Let's start with high-level and why I should trust this process for starters." Diego looks a bit frustrated and is taking this very seriously.

David strikes a more serious tone. "I am obviously well-connected inside the CCP. There are plenty of rich Chinese elites who want to get their money out of China and into US dollars so the CCP can't get to it. The very high-level version is that we make our money, our 15 percent commission if you will, from those elites trying to move money out of China. You are simply covering our costs of physically delivering your drug trafficking dollars to the elites skirting CCP rules. The 1 percent we charge the cartel goes to our couriers, but if they screw it up, then they owe us that money, or we'll kill them or their families. We are always paid back in a day or two in the very few cases they have lost the suitcase of cash."

"This still doesn't make sense to me. We probably need to go into some more details so I can explain this to my boss as well," Diego says with a rather confused look on his face.

David hands Diego a piece of paper with boxes and lines on it, and then he methodically explains his diagram, pointing to each of the blue boxes. "Okay, but this gets complicated quickly. I sketched out the simple flow of the drugs to cash to the Chinese elite to the CCP and ultimately back to the cartel. Rinse and repeat. See if this helps."

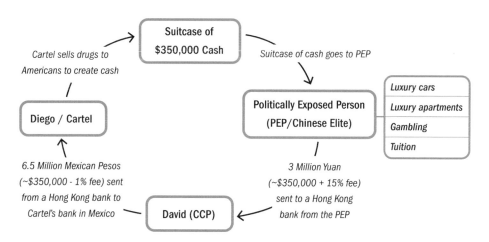

Diego looks over the piece of paper and studies it for at least two minutes. David turns to Z and says, "Maybe this did help?"

"Looks that way, boss. Good job. I never understood it myself."

David patiently waits and looks at the tractors and combines and studies the "Half Century of Progress" marquee sign in the corner. He pulls out his phone and Googles "Half Century of Progress" out of curiosity.

Z goes back to looking at the antique tractors too. "'Half Century of Progress?' What's that all about, David?"

"I just looked that up, Z," David explains. "Local farmers have these super old tractors, combines, and plows for people to come and look at right before harvest kicks off every odd year. No joke, thousands of people show up for this event, and many of these tractors are stored in these old hangars. They use them to farm a small area about five hundred yards from here to show kids how things used to be done."

Z kicks one of the tractor tires. "I admit that many of our Chinese farmers aren't using much more sophisticated equipment than what we're seeing here. See that bright red combine with only three rows on it? I've seen that in the fields before. Some are still using oxen."

Diego finally looks up at David, squinting. "Why didn't you start with this diagram first? If I'm reading this correctly, we're not even the real client here. These PEP folks are the real clients, and we're the source of the cash."

David's eyebrows show his surprise. "Goodness, Diego, you do understand it. That's exactly right and why we simply charge you the cost of the courier. Do you want me to go into more detail so you can explain it to your boss? We'll obviously need to burn that piece of paper when we're done. I'm truly here to answer any questions you have. We want implementing this new program to go smoothly for all of us, then we'll scale it from there." David genuinely wants Diego's buy-in and for him to understand the new program.

"I do appreciate it. I'll save my questions for now, but please explain more of the details," Diego says, looking intently at David.

"Raul. Memorize this diagram." Diego hands the paper to Raul, who is noticeably confused.

David holds back a laugh at Raul's confused expression. "Sure thing. Here's how this works: The PEPs are wealthy Chinese located around the world, including inside China and the US, who have handlers at Chinese banks. The banks help them transfer Chinese yuan, or the base currency of China. Still with me, amigo?"

Diego quickly confirms with a smile, "Si, hermano."

David smiles back, then continues. "The yuan are moved into Hong Kong banks where the Bank of China can't control or seize the funds. These Chinese elites are desperate to move their yuan offshore because the CCP only allows citizens to exchange fifty thousand US dollars per year. These PEPs are trying to move millions out of China every year. PEPs are all over the world, but many of them have agents inside the US for just this purpose. However, there is no limit for Mexican pesos."

"Still good?" David pauses.

"Hanging on, but by a thread. A whiteboard would help," Diego laughs.

"So, the black-market foreign exchange piece is what I just explained, and it's much more complicated than funds simply moving from Mexico to Hong Kong. We even hold actual auctions from time to time when these dollars are in high demand, which are heavily facilitated by our preferred messaging app, WeChat, which also allows for online payments. You don't need to be concerned about that at all, though. So, we charge the PEPs about 15 percent, convert their Chinese yuan to pesos, and transfer the funds to your bank in Mexico. The money is now washed, and you guys, the cartels, can use it as you please for manufacturing drugs, bribing officials, your own payroll, and acquiring weapons. And because of how much the PEPs pay, that 15 percent, we are able to charge you only 1 percent, which, again, is for the couriers, the risks, and the guarantee if we lose the actual cash. Still make sense?"

"I've never heard of this before." Diego's eyes widen with curiosity. "Keep going, but I am following. Basically, you're cleaning our money and helping rich Chinese get their money out of China and into US dollars. You're charging them what you used to charge us to stay level on your profit margin so you can reduce our charges." Diego looks to Pedro and Raul for confirmation, but they just shrug their shoulders.

"You're getting it," David confirms. "I receive your three hundred fifty thousand dollars in cash from you selling drugs to the Americans. The Chinese investors wire us three hundred fifty thousand in yuan into our Chinese bank accounts. We courier them, or their US agent, about three hundred thousand in US dollars, in cash, and our profit is the fifty-thousand-dollar difference. The cartel only pays thirty-five hundred dollars to wash the drug money, and the revenue goes into your bank accounts in Mexico as pesos within days, if not hours. There are several other ways to do this with front companies, personal deposits, and black-market foreign currency exchanges, but this is the main method to wash the cartel's drug money."

Diego is blown away by the scheme, "I sort of follow that, but two questions: One, why would the Chinese government allow that much money to flow out of the country? I assume they know this is going on. And two, what do the wealthy Chinese do with all of that cash? Don't they have an issue now since you can't just deposit three hundred thousand dollars into a bank without throwing up red flags?"

"That is why this is such a great relationship," explains David. "The CCP are all playing the long game of the US's demise: massive drug abuse, fentanyl, open borders allowing millions of Mexicans and Central Americans into the country who receive federal and state support. It's the perfect way to continue to weaken the US over time. We even supply the fentanyl precursors to the cartels on the front end and make money there. Then, these profits make it back to CCP leadership. And you know there are plenty of politicians, especially here in Illinois and the coastal states, who believe illegal immigrants will ultimately be allowed to vote, and the vast majority of them will vote for a larger government. That works just fine with our friends in Chicago. Those politicians only want to hold onto their power and under-the-table revenue streams at any cost. They couldn't care less about how that happens," continues David.

"That's incredible, bro!" says Diego. "That is true, especially around the aldermen and city council dudes around Chicago. We contribute to their campaigns to fund all sorts of fun for them: cars, girls, boats, and even upgrades to their homes. But you didn't answer what happens to the actual cash that's with the Chinese PEPs."

"When was the last time you were at the University of Illinois, Diego?" asks David.

"Champaign, you mean? I go there about once a month to check on operations. Why?" asks Diego.

"Okay, you ever notice how many extremely nice and crazy expensive cars are on campus, especially around the engineering campus?" asks David.

"Well, I noticed the cars, and those luxury apartments just keep going up, but I'd be lying if I told you I knew much about any of that," replies Diego as he points to his Harley. "They need more motorcycles there."

"Well, those same Chinese PEPs use their cash to gamble, turning the cash into chips. They buy expensive cars, and almost 70 percent of US homes bought by Chinese who aren't US citizens are bought with cash too. But get this: they also send their kids to colleges all over the US and pay for those kids' cars and apartments . . . and tuition," explains David.

"You have to be kidding me; this money laundering scheme involves the university?" Diego shakes his head in disbelief.

"Diego, this has been going on for decades. It all started in the mid-nineties when colleges were looking for ways to make more money and they started to accept so many more international students who pay full tuition," explains David. "For the colleges, they are just taking money orders or wire transfers from China, right? They aren't doing anything explicitly illegal. But you better believe they know what's up, and they aren't afraid to take the money. How many US kids who live right in the colleges' backyards get passed up so the colleges can accept Chinese students? Again, the CCP would never allow this to happen, and I don't care, obviously, but these universities and politicians from Chicago? They just want the money and power. It's a tale as old as time."

"Bro, that's a bit messed up. I'm going to stay in my lane, though. I love that seventy-two-hour guarantee at 1 percent!" Diego exclaims. "One more thing: all of these Chinese and international kids—agents, or whatever—get educated at the U of I, and then what?"

David grins and says, "Diego, you may be CCP after all, hermano. That is why this is the gift that keeps on giving, and the CCP doesn't really care about the money flowing into the US universities and out of China. In addition to the CCP making millions on the fentanyl trade here in the States with you, the Chinese kids are legallyrequired to go back to China to put their knowledge to work for us, or they are required to stay and continue to run the programs. Just as an example, we have a very good agent right now in the Illinois biochemistry department. Back in China, these students get huge bonuses for the trade secrets and intellectual property that they steal from their time over here. Like I said, hermano, we're playing the long game."

Diego motions to Raul and Pedro that it's time to leave. "I have to hand it to you, David, this is impressive. I'm going to talk to El Jefe to see what else we can start to move if you want to try to do even more. Heroin, human trafficking . . . you need any weapons?"

"We can always use weapons. The more advanced the better. One more thing, though, Diego." David shows him the lighter in his right hand, smiling at Raul.

"Raul." Diego points to David's hand.

David takes the money laundering diagram and lights it on fire. "Always hide the evidence. And I appreciate you handling our little issue with that lab analyst who was asking too many questions."

# CHAPTER 4
# SMALL TOWN LIVING

ERIC navigates his truck with the windows down through the "Royal S curves," about a half mile of banked pavement with two opposing curves. One curve maneuvers around a gravel pit and an old, dilapidated farmhouse, and the second straightens out the road leading into town. It felt more like a NASCAR road course for Eric and his friends back in high school. He reminds himself he must still control his "need for speed" these days and drive like a sane person because that wasn't always the case. From here, his hometown of Royal is just up the road, a half mile away, where he is going to meet up with family and old friends at the spring Royal Days gathering.

Eric moseys into the quaint town, looking for any small changes to people's homes, like landscaping, because he and his brothers mowed so many of the lawns at one point. As soon as he pulls off Main Street and takes a right into the large gravel parking lot just before crossing the railroad tracks, he smells the fried chicken that signals a town event is in full swing at the Royal Community Building (RCB). He immediately sees the baseball diamond where he played so many summer games in his youth and has great memories of his dad coaching. Eric remembers from his younger days that he needs to drive slowly on the gravel as he heads to park his truck; otherwise, he could spin his tires out and get in trouble with anyone over fifty who happens to see it.

Eric still proudly remembers helping town elders construct the RCB. It was largely built by volunteers with donated supplies and by the children who cleaned the dirty bricks donated by his parents, Les and Sheila Buchanan. The bricks were upcycled from an old elementary school his parents had bought. They turned it into apartments not too long after the RCB was completed in 1985. It was such an incredible honor for the whole town when the State of Illinois Governor's Award was presented to them in 1986. It was hand-delivered by Lieutenant Governor George Ryan after his helicopter landed in right field, just a few hundred feet away.

Eric parks his truck and is sure to back it up perfectly in line with the others to avoid disapproving glares from the town elders. He gets out and starts to walk toward the front doors, noticing a bouncy house in left field and a kids' hay maze in center field. A few dads are also on the infield with stopwatches timing "home-to-home" base running to get the kids ready for the spring baseball season. As everyone around town knows, this is the dividing line to root for the Chicago Cubs or St. Louis Cardinals. The rivalry can get a little intense—some may even say obnoxious—but that's small-town living. Spring training is wrapping up, and Opening Day is coming soon, so let the smack-talking begin!

Eric strolls into the RCB through one of the two sets of double doors. The building is filled with the smell of home-cooked dishes made from recipes handed down over generations. Eric sees a familiar community scene: people sitting around, gossiping, and playing Euchre. Euchre is a Midwest card game that dates back to 1810 but is rather easy to play. Feelings can get very hurt if someone "reneges" and doesn't play a card that is required, or a partner stops paying enough attention and trumps their own partner's winning card. That can turn ugly quickly.

Eric continues walking into the building and sees his dear old family friend and cousin once removed, Mitch Osterbur, sitting at a round table near the entrance. Mitch is clearly annoying his boisterous wife, Marsha, by drinking her coffee instead of getting his own.

This is very much par for the course. Many years ago, Marsha was actually Eric's confirmation teacher at the church.

"Mitch!" yells Eric. "How are you?!"

"Well, I'm above ground, buddy, and feeling really good. The doctors tell me they are happy. How are you doing?" Mitch stands up to shake hands.

"So, the cancer is in remission?" Eric jokingly pokes his arm as if looking for cancer.

"The first round of cancer didn't get me five years ago, and this round didn't either. I'm too stubborn to have it any other way." Mitch sits back down at the table.

"That sounds about right, Mitch. So good to see that you are still kicking even at eighty-five years old," Eric jokes.

"Seventy and a half, son. I'm not even seventy and three-quarters yet. Still a young buck." Mitch looks at Marsha as she makes it very clear that she's rolling her eyes.

"And how are you doing, Marsha?" asks Eric as he gives her a huge hug that engulfs her small five-foot frame.

"Same ole Marsha here, Eric." Marsha jokingly poofs up her grey hair and then sits back down. "Just carrying around this old bag of bones."

"Well, you both look great, and it's great to see you, too. What's the plan for the day?" asks Eric, sitting down at the table.

"Mitch is probably going to play horseshoes at Herbie's Hideaway, then go uptown to Freeman's Tavern to complain about something with the rest of 'em," smirks Marsha.

"So, I see not much has changed since the last time I saw you," Eric says with an ornery grin.

"No, no, we have a very busy day," Mitch pushes back. "I need to drive the kids around again with the tractor and wagon here in a bit, play horseshoes after that, and *then* go uptown to complain and have a beer. I'm carrying a very busy schedule today."

"I do miss 'uptown' being two bars in a three-hundred-person town . . . that never gets old," says Eric. "But it's coming up on planting time here, Mitch. You ready to go?"

"I'm on it, boy. Don't you worry," smiles Mitch. "I've slowed down a bit recently from the treatments and do less farming, but who doesn't love riding around in tractors?"

"And you need to get out of the house," Marsha chimes in.

"Yes, in order to protect myself and our fifty years of wedded bliss, I do leave the house from time to time." Mitch shrugs, then he loudly whispers to Eric out of the side of his mouth, "And I'm too old to start dating again."

Eric waits for Marsha's reply, but she just gives Mitch an "I'm going to kill you" look.

Eric changes the subject while making sure Marsha is joking. "I was told you are still quite the seed salesman, though, and getting a bit nerdy even?"

"A bit nerdy?!" Marsha pushes Eric's arm to get his attention. "He's a full nerd, making his own YouTube videos and testing out his homegrown plots of various corn seeds. He thinks he's like you in a big high-tech lab these days."

"That's impressive, Mitch. What turned you onto that?" asks Eric.

"Well, once again, Marsha telling me I have limited time to spend in the house or she'll throw me out." Mitch gives Marsha a hug. "But also, over the past decade or so—I lose track of time from the chemo, to be honest—I'm just seeing some things that I haven't really seen before on the seed yield side of things, so I wanted to run my own tests and plant my own corn plots. Did you know that some of my chemo treatments contain an alkylating agent that can be made from mustard gas, Eric?"

"I did know that," Eric says, impressed. "It's called Mustargen, and we run trials and tests on that chemical in one of our labs. Not my lab, but one of the labs in our building. We even have another project involving pantaphos that may have an impact on brain cancer, but it's early. That is fascinating about the food plots and yields, especially to the U of I, where ag and biochemistry converge in a way that is almost impossible to duplicate at other top-tier schools. What yields are you expecting this year?" asks Eric.

"For corn specifically, most seeds and soils will produce around two hundred fifty to two hundred seventy-five bushels with the right hybrids . . . that would be your Beck's, Cordova, and Wyffels. But Elevation has been pushing more like three hundred and sometimes three hundred ten, or so I've heard. Granted, these farmers will lie about their yields more than they lie about their golf handicaps." Mitch sternly points at a man at the table next to them. "Like that farmer right there."

Marsha shakes her head. "Eric, that guy beat Mitch at last year's horseshoe championship. He is still not over it."

Eric takes a quick peek at the farmer in overalls and quickly moves on. "Interesting. Anyway, we're running some similar tests in the lab, but if I told you about them, I'd have to kill you," Eric jokes as he looks around. "Spring Royal Days is really well put together this year, though. I'm loving the bouncy house and gourmet food," Eric says with a slight tinge of sarcasm.

"Yeah, it's not Michelin-rated, but it's being sponsored by Elevation Seeds. They have been doing similar things all over the area. Football games, St. Joseph-Ogden High School Hall of Fame celebrations, softball pregame dinners, and even awarding ten detasseling internships." Mitch explains the continued involvement of local businesses supporting local events, including at the local St. Joseph-Ogden, or SJO, High School.

"I do remember always wanting a detasseling job back in the day. They always paid the best. Now it's mainly done by machines in the field, though, but good for them," says Eric. "I guess as I look around, Elevation really does have a lot of posters and branding stuff up around here. Hadn't seen that before."

A small, middle-aged Asian lady strolls up to the table to say hi. She is well-dressed and alone but comfortable in the room like she has been there before.

"Speak of the devil, Eric," says Mitch. "This is Thao Te. Thao is the CEO of Elevation Seeds, and she came in to say hi to us today. She's from Springfield but made the trip anyway. Thao, this is Eric. Eric works at the U of I in the biochemistry department and can probably speak your language regarding corn seeds."

"Nice to meet you, Eric. Are you from here?" Thao looks up at Eric as he stands to shake her hand.

"Yes, ma'am, I was born and raised in Royal," replies Eric. "Mitch was just telling me that Elevation is performing really well these days. Congratulations."

"Thank you, Eric. We have a great sales force, and I've been trying to hire Mitch for ten years, but he's loyal to Beck's. Great company as well, but we'd love to have him join us," replies Thao. "Mitch, do you remember when seventy to eighty bushels an acre was a great year?"

Mitch concurs, "I do, and these numbers are just crazy to me still. Just think about the sheer amount of corn we're talking about, too. A bushel of corn weighs about fifty-six pounds, depending on moisture content. So, two hundred fifty bushels of corn produce fourteen thousand pounds—about the weight of an African elephant—of corn per acre. Here's the challenge though, sort of: a semitrailer holds about fifty-six thousand pounds, so that's only four acres of corn to fill each trailer. That doesn't take very long these days, but back in the day, it would take fourteen acres to fill up a trailer."

Eric looks at Marsha. Now she's really rolling her eyes. "Tell us more, Mitchell," says Marsha as Thao and Eric laugh.

"That's all correct," Thao continues, leaning on a chair. "And we're still working hard to get to three hundred bushels an acre.

We need to make sure we don't have too much degradation from corn rot or other fungi and diseases, and we should be getting there soon."

Eric looks at Thao and is fairly confident he sees a flash of scorn in her eyes as she looks at Mitch but can't quite tell.

"Very nice to meet you, Eric." Thao gestures for him to stay seated as she shakes his hand. "Great to see you as always, Mitch and Marsha. I hope you get to enjoy the beautiful day soon," says Thao before she moves along to another table.

"Well, I wouldn't have expected an Asian female to be the CEO of a seed company. What's up with that?" Eric looks at Marsha. "Is she local? Elevation couldn't have hired an engineer, chemist, or executive from Illinois or at least the Midwest?"

Marsha puts down her iced tea and then jumps in. "Mitch will try to be politically correct because he's working for their competitor and doesn't want to ruffle any feathers. She was put into the head role when Elevation was sold to a company out of Springfield. I can't remember the name, but they really started to brand themselves heavily after that and seem to be making serious investments in their product. I don't like it at all, and farmers need to know the real people and investors behind these companies. I mean we're literally talking about our food supply. Mitch thinks I'm a conspiracy theorist, though." Marsha props her bent arms, palms up, into a "whatever" pose.

"Well, you are," adds Mitch with a laugh.

"Love you guys!" says Eric. "I'm going to head over to Freeman's and see what's up over there. I'm guessing the boys will be there?"

"I would bet at least a dollar you're right. See you soon, I'm sure," says Mitch.

"Oh, wait, Eric!" Marsha jumps to her feet.

"What?" Eric laughs at her suddenness.

"Well, there's someone I'd like you to meet," Marsha says softly.

Eric musters the strength to stand up to Marsha, which never works. "As Grandpa Buchanan taught all of us many, many years ago, Marsha, learn to say *no* for an answer!"

Marsha isn't fazed. "Look, I know that last girl didn't quite work out well, and she may or may not have keyed your car. And I'm deeply sorry about that. But this girl, Christine Pyle is her name, is very attractive, and she's literally cooking in the kitchen."

"Come on, Marsha. Let's not do this, pretty please?" Eric pleads.

"It'll only take a second, but I do think you'll like her. She's super smart, works at Busey Bank in cybersecurity, and isn't even a distant cousin like everyone else in Royal!" laughs Marsha.

Eric looks to Mitch for help or a way out. Mitch instantly busies himself with looking up the price of corn on his phone and tries his hardest to stay out of it. "She is rather cute, Eric," murmurs Mitch.

Eric looks back up to see Marsha rushing across the concrete floor, dodging the eight-person round tables like she's in a game of Frogger. Eric sits down and grabs an iced tea from the table.

"Mitch. Why do you let this stuff happen? I should make a break for it and let you deal with the fallout." Eric takes a serious look at an exit door behind him.

Mitch just shrugs and doesn't look up from his phone, giggling under his Beck's trucker hat. "I would appreciate it if you don't do that."

Marsha quickly returns, dragging an apprehensive young woman.

"Well, she was right. She is incredibly attractive. Didn't see that coming." Eric mumbles under his breath.

Marsha says, "Eric, this is Christine. She's friends with Katie from Champaign."

"A friend of my cousin Katie O. is a friend of mine. Nice to meet you, Christine." Eric stands up and looks into the green eyes of the fit blonde who obviously works out—Pilates, he guesses. He then extends his hand. "I have to warn you that once we have said 'Hi' here in the Royal Community Building, we may as well be married as far as the Royal gossip circle is concerned."

"Nice to meet you, Eric. I'm Christine." She extends a soft but firm handshake as her cheeks blush.

"Marsha," Eric turns to Marsha to deflect some attention off himself. "Do you remember how my brothers and I would get into trouble on the west side of town, and Mom and Dad would know about it before we even crossed the railroad tracks that split the town in half? It was super impressive, and I believe the gossip circle has only increased in efficiency, but not accuracy, with everyone having cell phones."

Eric turns back to see Christine has an enormous smile on her face. She's wearing what Eric can gather would probably be the closest thing to rural attire in her closet: a flannel shirt that is more Florida Georgia Line country, jeans, and Nike tennis shoes. Eric assumes this isn't her standard choice for her Saturday wardrobe but appreciates the effort. Her hair is in a ponytail, and he can smell fried chicken as she stops at the table.

Eric, always trying to be a gentleman, moves toward the table to try to pull out a chair for Christine to sit in and briskly knocks his iced tea onto the floor.

"Well, there you go. That's why I played defense," says an embarrassed Eric.

A frantic movement catches Eric's eye, and he notices Katie bounding out of the kitchen and running over.

"What the hell happened here?!" Katie grabs some rags and helps to clean up.

"Well, you see what had happened was," laughs Eric. "Your friend Christy here."

"Christine, Eric, you dummy." Katie looks at Eric in disapproval and rolls her eyes.

"Yes, Christine was trying to leave because she's tired of listening to the town gossip, I'm guessing, and knocked over my drink!" Eric fibs.

"Well, first of all, the town gossip is always spread by the men," retorts Katie.

"That's true," chimes in Mitch, feeling a bit more certain that he won't get in trouble. Then he sits back to watch the show unfold with a wry smile on his face.

"And second of all, you're such a klutz. I know that was you. Have you met Eric, Christine?" asks Katie.

"Just did," smiles Christine.

"Eric, I'll tell you when to speak and what to say, okay?" Katie continues to give Eric a hard time.

"I'm so sorry. I am a klutz. That's true, too. Yes, my name is Eric Buchanan. Marsha tells me you work for Busey Bank? So, why are you here at the Community Building?" asks Eric.

"Yes, I work in cybersecurity at Busey Bank, but I love to volunteer as well," Christine smiles at Eric. "And Katie said she could use some help in the kitchen today. So, we drove over here to check out her super cute town."

Eric, using paper towels to clean up the iced tea, is still trying to understand how Katie and Marsha are introducing him to a girl like Christine, and his words aren't working so well for him. "Well, it's technically a village because it's only three hundred people . . . not a town. It's the Village of Royal," explains Eric, but then he realizes he's done it again.

"You are such a nerd, Eric!" laughs Katie. "Stop!"

"That's very interesting, Eric. Do you always correct everyone?" Christine asks sarcastically as she winks at Katie. "I didn't know there was a difference. I should probably go back to the kitchen to make sure everyone knows the difference between a chicken and a turkey."

Mitch briefly looks at Eric, shakes his head, and goes back to his phone, laughing under his hat.

"Very nice to meet you, Christine. You're in good hands with Katie, but just don't do what she does," Eric pokes fun.

"Don't you worry about me!" exclaims Katie. "I'm sure we'll see you on campus soon. I'll shoot you a text."

"I'll be waiting with bells on!" Eric laughs, glancing at Christine again as she walks away.

Katie calls back, "Don't think I'm not paying attention there, big guy!"

Eric turns to Marsha. "Well, maybe a heads-up next time? Not sure I could have screwed that up much worse. I'm going to head over to Freeman's and find some guys who don't make me as nervous as Christine just did. Love you guys."

"Love you too, Eric!" says Marsha as she jumps up to give him a big hug goodbye. Mitch tips his hat with a frown on his face.

"You really crushed it. No wonder you're still single at twenty-nine." Mitch shakes his head.

"Thanks, Mitch."

# CHAPTER 5
# BELLYING UP

"**B**EERS all around!" Eric announces, spinning his finger in the air as he walks into Freeman's Tavern. "What's up, boys?!"

Eric heads straight over to his cousins and some friends, who are taking a break from spring planting. Due to heavy rain, their farming equipment would get stuck deep in the mud.

Royal, IL, has two taverns that work well together. The locals are excited about the bands that come into town now and how the bar doesn't smell like fried food, a scent that would stick to your clothes for hours, if not days. Freeman's now has that new flooring and paint aroma, which is sure to fade soon. Regardless, everyone is very proud of their new watering hole.

"Eric! Grab a beer, brother!" says Brian, who has an oddly scrawny frame for a police officer but a slight beer belly, nonetheless.

"Aren't you supposed to be on duty or something?" asks Eric as he slaps Brian on the back.

"It's Saturday, man. I ain't on duty!" replies Brian as he waves to the bartender for a round of Busch Lights. "Busch Light work for you, Eric?"

"Heck yeah, man. Thanks," replies Eric. "So, who's the new guy?" asks Eric as he points to the rather tall, broad-shouldered, dark-haired bartender standing behind the deep counter with large cup holders built into it.

"This is Chad Goldenstein, the new bartender for Freeman's when Michelle isn't working. She's been putting up with us for over ten years, so I'm guessing she didn't feel like hearing our stories for the hundredth time. He's been here for a few months, but he talks real funny," his cousin Danny says in his odd Illinois-Texas drawl.

They all start laughing, but Eric looks at Chad with a confused look on his face.

Chad reaches out to shake Eric's hand. "Hey, man. Chad."

Eric is surprised to feel a very strong grip.

"I'll get it out of the way for ya: I went to Haa'vad ya'd to pa'k ma ca'," Chad says, using the old, self-deprecating Boston accent test to everyone's delight. "Here's your beer, brother."

"Say hi to your mother for me!" Eric responds with a chuckle.

"Nice." Chad nods in approval at the reference to Mark Wahlberg's *SNL* skit.

"What's up, buddy? How the heck are you? Time to get into the fields, I'm assuming?" Eric turns to his other cousin Jeff, and Danny's brother, who is wearing the same Case IH Ride or Die shirt he's been wearing for ten years and Lee jeans he's probably had for even longer. Eric can see that Jeff's hands, which are outsized from working on tractors—and probably a few extra pounds—continue to be lined with grease and dirt.

"Yup, we started about a week ago, but it rained the past couple of days, so we're, ummm, planning right now," Jeff says in the local drawl that's even a bit slower than Danny's. Both start to crack up since they appear to have been at the bar for a minute or two already.

"Did you drive a tractor up here for Happy Hour?" laughs Eric. "I always remember tractors during the spring and harvest being lined up outside. The original Uber."

"No, we left them in the fields to not rut them out. Remember, those things weigh about thirty thousand pounds and pull a five-thousand-pound planter for what we farm. We need solid fields to get our stuff around." Jeff dryly shows his command of farm equipment.

"I was raised in this big urban center of Royal, but it's still amazing to me how that whole process works. Next time we're at the farm, can you explain it to me a bit more?" asks Eric.

"No problem, and happy to help. But like the rest of us, you'll have to tip over a cow before we show you behind the curtain," Jeff laughs.

"I'm not that 'city' now, Jeff. Remember, I did walk beans for Uncle Skeeter." Eric drinks his beer. "But he always drilled his beans instead of having nice rows. Man, that was tough getting our feet through those beans."

"Yeah, those were the good ole days," Danny adds. "We don't do none of that anymore."

"What is 'walking beans?'" Chad pulls up a barstool next to their table and sits down.

Danny explains with the excitement of reliving his glory days, "Back when we were kids, either the planters would lay down seeds in a row, or you could drill the beans into a bunch of holes that were not in easily walkable rows. The beans didn't get as tall in when they were drilled because they were closer to each other, but yields would be higher overall. So, Dad would drill, or not plant in rows, most of our acres." Danny drinks his cold beer. "Eric, his brothers, Jeff, and I . . . okay, fine, and my older sisters too, would walk through the beans and use a sharp hook to pull out weeds, like buttonweeds."

"Okay, I gotcha, but why did that stop now?" Chad is really interested.

"Well, Mr. Scientist over here can help with that." Danny looks at Eric.

"I know, I know," Eric replies with a tinge of nostalgia. "Roundup is the short answer."

Chad looks confused. "Like the weed killer we use around my house?"

"Pretty much." Eric sits back. "Most crops are resistant to so many things these days. Disease-resistant. Fungus-resistant. Even wind-resistant from increased stalk strength. But also, resistant to weed killers, like Roundup, that prevent the weeds that we used to remove with hooks from even growing without killing the crops."

Chad nods as he follows along. "So, you do this in your lab at the University of Illinois?"

Eric cocks his head and looks at Danny. "Yes, but did I tell you I worked at a lab at the U of I?"

Chad's eyes widen slightly. "No. I'm sure one of these guys mentioned it at some point, and I thought it was interesting."

Danny finishes his beer and pulls the tab off. "I'll need another one here soon. Remember, guys, I collect these for the Ronald McDonald House, so don't waste them."

"Gotcha," Eric continues. "So anyway, our technology produces GMO hybrids, specialized seed treatments, and targeted weed killers. These modifications are at the DNA level inside the seeds. So, we can turn on—or off—attributes at a very specific level. I was just chatting with Mitch, and he's thinking you'll push two hundred fifty an acre this year, which is incredible."

Jeff sinks lower in his chair. "Yup, that's about right, but we'll see what the weather does for us too."

Eric asks, "How many acres are you boys farming now?"

Danny says, "Oh, maybe about twenty-five hundred acres or so—combination of our land and rented."

"Goodness, that's a lot," says an impressed Eric. "How much does that produce?"

"Hmmm . . ." Jeff murmurs while doing some mental math. "I guess if it's about fifty-fifty corn and beans, then it's around two hundred fifty thousand bushels of corn and another hundred thousand bushels of beans?"

"Chad, not sure if you are aware, but these boys are part of a multigenerational conglomerative farming industrial complex," says Eric with a smile.

"Conglomerative, huh?" Chad heads back to the bar. "Tell me all about it, but let's get another round out before you kick this off. Seems like it may take a minute."

"Chad, I know you're working, but when Eric starts to tell a story, make sure you're comfortable and have a beer in your hand . . . maybe three." Danny pushes Eric.

"Well, Chad," Eric takes a healthy sip and then grabs a new beer, "our Grandpa, Lorenz Buchanan, built the grain elevator back in 1945, and my dad, Les, ran the elevator until it sold in 1990. He and Mom, Sheila, moved back to Royal after they graduated from the University of Illinois in 1969. Mom graduated in business, and Dad played basketball and baseball for Illinois and graduated with an ag degree." Eric looks around to see if he has permission to continue.

"Go ahead. You're doing fine." Danny adjusts his glasses and rubs the top of his buzz cut, which is slightly longer than his brothers'.

"Now, our Grandpa Buchanan was a newbie around town, and our Grandma Buchanan, Anna, was an Osterbur before they got married in 1940. The town was started by four Osterbur boys back in 1885 who were Grandma Buchanan's great-uncles. Those Osterbur boys were drawn to the marshy and swampy farmland that they knew well because their ancestors grew up in East Friesland, Germany. They knew how to drain the land properly, grow all sorts of crops, and use oxen to pull planters and plows." Eric looks at Jeff for approval, and Jeff nods to go ahead.

"I don't like dealing with my Case IH tractors, and I'm watching Netflix half the time while driving them in the field. I can't imagine having to deal with eight oxen that don't follow instructions well." Danny's laugh jostles his belly. "That's also why I'm not married."

"You see, Chad, this is why my stories take so long. No distractions please." Eric pauses to make his point to Danny.

"Your stories take so long because you take forever to tell them," Brian chimes in. "Chad, in his defense, there's a lot of family history for these guys around here."

"Fair enough, but I'll continue," laughs Eric. "The grain was then stored in grain bins over the winter so they could use it for their livestock and feeding their families through our cold winters. However, there was typically too much food, and they needed to sell the crops, or they would rot and be worthless. Some of this land had other uses as well, like for raising sheep or goats or even for hunting. And our Grandpa Buchanan's twin brothers, Edwin and Edward Buchanan, and then their kids, owned a dairy farm for about seventy years around ten miles north of here in Flatville." Eric points to the south.

"That way." Danny corrects Eric's terrible sense of direction.

"I've seen that Flatville church, Eric. Largest rural church in America, I'm told," says Chad.

"That's right," says Jeff. "Our family has been attending church there almost every Sunday for about sixty years, as far as I know."

Eric jumps back in. "Jeff, I always get lost on the Harms kids' situation. After all these years of farming and livestock, I'd think you guys would have figured out what causes this. Maybe you take over explaining your family tree." Eric sits back and drinks his beer, then pulls off the can tab and flips it to Danny.

"I got it, Eric," Jeff helps out his cousin. "Farming still runs deep in our family. My mom and dad, Lisa and Skeeter, are the fifth generation and are farming the ground that Grandpa, we called him Opa, started farming in 1910."

"I'm with you, but barely," Chad nods to Jeff.

"We still run the farm with a lot of help from our sisters, Anna and Tina, which is usually not wanted at all."

Eric jumps in, shoving Brian. "Danny and Brian here are the playboys of Champaign County and haven't made it down the aisle yet! They are in high demand, let me tell you!"

"Neither have you, Eric! We ain't that dumb!" Brian shakes his head.

Eric then says, "I'll wrap it up, Chad. My folks, Les and Sheila, live here in Royal and have four boys: me, the twins, Jason and Joel, and Cory. Jason lives in Texas, and Joel lives in Tennessee. They turn fifty next year. Cory is forty-seven and lives in St. Joseph, about ten miles away, where we all went to high school. I'm sure you've met Cory."

"He's definitely been here before. I've never seen anyone complain so much about sports and umpiring," Chad confirms, shaking his head.

"Yup. That's Cory." Eric laughs.

"Eric is the youngest of the four, but the family joke is that Eric is a younger version of Jason, just on a different path," Brian interjects.

"You nailed it, Brian. Cory is probably my favorite, though." Eric sets down a twenty-dollar bill as he starts to head for the door. "Time to head home. You boys should probably do the same . . . or maybe stick around for a few more hours—if you're allowed to, that is."

"See ya later, Eric. But I don't think we're quite done planning here yet." Danny waves his finger in a circle to ask Chad for another round.

Eric walks through Freeman's double doors and back out to Main Street. His phone dings, and he reads a text message from his lab analyst, Chris Lee: "Boss! Steve was in a car accident last night. He's dead!"

# CHAPTER 6
# PLAYING THE LONG GAME

"I PROMISE you there will be serious consequences if anyone isn't prepared for this call with MSS." David looks around the conference table at the Union and begins to dial into the conference call that General Houbin demanded.

The Union is the CCP's operational headquarters, or HQ, and has been named as such in order to blend in with University of Illinois vernacular. In contrast, the proper Illini Union on the University of Illinois campus is a place where students mingle, study, and can have open but private conversations. Many of David's agents inside the university—lab analysts, professors, assistant professors, etc.—use the Illini Union on campus to freely flow among their peers while hiding in plain sight. It's easily done given the university's code of conduct surrounding "foreign relations" and working very hard to make sure no feelings are hurt, regardless of the underlying intent.

General Houbin likes to periodically reiterate the party's long-term plans and make sure he's up to speed with current progress. The reality is that he also likes to assert his authority over the group and acquire project knowledge to safeguard himself inside the CCP. Like most Chinese generals, Houbin is in his position because of blind allegiance as opposed to any true skill set. He just happened to pick the right horse in President Xi decades earlier.

The general likes to work over the phone, not Zoom, because, as David surmises, he can zone out on answers without participants seeing he's not paying attention. It's easy to tell when he has stopped caring because he will simply say, "Interesting." Regardless, the general is a senior leader in the Ministry of State Security, so when he asks for a meeting, he gets the meeting. David has briefed his team to be extremely professional and formal on the call and to not mock the general in any way. He is less than convinced they will comply.

David kicks off the call, speaking in Mandarin. "Hello, everyone, especially General Houbin and his team in Beijing. Our team here is working hard after traveling from the mainland. Their dedication to the MSS is unwavering." David highlights the sacrifices of his team on the ground and that the group in Beijing has not made that sacrifice. He tires quickly of the stoic pandering to his commanders, though. He would prefer to just be left alone to run his programs as he sees fit.

"As we know, we are doing extremely important work on behalf of the Chinese Communist Party," David speaks with a sterner tone than usual. "To start, let's celebrate our recent victories."

David continues with their largest success to date: "General Houbin, we have full access to the US cellular network. We had a highly successful trial run with wireless providers AT&T and Verizon, dismantling their networks for over eight hours. As expected, they blamed software bugs during an upgrade rollout, and the US media fell in line as planned. I cannot stress the level of this project's success." David takes a drink of water but is really pausing for effect. "It wasn't publicly reported, but key military communications tied to those networks were also disrupted. There is apparently no clear backup system for the military comms other than satphones, which are very limited. As predicted, affected citizens and companies panicked at their loss of communications. This resulted in a tremendous loss of productivity while confirming there are limited backup plans for citizens and companies alike."

General Houbin jumps in. "Excellent, David. Incredible test run for future projects. Did those results alter any future projects?"

David nods to Tom, silently accepting the compliment but a bit shocked the general is still following along. He continues, "We

# PLAYING THE LONG GAME

still believe that knocking out US comms along with even one of our many other projects we'll discuss here is enough to send the majority of the US into disarray within a couple of days. As we have discussed, our goals here are to cause panic and confusion for now and not elevate our projects into a direct war with the United States yet. We will be disciplined and remain inside the gray zone." David eyes his team to accentuate the point. "I can go around the room for updates from our team now, General, if that suits you?"

"Please proceed," the general curtly responds.

David says, "Go ahead, Tom."

"Thank you, Mr. Lee." Tom clears his throat to begin his explanation. "We worked for ten years on infiltrating the software for AT&T with dormant malware, then used that malware to increase the potency of our attacks. As you can see, we had our greatest success with AT&T, but this is highly repeatable across all US carriers. We confirmed that many military phones are also running on the AT&T network for when we need to shut down domestic military comms. In addition, 9-1-1 comms were disrupted, as predicted, in major markets where we tested this program, including Houston, Chicago, Dallas, and Atlanta. Very successful by all accounts, and we're ready to ramp it up upon your order."

David smiles broadly. "Yes, Tom. Please keep improving the cyberattacks and making them less detectable by US cybersecurity protections, including both federal and private company efforts. Work to attack along the paths of least resistance, which include older systems, routers, and programs that are out-of-date and not receiving security patches."

"Yes, sir," says Tom. "The FBI did finally identify our offshore Volt Typhoon operation this month, which is the program used to install extremely high-stealth computer scripts onto old Netgear and Cisco routers. Those scripts install a command control program onto thousands of computers' memory banks, then leave no trace and are virtually undetectable. I am still a bit amazed that most government organizations are oblivious to how vulnerable their systems are to attack. And they still can't repair those wormholes any time soon. The media is just now reporting on the vulnerability of the water infrastructure, but we're well past setting the trap for water. We have moved into setting the stage for disabling nuclear facilities."

"I'm aware, Tom. It's an amazing opportunity for us to exploit, and it seems like we still have a long runway to continue wreaking havoc at the time of our choosing," confirms David.

"Please update us on the nuclear capabilities," David directs Tom.

"Yes, sir," Tom replies with a tinge of excitement. "It's remarkably easy to get access to their nuclear facilities' programs, but the challenge is to do damage before manual overrides can be used. Do you remember the US/Israel attack on an Iranian nuclear facility back around 2005 to 2010?"

"A bit, but that was a while ago. Refresh our memory," David says.

"Yes, sir." Tom sips his water and leans toward the speaker. "The CIA and Israel Defense Forces, or IDF, created a software worm that was aggressively attacking Siemens-built programmable logic controllers, or PLCs, focused on Iran. This gets rather technical, but the Iranian PLCs were Microsoft Windows-based, and the worm infected over two hundred thousand computers, which caused over one thousand computers to become worthless. Ultimately, the CIA and IDF used their control of the PLCs to initiate the uranium centrifuges to spin at such a high rate of speed that they destroyed themselves. Our intelligence claims that 20 percent of the centrifuges were destroyed in Iran, setting their program back at least ten years."

"Interesting," General Houbin blandly replies.

Chinaloa covers her mouth, laughing at the well-known stock answer from General Houbin, and ducks under the table to conceal her noises. David sees this coming, glares at Chinaloa while motioning for her to get it under control with a curt slide of his hand under his chin, and mouths, "Cut it out."

Tom shakes his head at Chinaloa's antics. "General, that's the short version, but the point is that we are doing the same thing here in the US by attacking vulnerable areas inside the reactor software. We are probably a year away from being able to debilitate the Clinton, Illinois, nuclear power station. The plant provides power to over eight hundred thousand homes in Central Illinois. It would take months to recreate that power from their coal plants. Layer on a total loss of comms, and Illinois will fall into anarchy within days."

"Excellent, Tom. I still can't believe how deeply you infiltrated American politics," David pats Tom on the back, also reminding the general that his team is highly experienced, with some very significant wins in the past.

"Well, I had to work hard, and this is why we all need to act 'Americanized,'" Tom says with air quotes. "It took hundreds of thousands in cash, but we got great intelligence, great leverage, and a model for others to use to generate political access," Tom says with pride. "I don't quite have the . . . *gifts* that Christine Fang had, but she, too, did a great job of 'infiltrating,'" more air quotes from Tom, "that congressman from California."

"Eric Swalwell, yes, yes. He was a remarkably easy target and easily, well, persuaded," David says with a grin. "Very good job, though, Tom. As one of our most senior associates, you are doing a great job. As always, let me know what else you need to continue your success."

"Yes, sir," says Tom, sitting back with a smile and resting his hands on his belly.

David looks over to Chinaloa to give the next update. "General Houbin, Qiyun Yi is up next. You hear us call her Chinaloa because of her time working with our other associate, Ziqi, in Mexico and Guatemala. Together, they created the most effective money laundering scheme of scale for the Sinaloa Cartel. The program has been further refined to avoid US banking detection and is responsible for laundering over one billion dollars in cartel drug money so far. This has provided almost two hundred million US dollars for the CCP so far, including funding these current programs. Chinaloa is a dedicated CCP member who ultimately got caught by the DEA in Memphis, but it was not her fault. She was tied to El Chapo through her operations in Memphis, and El Chapo's associates got busted by being sloppy on the phone. Then she got snagged in the sting operation. She has returned to help the CCP with our goals of destroying the US from the inside," David summarizes.

"Very good," General Houbin says with very little vigor.

David looks over at Chinaloa, who has collected herself and hasn't repeated her earlier antics. "Okay, Chinaloa, would you like to go next? Start with your work to contaminate the Mahomet Aquifer. Since that aquifer is only twenty miles west of here, it's an easy place to start. Where are you currently on that project?" asks David.

"Yes, sir," replies Chinaloa, back to being a true professional. "We still have American relations inside the US via our heavily shielded holding companies, mainly WH Group. We are using subsidiaries of WH Group to acquire land around the Mahomet Aquifer. We keep all transactions as difficult to trace and low-key as possible. We've used Smithfield Foods before, but now we use a new acquisition model. This firm is distantly tied to Archer-Daniels-Midland Company, a very large US conglomerate. One of the cousins of the Daniels family, Charles O. Daniels, started his own company a couple of decades ago called CO Daniels. That business is now the holding company for Shafer Chemicals and Elevation Seeds. So, ultimately, we'll continue to acquire the land around the Mahomet Aquifer through CO Daniels."

"Very good. The deep levels of these company structures are hard to track. Ultimately, we'll probably need to use one or more of them to buy the chemicals for the aquifer, right?" asks David.

"Exactly," Z confirms as he jumps into the conversation, finally failing to contain himself. "Our plan is to continue to assemble land outside of Mahomet, only about thirty miles west of here, under the guise of farming and purchased in the name of real US entities. This also works for my projects regarding spraying chemicals to damage farmers' lands that are not using Elevation Seeds."

Chinaloa jumps back in with a stern stare at Z. "Z, I wasn't done yet."

"Apologies, Chinaloa. Please continue." Z ducks his head down with a scared look on his face.

Chinaloa glares at Z, then continues, "Through Shafer Chemicals' licensing, we are purchasing Mustargen, which is used to treat cancer, so it is common in many US labs. Shafer provides a nominal amount of Mustargen to the biochemistry lab at the U of I, where we have stationed 'researchers', our internal agents. They are working to blend it with a polymer that is durable enough to support adding the Mustargen into the Mahomet Aquifer. Once the polymer enters the water, it eventually dissolves and releases the Mustargen into the water supply as a carcinogen. We do have other options, but the primary goal is to make the water nonpotable. As we know, Mustargen is a nitrogen mustard that was originally used as mustard gas for chemical warfare in World War II, so it is highly regulated. We acquire our other needed chemicals, specifically pantaphos, in a similar manner. Just like mustard gas, the chemical pantaphos has cancer-related applications and is studied for how it can break through the glioblastoma cell wall of brain cancer cells."

"Very, very good detail, Chinaloa, but maybe a little higher level." David gestures to Chinaloa, raising his hands palms up.

"Understood, but this is important," explains a slightly defiant Chinaloa. "The main thing is that our researchers at the U of I need to get access via Shafer Chemicals. Shafer buys pantaphos for both cancer research and to eliminate rot in onions and corn. We acquire a surplus of it through fake shipping manifests and have thousands of gallons of it on site here. We spray the pantaphos chemical solution onto neighboring crops that are not using Elevation Seeds to reduce their yields. This facilitates an accelerated transition to Elevation for farmers buying from other seed manufacturers. And our seeds do not play nice with other seeds, so they are stuck using ours. We call them 'terminator seeds.' And then we control the supply of corn."

"Extremely impressive, Qiyun," the general says, using Chinaloa's formal name. "I don't think I'm following the plan for the water aquifers though; those are essentially underground lakes?"

Chinaloa gestures back to David with the proverbial 'bird.' "See!" she mouths at him. David shakes his head at her insubordination.

"From a high level, General Houbin, yes, they are underground lakes," Chinaloa continues. "The main thing is that Shafer Chemicals has access to many chemicals that can ruin a water supply source for decades, and the FDA doesn't test for most of those chemicals in the aquifers. CO Daniels buys titles to farmland that is around or on top of the Mahomet Aquifer, then we drill straight down into the aquifer and can slowly—or even not that slowly if war breaks out—turn those aquifers, or even lakes, into pools of cancer-causing water. This is accomplished through direct injection from our advanced cell technology, which we have stolen from the fracking industry in West Texas. We will know what is contaminated or not, so we're not at risk."

"Yes, very impressive, Qiyun. You did a great job with our money laundering operations about a decade ago as well," says David, smiling at Chinaloa while shaking his head at her flipping him off. "Anything else?"

"Thank you. Just like our money laundering operations, there's always a way to accomplish our goals by being creative. With technology continuing to evolve to support us, we will always be a step ahead of the US government," explains Chinaloa.

"Agreed. And what do you have, Z?" asks David.

"General Houbin, I am Z, and I'm working with Tom on money laundering and drug trafficking. We met with our equivalent of a director in the Sinaloa Cartel last week to aggressively increase our business with them. In the past week, Sinaloa has tested the process and found it works extremely well, as we expected, and they received their pesos from our underground banks within forty-eight hours. We've had no issues with couriers or our main clients, the mainland PEPs."

"Thank you, Z. I'm aware of the black-market foreign exchange program for our PEPs. President Xi's cousin gets monthly reports, so I assure you this has the attention of the party. This drug trafficking program is important for not only funding our projects but to the demise of the United States from within. I'm not sure if I have mentioned that I'm quite a history buff. I'll give you the high-level summary, but the Opium Wars of the nineteenth century—and what the British did to us—are lessons learned that we are now using to crumble the US from within," General Houbin drones on.

At the same time, David, Z, Chinaloa, and Tom all drop their shoulders and heads, as they have heard this Opium War example from the general many times—and with increasing frequency as he ages.

"The old guard," the general begins, "remembers the stories well from our grandparents. The streets were in ruin. You had to walk over zombies that used to be friends. Family members would just look through you as if you weren't there. That is the power of opium. The Chinese economy was initially boosted by the opium trade but then quickly degraded when the citizens became lazy. In turn, as the people smoked more opium, they would become dependent on the state. Ultimately, they became criminals and finally, would die," the general says with his usual dramatic flair.

David puts them on mute, as the group is cracking up at Chinaloa mockingly banging her head on the conference room table. David thinks to himself that he is giving this team too much leeway and needs to tighten up the discipline. But in her defense, it's pretty funny.

"First, I'll remind everyone," the general repeats the well-known story, "the British burned the old Summer Palace to the ground on October 18, 1860, in the second of the two Opium Wars at the beginning of the Century of Humiliation. Only seven of those twelve beautiful bronze heads have ever been recovered to this day. A true travesty. Since that day, the CCP has been committed to never suffering defeat or shame like that again. However, . . ." the general pauses for his big finish, "we did learn to turn the tables on the gweilo." General Houbin uses the old slang description for white people that means 'foreign devil.' "And now, we will use all our power, our supply chain, and our influence inside Central America to push that poison into their countries. They will suffer the disgrace felt by my ancestors."

David works to wrap up the call. "Very moving, sir. And thank you to my team—excellent updates. General, do you have any questions for us?"

"I do not, David. But please tell Helen I said hello," the general responds then quickly disconnects the line.

David shrugs, then he tells his team, "I know the general tells the stories of the Opium Wars, but in his defense, that's exactly what we're doing to the Americans, and it's working extremely well. The party is very proud of what you are accomplishing and will continue to expect great results. We *will* be victors in these endeavors as long as America continues to be apathetic and greedy about taking our money and turn a blind eye to what they know is occurring. As long as we remain in the gray zone of our warfare where they can ignore us. This is what I keep working to teach all of you."

David pours himself a glass of water. "As you know, I've studied the US for most of my life to look for weaknesses and fault lines, and they are almost everywhere, but as former President of the United States Ronald Reagan once said, 'Nations crumble from within when the citizenry asks of government those things which the citizenry might better provide for itself.' And from what I can tell, rural America doesn't seem to be waking up anytime soon to the fact that their federal government is not going to do anything at all and that it's only up to them to really protect their land."

# CHAPTER 7
# FRIDAY NIGHT LIGHTS

"Chris, I have no idea what happened. The police tell me it was a drunk driving accident and that he passed out at the wheel. I know he loved his Miller Lites from time to time, but get this: the police randomly mentioned that there were a number of Coors Light bottles in his car at the time of the accident. I know it's weird, but that makes no sense to me," Eric emphatically updates Chris Lee on what he knows about Steve's death.

Over the course of the summer, and now into early fall, Eric and his team have worked many overtime shifts on their specific projects: corn yields, seed treatments, field site visits, hybrid analyses, and coordinating with other labs for cancer research. Eric is ready for a break and needs to spend more time with Christine, as their relationship has really progressed over the summer. Helen is incredibly resilient, maybe due to her age, and works more than everyone else.

Chris has been somber all summer from Steve's passing and can't figure out how it happened, as drinking and driving is way out of character for Steve, especially with Coors Light rather than Miller Lite. Eric has been giving Chris a wide berth for many months but is also perplexed by the tragedy.

"Helen! It's time for Friday night lights!" Eric bursts out of his office, pumping his fist in the air. "You've been working way too many hours and need a break."

Helen jumps in her seat.

Helen, pulling down her safety glasses and rolling her eyes at Eric, wearily says, "There's no way I have time for that, Eric, and I'm not even sure what you are saying."

"Helen! Friday night lights! Fall football at my high school, St. Joseph-Ogden!" Eric pauses, then pleads. "Come on, Helen, this is where my glory days were, and I was king of the world. I bet when we show up, they'll carry us to midfield, and we'll call the coin toss. Better yet, we'll probably get to run through the banner while they play the theme song to the movie *Rocky*!"

Helen rolls her eyes again and puts on her glasses to return to the microscope and keep working on her charts. "Eric, you know this is the best time to get our most accurate results and plot our findings."

"Okay, as your boss, I command you to go home, get ready, and put on a fun football outfit. I'll pick you up in an hour." Eric laughs and points to the exit. "You are going to love it, and I'll introduce you to some wonderful people, more of my family, and . . . wait for it . . . Christine is joining us too."

"If she's coming along, I do not want to be a third wheel and make things awkward." Helen makes her excuses, then she points to Chris, who has still not looked up. "What about Chris? Will he go?"

"I don't think Chris is in the mood, but I'm going to send him home to get some sleep. He's had a long summer, and I'm a bit concerned about him, honestly."

Eric turns to Chris and softly and kindly says, "Chris, you are more than welcome to come to the football game at St. Joe, but if not, why don't you shut it down and go get a good night's sleep and some rest this weekend?"

Chris turns off his computer, his head sagging. "Sounds like a plan, boss. I'll get some rest this weekend, I promise. You guys have fun at the game."

Eric pats Chris on the back, then he turns back to Helen. "Okay, Helen. You have a deal. You drive yourself to Monical's in Saint Joe. I'll pick up Christine and meet you there. We can grab a bite to eat, maybe a beer, and then we'll head over to the game. We're playing those losers from Unity. You know, the ones who date their sisters and all have cats as pets!" Eric laughs out loud and leans on her station, showing he's not going anywhere until she says yes.

Eric sees Helen crack a smile and senses she's truly happy to be invited. "Okay, fine. I'll drive myself, then I can leave early and go to bed. I have been really looking forward to meeting Christine too. I'll wrap up here and meet you at . . . where again?" asks Helen.

"Monical's Pizza. I'll show you how to properly mix the white dressing with the red dressing. It's like mixing shampoo and conditioner; you have to have the proper balance. And then you need a Coors Light to make sure it's really balanced," explains Eric with as much sincerity as he can muster.

"You need to get out of here, Eric," says Helen, rolling her eyes. "Monical's is coming up in Apple Maps for me. I'll see you there at 5:00 p.m.?"

"Sounds like a plan," says Eric as he takes off his lab coat and chucks it over her computer monitor. "I can't wait. You're going to love it."

Helen powers off her computer, grabs her backpack, and heads out the door with a little pep in her step, excited to finally meet Christine.

Eric texts Christine again: "Are we still on for kicking the crap out of Unity High School?"

"You make no sense most of the time!"

"So yes?" texts Eric.

"Sounds good. 4:30?" texts Christine.

"Yup!" texts Eric.

Eric heads home to shower and change into his SJO spirit wear, then he drives his gray F-150 Platinum pickup truck over to Christine's apartment on the corner of University and Lincoln Avenue. Eric thinks it's a little serendipitous that she lives at Lincoln

Place Apartments, which his parents built with his Grandpa Pusey back in 1985. Grandpa was an architect, a World War II veteran, and a professor at the University of Illinois. Eric's Grandma, Leota Mae Pusey, owned about thirty single-family homes at one time. Even Eric's mom, Sheila, operated these apartments for many years. Oddly, Eric didn't have much desire to get into apartments, much like his Aunt Toni, who has lived most of her life in Indianapolis.

Interestingly, a middle school used to be on this land, but it was torn down, and the bricks were used to help build the Royal Community Building. He decides to skip the history lesson with Christine this time around, as he had told her some of this before. Eric reminisces about his fond memories of push-mowing the private yards and how that fresh-cut grass smell never leaves you. He thinks about moving those older kids in and out of the apartments in August, how much he hated cleaning up after those disgusting students (another smell that also never leaves you), and navigating beds inside the narrow hallways while it was ninety-five degrees outside. He chuckles to himself about how he was mainly paid in Dairy Queen ice cream cones and that his parents probably owe him some interest.

Eric walks up to Christine's apartment and knocks on the door. She opens it. She's shockingly well-prepared for the game. She has her hair in a bun and is wearing a maroon and blue SJO shirt and blue jeans with super cool maroon Nike low Dunks.

"Where did you get all that get-up? It's very on point!" asks an impressed Eric.

"Katie O. hooked me up last night." Christine shows off the awesome shoes she bummed from Katie.

"Well, okay. Let's head out then!" urges Eric.

Eric and Christine drive along Route 150, and Eric points out the highlights along the way. "Do you see that house all by itself?" Eric points to a house about two miles away across a bean field.

"Off in the distance there?" Christine points to the correct house.

"Yup, that one. That's where Mom lived from when she was only ten years old. Grandpa Pusey lived there for the next fifty-five years," says Eric.

"Well, that's interesting given he did so much. The guy got his black belt in tae kwon do at seventy-six. I would have thought he lived in Champaign and not so much in the country," says Christine to Eric's total surprise.

"You do listen. My goodness!" says Eric. "Why not the country, though? And what's wrong with the country?"

"I do listen, silly! At least the first time or two you tell your stories," Christine says with a warm smile. "There's nothing wrong with the country at all. I even remember that Grandpa Pusey was shot through his arm in World War II and killed the German that shot him—then even got the Luger afterward. Architect, captain in the army, professor—just feels like he's a city guy to me."

Eric considers that perspective for a second. "I can see that."

They drive into St. Joseph, past the high school that takes up a city block, then meander through a neighborhood with well-maintained Victorian-style homes and pull into Monical's parking lot.

"Now, what's the most important thing that I told you?" Eric turns off his truck and then stares comically at Christine.

"Don't overdo the white sauce in the red sauce," Christine says matter-of-factly, humoring Eric. She gets out of the truck, shaking her head.

"Exactly!" Eric thinks he's so funny. "But also remember that Helen is a bit shy, so you'll have to help her out of her shell a bit," Eric softly says over the truck's hood as they walk toward the entrance.

"On it." Christine gives him a thumbs up.

As soon as they walk through the front door, Christine rushes to Helen for a big hug like two old friends, and Helen easily reciprocates. Relieved, Eric takes a deep breath, as it appears the introduction has gone well and may lay the groundwork for a future friendship.

"Hey, Helen! So glad you could make it," says Eric. Then he asks the hostess for them to be seated.

"So nice to meet you, Helen," Christine stands back next to Eric. "I've heard only incredible things about you from Eric."

The hostess leads them to a table in the back of the classic pizzeria dining area, and they sit down at a table covered in a checkered red and white tablecloth. Eric chats with the hostess for a second while Christine uses her hand to push off the pizza crumbs left over from the prior patrons. Eric notices her need to clean the table. "It's part of the ambiance; please don't mess it up," he jokes. "But seriously, why do the crumbs stick to that tablecloth so much?"

Eric notices that Helen isn't overly shy with Christine as she says, "Truly, so nice to finally meet you in person, Christine. It's been a long summer for all of us, but we are working on important projects. Eric tells me that you two were able to spend a lot of time together this summer, too. He is very fond of you, that much I can tell."

"Yes, when it works out for our schedules. He's working a lot, as you know, and I've been slammed at work, too. We're making it a priority to spend time together, so we meet each other a few times a week. I'm not sure his buddies are overly excited about me taking up his time, but they'll have to get over it." Christine winks at Helen as breadsticks and a large bowl of house salad are delivered.

"Don't mind him, Christine. And definitely don't let his buddies worm their way into *your* time." Helen continues to look more comfortable. "How are things at the bank?"

"Things are going well," Christine says with limited excitement. "I think everyone knows banks are under constant cyberattacks. Since that's my area of responsibility, it gets old and a bit repetitive. I wish I could just put up a sign that says, 'Please leave us alone,' but I doubt that will work." Christine perks up a bit and smiles slyly. "I do like the forensic research part of our work where we investigate attacks and directly help people and companies that have lost money. We're getting better at exposing the true culprits, too, but it's still almost impossible to prosecute them."

"Fascinating. How do you investigate attacks?" Helen quickly asks with a more serious look on her face. "I don't think I'm following." She grabs a breadstick and looks intently at Christine.

"Well, we have access to . . ." Christine pauses, guardedly looking at Helen for a split second. "From a higher level, it could be a number of things, but it's mainly fraudulent transactions, money laundering, or even corporate espionage." Christine fidgets with her napkin as she talks about this level of detail with Helen. "But we don't need to go into work things and bore you to death."

"Well, that sounds very interesting," says Helen.

Eric sees Helen pick up on the cues and change the subject.

"I'm told that we need to be very thoughtful about what we're ordering here," Helen says.

"And the combo of sauces," Christine sarcastically interjects.

"Oh no, he went over all of that with you, too?" Helen shakes her head. "Come on, Eric, you have to do better. Girls don't want to hear about salad dressings."

Eric jumps in. "Everything is good, I promise, but the thin-crust pizza is what makes Monical's famous. And I ordered for us when I was talking to the hostess, so hopefully, you love their deluxe pizza: no cheese, extra sauce."

"Thanks for the no cheese. I hear you are dairy-free too, Christine?" Helen asks, knowing that most people think she's weird for not eating dairy.

"That's right. I cut it out a while back because I have a personal vendetta against dairy cows. Truly hate them and what they did to my family back in the home country." Christine laughs at her attempt at humor. "I knew we'd get along, Helen! Now, Eric, you can listen to Helen and me talk about shopping." Christine quickly moves to one of her favorite topics.

"That works for me. I'll be on my phone over here looking at high school score updates." Eric puts his head down and starts responding to text messages on his phone. "Also, I need to catch up on my family text thread about tonight."

"I've heard so much about you from Eric. You have a sister, right?" Helen leans in closer to Christine.

"Yes, one sister, and we're from the north suburbs of Chicago. I like it up there but am fine moving out of Illinois too. It's just so cold and drab here for way too long; I'm not sure I can take it much longer," Christine confides as their deluxe pizza is delivered.

"I get it, but it's such a beautiful state, too. Trees, water, wildlife, all the seasons. I sort of love it, to be honest." Helen grabs a piece of pizza.

"I can see that, and the people are just wonderful, too. How does it compare to your home in China?" Christine leans in to hear Helen.

"Well, my hometown has about one hundred thousand people, so it is not overly rural. But similar to here, we have a lot of agriculture around the town. Farms and livestock mostly, but the farms are nowhere near this advanced. We don't have the tractors, semis, or combines like the farmers have here. We're decades behind in terms of ag technology." Helen sips on her water. "But our lab is world-class, too, at the university."

"Please eat, Helen. I'll talk your ear off all night. But that's interesting. Would you go back and help to improve their farming?" Christine leans in a bit more.

"I do like it here, but I miss my family. To be honest, I'll need to see what jobs are out there." Helen trails off a bit.

"Jobs in China?" Christine asks with some confusion.

"Sort of," Helen rubs her ear and looks away. "For us Chinese, sometimes we get told what to do more than really asked, I guess."

"I see." Christine nods sympathetically. "Well, let's enjoy our time here. I'm always happy to go run around with you and shop or just hang out. I'll text you my number. Don't hesitate to use it," Christine says playfully. "I'm really liking the pizza, but I didn't even try the white sauce."

"I didn't either." Helen playfully leans over and taps Christine's hand, looking for an excuse to not try this concoction. "It looks weird to me. Eric, the white sauce is all yours."

"Weak! You at least need to try it. Fine, I'll go pay the bill." Eric quickly finishes his Coors Light.

"We just got here and started getting to know each other, Eric." Christine's stare is pleading. "I prefer not to compete for Helen's time over high school football, you know."

"I'm sorry, ladies, but it's time to go. Let's cheer on the Spartans." Eric jumps up to pay the bill at the front counter. "We'll have plenty more chances."

After Eric pays, the trio heads to the parking lot. Helen gets into her minivan and follows Eric and Christine about three hundred yards to the high school parking lot across Main Street. They park in two of the last spots toward the back of the lot, which is packed with people discreetly tailgating.

"You weren't joking about the crowd," says Christine as she looks around at the hundreds of fans in blue and maroon. "Katie O. says she'll be here tonight, too."

"Yup, it's impressive. And I'm sure she will be. This is a big game against Unity. Let's just hope she never ends up with a guy from there." Eric starts to pick up his pace and cues Christine and Helen to keep up with him.

Eric sees Katie O. a few cars away as they cut through the rows toward the bright lights of the field. "What's in the Yeti there, Katie O.?!"

Christine waves at Katie and motions that Eric won't let them stop for some reason.

"Don't you worry about it." Katie retorts, but let out her signature snorting laugh. "We'll see you two later tonight, okay?"

"Why is this such a big game?" Christine asks. "This is still high school, right?"

"I'll pretend like you didn't say that." Eric shakes his head at Christine. "As with most years, our head-to-head matchup against Unity decides who wins the Illini Prairie Conference. Plus, we hate them. And they hate us." Eric boxes the air.

"Gotcha. So, like, a bunch of high school boys who don't like each other because of girls then carry that insecurity with them the rest of their lives and tell everyone they're meeting up about the rivalry and some catch or something?" Christine does a great job of maintaining a straight face.

Eric stares at Christine, trying to figure out if she's serious, then sees a grin begin to crack. "You're picking up on this real quick!" Eric bursts out laughing. "But you're probably going to like this one a bit more."

Eric sees the brand-new LED lights that make the football field look like it's high noon. The stands on the left side are colored maroon and blue with SJO fans, and the cowbell clanging is already grating on his nerves. The band strikes up the Spartan fight song to finally drown out the cowbells for a minute. The opposite stands are colored in a darker maroon and white, the Unity fans showing their team spirit. The grass is a perfect shade of green with the Spartan logo at midfield and the bright white lines showing every ten yards. Eric looks for his closer friends and family while saying hi to the rest of the crowd he knows from growing up, playing football, and coming back to games. He can tell most of the fans are very charged up, and a few of the SJO and Unity fans exchange pleasantries that involve their mothers. He finally sees his brother Cory and heads straight over to him with the girls in tow.

"Cory! What's up?" Eric gives his brother a man hug.

"You know, just another packed day with people who keep running into me. My daughter won't stay around me, so I keep chasing her down, and I have no clue where my wife is," snarks Cory.

"Always a ray of sunshine!" jabs Eric. "Is Dad ready for halftime?"

"Seems that way. They'll meet by the entrance, then they'll walk onto the field." Cory points to the entrance to the field. "Mom and Dad are running late though; Dad was probably having a bad hair day." Cory jokes about their dad's receding hairline.

Eric then sees Mitch waving to him and powering through the crowd.

Cory says, "Oh, come on! Where did she go?!" and runs off looking for his eight-year-old daughter, Cameron. Helen, Christine, and Eric just laugh at Cory's dramatic expression.

"Hey, Eric. Great to see you. And who do we have here?" Mitch asks when he finally gets to Eric, then smiles at Christine and Helen.

"Mitch, this is my trusted lab analyst, Helen, and my, um, friend Christine, whom you met at the Community Building," Eric stammers out and immediately turns red.

"'Friend,' got it." Mitch laughs, shakes Helen's hand, and gives Christine a side hug. "Very nice to meet you, Helen, and great to see you again, too, Christine. Did Eric figure out your name isn't Christy yet?"

"He's gotten better since the Community Building, Mitch." Christine playfully hip-checks Eric. "But unfortunately, there are now other things he needs to work on."

"Come on, Mitch, help a brother out." Eric shakes his head with playful disappointment.

"Okay, fine, Eric. Sheesh." Mitch then nods toward Helen. "I'm glad your lab mate is here, Eric. I wanted to chat with you about some of the things I'm seeing in the fields as we come up on harvest."

"Wow, okay. Whatcha got?" Eric shrugs at Helen pulls in closer to hear Mitch better.

"Look, I understand that Elevation Seed employs a lot of people around the area, and they are great people, so I want you to be very cautious with this information," says Mitch, looking back and forth between Eric and Helen's eyes through his glasses.

"Okay, this sounds a bit ominous now. We're still talking about corn seeds?" asks Eric, half-jokingly.

"We are, Eric. I know it's weird, but here goes. You know I've been telling you that Elevation's yields are noticeably larger than other hybrids?" Mitch asks, twitching his decades-old mustache.

"I remember," Eric confirms. "Maybe ten bushels an acre. But I just assumed that was due to soil differences and maybe fuzzy math. Again, you can't trust these farmers to tell the truth about yields any more than you can trust them about the size of the fish they just caught," Eric teases, but he is truly interested in what Mitch is telling the three of them.

"Eric, I know it sounds goofy, but I'm just asking you, and I would presume Ms. Helen here, to take a closer look into the different yields and potential causes. I've been doing my own research by walking into multiple fields and looking at the current corn status. Things like ears of corn per plant, kernels per husk, and any signs of rot or other issues, like husks falling off the stalks too early. Elevation's yields appear to be closer to twenty-five bushels more currently, but it has to do with the reduction of some of the other hybrids. Meaning, Elevation looks to be coming in around 250 per acre, but the others are showing closer to 225. The cause appears to be more corn rot than I have seen in the past ten years. These hybrids are so resistant to many diseases that corn rot is just not a huge issue for us anymore, but I'm seeing it in the fields," explains Mitch.

"Hmm . . . that is odd." Eric rubs his rather large forehead. "Okay. Well, we'll take a closer look, but I don't believe that's jumping out at us in the lab. Do you, Helen?"

Helen shifts her feet slightly and briefly pulls on her ear, which seems to grab Christine's attention.

"I'm sorry, Helen. Mitch here is a dear friend but also a bit of a fellow nerd who likes to study crops more than most," explains Eric. "You can tell him what you're seeing."

"Um . . . well, I have not seen anything about advanced corn rot in our sampling so far this season. There could be a variety of explanations, but perhaps a new strain of disease is causing it, and we haven't identified it yet. We can look closer though, Mr. Mitch," Helen says sheepishly.

Eric peeks over at Christine because he knows this isn't exactly how the evening was supposed to start. He can see she's taking some deep mental notes as she listens intently to Mitch and Helen.

"We're on it, Mitch," confirms Eric, turning to Helen. "Helen, let's take a look next week in the lab. But as Mitch pointed out, Elevation Seeds is important to the town, employs a lot of locals, and supports a ton of events, so we don't want to jump to any conclusions until we're absolutely sure our testing is accurate."

"Thanks, Eric. Sorry to bother you with your new friends." Mitch extends his hand to Helen. "Very nice to meet you, Helen."

Helen shakes Mitch's hand.

"And Christine," Mitch gives Christine another side hug, "Eric needs some serious support, which we've all known for many, many years. Godspeed." Mitch slaps Eric on the back as he walks away.

Eric gives a half-hearted laugh, then turns to Helen. "That all seems so strange to me, Helen. You haven't seen any of that in your analyses?"

"Nothing at all, Eric, but I'll look more specifically into what he's saying tomorrow." Helen focuses directly into Eric's eyes with deep intent. "With our lab technology, we should be picking up on these issues before he would, though."

"I agree. Thanks. Look who is coming over now!" Eric frantically waves as he sees Cory, Cameron, and Cory's wife, Bobbi, walking back toward them. The intense bright lights over the football field make a halo behind them. A heavy murmur erupts from the two-thousand-person crowd as they wait in anticipation of the kickoff.

Bobbi strolls up, holding Cameron's hand. "Well, this is a cool family night!"

"Sure is. How are you doing?" Eric gives Bobbi a high five and drops to one knee to give Cameron a big hug.

"I'm doing well. Just running around making sure things are okay," replies Bobbi.

Les and Sheila Buchanan stroll up to the group as the game is just about to kick off, running unusually late.

"Hey, guys. Glad you made it," says Eric as he gives his mom a big hug and his dad a high five. "Whoops, kickoff!" Eric stops abruptly as the entire stadium roars.

SJO kicks the ball to about the five-yard line, and the game has begun. The kick returner for Unity dodges the first tackler, then gets destroyed around the fifteen-yard line, and the SJO crowd goes nuts.

"That's how you start a game!" Eric shouts, throwing his fist into the air.

Eric takes Christine by the hand and then turns to his parents. "Mom, Dad, this is my friend Christine."

"Very nice to meet you." Sheila gives a surprised Christine a big hug. "Sorry we're late. We had to meet with other alumni before the game."

"Hi, I'm Les." Eric's dad stretches out his hand to Christine as she looks up at the 'ex' six foot five inch frame.

"Is this your first time at a St. Joe football game, Christine?" Sheila gently asks Christine with a warm tone.

"It is, Mrs. Buchanan. I can't believe how packed the parking lot is. And the stands are shoulder-to-shoulder with fans! It's about as loud as what I would expect from a college football game."

"Yeah, it's not always like this for every game, but this is a big game against Unity. I am sure Eric told you this is quite the rivalry and has been for forty years."

"This one time in a basketball game against Unity when I was a sophomore," Les begins to tell a "good ole days" story.

"We can talk about that later, Les. We need to go for halftime," Sheila interrupts, patting her husband of over fifty years' hand and leading him away.

"Man, your dad is so tall, and your mom is so small," Christine demonstrates the over one-foot difference in their height.

"Yeah, Mom was a cheerleader here, and Dad was a really good athlete, but I don't want to ruin the surprise either. You'll find out more about that later," Eric says coyly.

"Okay, fine. But I can see they are still in great shape, too." Christine watches them briskly walk toward the SJO sideline.

"I know! Dad is still a good golfer, and Mom still makes those little legs go incredibly fast power walking 5Ks. I've done a few with her, and she literally puts her head down and even beats some runners. I have to focus to keep up with her." Eric mimics his mom's walking.

Eric gives Christine a little hug, then sees Helen over her head and can tell something isn't quite right.

Eric goes over to Helen as she fidgets with her hands. "Everything okay?"

"Yes, this is just all very, very new to me. I've never been to a high school football game before, and I can't believe how many people are here," Helen screams over the continuous dull roar of the crowd.

"I know it's a lot, but you're doing great. Can you hang in there until halftime?" Eric points to the scoreboard, which shows a few seconds remaining.

"I'll try." Helen apprehensively scans the parking lot, which has seen a marked change from ten minutes ago. She jumps as the clock runs down to zero and the halftime horn blares.

# SOWING DISCORD

"Okay, Christine and Helen, this is the highlight of the game," Eric says as he points out his dad walking from the midfield sideline to the middle of the football field.

"Welcome, SJO sports fans!" comes over the speakers. "We are now introducing you to our inaugural St. Joseph-Ogden Hall of Fame Class!"

The crowd cheers.

"Eric, your dad is being inducted into the hall of fame?" asks Christine.

Helen, wide eyed, looks around at the stands. "I'm not sure what that really means, but the crowd sure does love it. Congrats to you and your family, Eric."

"Yeah, I wanted to surprise you both. Dad was quite the athlete back in the day. He even went on to play four years of basketball and two years of baseball at Illinois."

"Les Buchanan. Basketball. Class of 1965!" says the announcer as the crowd cheers.

"Well, that is very cool. When are you getting inducted?" teases Christine.

"High school was fun, and we had some good success, but I'm not sure 'tackling dummy at Illinois' is an actual award. At least not yet," Eric says, shrugging. "But don't mention this to anyone, but Bobbi is going to be inducted soon too."

"But let me tell you the really cool thing about this field and more about Bobbi!" Eric points to a sign that hangs just below the scoreboard, showing the game is tied seven to seven.

"Okay, tell me!" Christine is super curious.

"Well, Bobbi Buchanan was Bobbi Duval before she married Cory. And this field is named after her dad, Dick Duval. It's literally called Duval Field, and a little-known fact is that the font is the same one used for his favorite beer, Bud Light. He coached football and baseball, was the AD for the past thirty years, and went to the

State Championships five times. He's in the Illinois Coaching Hall of Fame, too," explains Eric.

"You're joking. Really?" Christine seems suspicious that Eric's sarcasm is in play here.

"Nope. Dick and his wife, Lynda, moved from the Kankakee area when we were very young and stayed the rest of their days here. Dick got cancer a while back, and the field was dedicated in his honor when he was really sick. He's such a tough dude that Cory drove him around with the family in a golf cart when he could barely walk. He still gave all of us former players and students a hard time up to the end. He passed away about a week after the dedication," says Eric.

"Oh my goodness, that's an incredible story." Christine looks off into the crowd. "It's really special how connected small towns are. Very different from where I grew up in the suburbs of Chicago. Almost everything here is related, from sports to school to businesses to family," Christine observes.

"It really was. Super special and a bit emotional for all of us." Eric stands up a bit straighter. "You'll hear me say some 'Duvieisms' from time to time, but a great one is 'You know what happens when you assume, Buchanan?! You make an *ass* out of *you* and *me*.' He always said that while stomping his foot and spelling out the words with his hands."

"Ah," Christine chuckles. "I like 'you make an ass of me' a bit better."

"Well, aren't you creative now!" Eric becomes a bit uncomfortable, as he likes Christine more than he intended.

 Eric gives her a side hug, eyeing what seems to be an uncomfortable and distracted Helen. "Okay, Helen, you did great for your first Friday night lights. Thanks so much for coming."

"This has been so much fun, but I do need to go. Sounds like Mitch wants some extra work in the lab. I'll handle it in the morning." Helen smiles pleasantly, then gently pulls away from Eric.

"I'll see you Monday, but I may try to come in tomorrow as well," says Eric.

"Sounds good. It was such a pleasure to meet you, Christine," says Helen.

"So nice to meet you, too!" says Christine as she moves in to give Helen a hug. But Helen only gives her an odd side hug and pats her on the back.

"Oh, okay," Christine says with a smile. "We'll work on our hugs next time."

Just as Helen is about to walk away, Eric's cousins, Danny and Jeff Harms, come up to say hi to Eric too.

"Congrats to Uncle Les on the Hall of Fame. That's pretty cool," Danny says, then jokes, "I'm sure Sheila will love hearing the glory days stories."

"Mom will be thrilled." Eric shakes his head in amazement at how his dad can recall every moment from every baseball and basketball game he ever played in his life. "How does he remember every detail from his career?"

"Oh!" exclaims Eric, remembering to introduce the girls to his cousins. "Guys, this is Helen. We work together in the lab. And this is Christine. We met at Spring Royal Days. Katie O. introduced us. That was right before joining you guys at Freeman's."

Danny, Jeff, Helen, and Christine exchange hellos and handshakes. Eric notices Helen nervously scan the parking lot.

"I need to get to work early in the morning, everyone, but it's been really nice to meet you," Helen says, abruptly turning to leave.

Eric stammers, "Are you good?"

Continuing to move away from the group, Helen quips, "Yeah. I'm fine. I'll just see you at the lab."

As Helen anxiously walks away, Eric peeks back at her, confused by their odd exchange. He sees a stout middle-aged Asian man behind the end zone staring at Helen. The man, is rather far, but appears to watch Helen get into her car, then looks back at Eric. Eric tries to focus on him for a split second through the lights. The man quickly turns and walks toward the Unity fans on the opposite side of the field and disappears behind their stands.

*Well, that whole thing was a bit weird,* Eric thinks to himself. He then turns back to the group. "Well, gang, where are we going after the game?! As Coach Duvie taught us, 'Win or lose, we booze.'"

# CHAPTER 8
# DUTY TO PARTY

"You look like you had some fun after I left!" Helen lifts her head from the microscope and snickers at a rough-looking Eric walking into the lab on Saturday morning.

Eric is not dressed in his usual golf shirt and dressy jeans lab attire. His lab mates constantly haze him for his lack of wardrobe creativity and Salvation Army vibe. This morning, he's wearing something very different and really mixing it up—a golf shirt and *casual* jeans. He has accessorized with a blue Cubs hat pulled down a bit to hide from some of the brighter lab lights in the ceiling. Eric pulls up a lab chair at the station next to Helen and spins around in a circle like a kid who just ate a sugar-filled Twizzler. He grabs the station counter to stop himself, quickly realizing the move was a bad idea.

"Guilty. Christine and I ended up running around with some old friends. We found our way to Bunny's Tavern in Urbana, then closed it down. We had a great time, though. I'm nervous to say it, given my aversion to girlfriends, but I'm really starting to like Christine."

"I'm not even from here, and I can tell that you two are genuinely hitting it off. You make a great couple. I'm happy for you." Helen smiles warmly. "Can we chat about this experiment that Mitch mentioned? The pantaphos is attacking the glioblastoma cell wall inside the brain cells of our test mice. It is also very toxic to the cells, which is very exciting because those cancer cells are difficult to kill. We should let the cancer research group know we are seeing positive results and may need quite a bit more pantaphos."

"I'll let them know. Good work." Eric labors to articulate. "Helen, thoughts on wrapping up this test set and grabbing breakfast at Merry Ann's Diner again? I could use some coffee. I'm not going to be overly engaged until I get something to eat soon," Eric says, clearly failing to pay close attention to Helen's comments.

"Agreed! I'm starving, too, and I'm at a good stopping point. I'll drive," Helen says with a smile. "Usually, half of Merry Ann's customers are students who haven't gone to bed yet, so you'll fit right in."

"I just need some coffee, Helen! I'm not that tired."

"Not tired, huh? Sure."

Helen drives the five minutes from the lab to Merry Ann's and only hits one curb along the way. Eric and Helen walk in and plop down in a booth.

"Hello, Eric and Helen," Virgina, the super-spunky middle-aged waitress greets them. "Glad to see you again. What will you be having?"

Even before Eric starts to speak, both Helen and Virginia stare at him, waiting for his customary joke stolen from the cult classic movie *Swingers*. "Ma'am, says here I can order 'Breakfast Any Time.' I'd like to order pancakes in the Age of Enlightenment," he says with a big smile, slowly looking up at Virginia.

Virginia groans and rolls her eyes, "You got it, Voltaire." Then she cracks a big smile.

"How about you, little lady?" asks Virginia.

"I'll just have some pancakes with a side of medium eggs."

"Coffee for both of you?"

"Yes, please," both Eric and Helen respond in unison.

Virginia quickly returns with the coffees and says with a smile, "Here you go, guys. Enjoy."

Helen pours a generous amount of cream and sugar into her coffee.

"I still don't know how you call that coffee. That's a dessert." Eric shakes his head.

"It's much better than the motor oil you drink, but you are quickly perking up. Well done," Helen says and sips her coffee.

Helen fidgets with the silverware and straightens out the paper napkin for the second time. Eric sees that Helen has something on her mind and gets more comfortable in his seat.

"Eric, when we are in the lab and helping to create these hybrid corn seed strains, do you have any thoughts about whether that it's okay, not okay, or maybe just doesn't matter so much?" Helen ponders.

Eric sips his coffee and looks at Helen, puzzled. "I'm not sure I'm following. What do you mean? Like, is it okay or not okay from an ethical perspective?"

"I just mean our jobs are to improve the quality of these seeds—corn, beans, wheat, alfalfa, etc. Do you ever get concerned that we're creating a situation where seeds—and I guess America's food supply—are designed in a lab and will ultimately cause some issues down the road?"

"That's a very interesting question. It seems like we're not just going to have a nice low-key recovery breakfast, huh?" Eric rubs his temples.

Helen throws up her hands and says, "I'm sorry, it's just been bouncing around in my head. We don't have to talk about it. Tell me more about the football game. Did you win?"

"No problem at all. I'm just giving you a hard time. But, yes, we did win!" says Eric with some more pep. "But to your point, I do have concerns about creating super strains of diseases. Some of those strains that mutate on their own outpace our research and modifications to our own individual genetic makeup. For example, we could easily be changing human DNA, our genetic makeup, through our food supply. We play a vital role in that. We also know about the issues and lessons learned from several examples where labs have contributed to severe destruction—including biological warfare in World War II. Scientists have created or spread all sorts of diseases through weapons, such as smallpox and anthrax. Even COVID showed us that a virus created in a remote lab can spin out of control into a global pandemic."

Virginia brings their stacks of pancakes and eggs.

"That cook is so fast; always has been." Eric loves to compliment the service here.

"Yes, thank you so much." Helen grabs the maple syrup.

"Right. That's the stuff I'm talking about," Helen says as she pours about 5 seconds of syrup onto her pancakes. "I know many researchers from Wuhan, and they are having very real regrets about their work on the MERS virus that turned into COVID. China—and even many people inside the States—have worked very hard to cover that up for years. The truth has finally come out, along with the many failures associated with that pandemic. Ultimately, I think many people finally realized our governments do create nefarious viruses and then use them to increase control over their citizens. I personally believe that part of our responsibility in the lab is to create and incorporate stringent safety measures. This also works to limit the damage governments can inflict on their very trusting people and around the world."

"As healthy as you are, I can't believe you drown your pancakes like that. You'll have diabetes by the time you're thirty," Eric ribs Helen's food etiquette again. "But go ahead. I agree and am following."

Eric's comments don't even register with Helen as she continues. "But as you know, when bird flu and anthrax leaked from a US lab in 2014, many of our current protocols were updated to prevent a recurrence. We keep updating our safety procedures, documentation, and communication between labs. We also need to be very careful with our role in 'playing God,'" Helen uses air quotes, "and be focused on helping, not hurting, humanity. I think that is where I struggle a lot when I see labs being used to weaponize a country."

Eric stops joking, seeing this is rather personal for Helen. He realizes that Helen has a soul searching conflict she's trying to work out. "Helen, these are very heavy considerations for our work. I must admit, I haven't thought this deeply about what we're doing in our lab."

Helen is still distant in her own thoughts. Trying to contemplate what appears to be an internal battle, she continues. "Helping to feed the world with high-yielding, disease-resistant corn is a great goal, to me at least. But using our technology and knowledge to create terminator seeds to restrict all other seeds from growing should be forbidden because it does real harm to our international food supply. And for what? For the benefit of a ruling class or a dictator?"

Eric waves for Virginia to top off his coffee while staying very engaged in Helen's well-thought-out concerns. Virginia ducks in to fill up his mug, sees the serious mood, then gracefully continues to another table.

"I know that many people—maybe even you, Eric—believe COVID was intentionally released from that lab in Wuhan in order to do serious global damage." Helen shrugs. "I don't know for sure, but I highly suspect it was a lab leak from poor safety measures. However, I do know that immense global damage was done. How do we prevent that from happening again?"

Eric sets down his coffee mug and looks intently at Helen. "Well, the release of dangerous chemicals, viruses, and even dangerous pathogens is different than what we are doing in our lab. Although, those guys up at the University of Michigan need to get their labs on lockdown for agropathogens it seems. For us, our goal is to make crops resistant to specific attacks. We can't stop a tornado from going across a cornfield, but we can increase stalk strength to make them stronger in high winds."

"That's true," Helen agrees, pushing her food away.

"No more, huh?" Eric, seeing that she's done, continues. "One of my main concerns is that we need to be cognizant of our resistant strains that force Mother Nature to create super diseases. These are the strains that attack our food supply at an existential level, and we have no way to stop them. As a world, we don't have enough food stored for a famine-level event, like say, the Irish Potato Famine in Europe in the 1800s or the Dust Bowl of the 1930s."

"That's all true, and there are literally billions more people now than back then." Helen nods in agreement.

Eric continues, "We have a legitimate concern, like you are correctly questioning the genetic modification of anything living—viruses, seeds, etc. This includes the chemicals that we use to modify them, such as antifungal and antidisease chemicals impacting growth and productivity. In theory, we do our best to ensure our modifications are safe, but we can't be 100 percent sure by any means. Now, here's an interesting question that you may not have thought about." Eric pauses.

"Okay, let's hear it!" says Helen, refocusing on Eric's comments.

Eric appreciates that she loves to be challenged. "Let's consider American businesses, universities, and landowners. What processes are in place for giving intellectual property to non-US citizens?" Eric narrows his eyes. "Meaning, you personally have incredible access to US trade secrets, data, processes, and even people."

"Are you asking me if I'm a spy?" Helen smiles.

"I'm not concerned about you being a spy at all. It's just a thought: how much access would I get in China if the roles were reversed, for example?" Eric picks up his fork to finish his omelet and let Helen contemplate his question.

Helen pauses for a few seconds. "Well, good point. There is almost no way the CCP would give you this level of access in a Chinese lab. Everything is on full lockdown and heavily controlled in China, especially in research labs. That's why many of us work so hard to come to the United States. Here in America, we are allowed to learn, study, and gain vital experience. Back home, we don't have access to Chinese secrets because the CCP is concerned about US espionage. What we learn here in the States takes many years; however, in China, it could take decades, if it were even possible."

Eric pauses to consider what Helen is saying. "Well, that is interesting and what we generally call fundamental research. Chinese students come here to learn at a heightened pace because the risk to the information—and, I guess, the risk of espionage—is only an American risk and not a Chinese one. Then, the students return to China with a much higher skill set because of it. It's a sandbox of sorts where you can learn and not be concerned about breaking anything or compromising lab research, like in Wuhan. If you were to mess up, then you would only be breaking American research, right?" Eric asks in earnest.

Helen shifts in her seat, a bit agitated. "Well, that's not really the point of studying abroad. I promise you that I'm just trying to learn as much as I can from you, the other analysts, and professors, in addition to having access to the best technology available in a university environment."

Eric addresses her concern. "I know that's not what you are trying to do, but what about people or students who have different goals or intentions? Maybe even goals to hurt the US from within. How do we manage those risks? To me, frankly, our federal government needs to step in to install a little common sense. We should be protecting our trade secrets and our latest advancements. Otherwise, Illinois, and many other universities, will continue taking international money while educating international students and professors. They could then return to their home countries to find ways to hurt the US from inside and outside. Wouldn't you agree?"

"I highly doubt any of that could happen. There are people, including you, who are watching us international analysts rather closely," Helen pushes back.

"Sort of. I trust you and have for some time. You are a good person, which is very apparent. However, there are other folks around here who seem shady to me. I think I called them 'goofy' before. It's just not that hard for them to do nefarious things in our labs. They can steal data, take lab results, upload viruses, and transfer intellectual property. All sorts of things can be done without anyone really knowing. I'm not in charge of any of that for our lab, and we follow strict protocols, but it's not too hard to get around those either. In addition, the university administrative folks obviously love other countries' money and have for decades. International students make up about 20 percent of the total college population and maybe half of the engineering colleges."

Helen seems to be getting a bit more nervous and starts to wring her hands when she's not stirring her coffee over and over again.

Eric waves to Virginia again and asks Helen with a warm smile, "Are you okay? I promise we are just playing philosophical Jenga to see what stays up. This is all well above our pay grade."

"I'm fine. I just know many people believe that many of us Chinese are here to steal information and trade secrets," Helen says shyly.

"Well, let's change course to another philosophical dilemma that has bothered me for a minute," Eric offers a verbal off-ramp.

"Okay, I'm feeling a bit sorry about bringing this up, but at least we can continue to talk about this over breakfast while you recover. And you look a whole lot better too," Helen says kindly as Virginia arrives.

"What do you two need?" Virgina asks.

"No rush, but the check whenever you get a chance, and probably some more coffee for her. She's stirred the sides off the mug," Eric jokes. Virginia leaves.

"Thanks, Helen. I do feel much better," Eric says with a smile. "This is something America's farmers need to consider. These are very real dilemmas for our farmers and their families—and it will only continue to get more concerning for them."

Helen tilts her head in confusion. "How so?"

"Back to the source of the money that the U of I has become dependent on from China and other countries. We have all of these new buildings, programs, staff, etc. That comes with a hefty price tag, like we discussed. For farmers, they ultimately have a duty to their families to make money, send their kids to college, make a living, all of it, right?"

Helen narrows her eyes, contemplating the question, then nods in agreement. "I'm following."

Eric nods back and continues, "They have many alternative opportunities for their farmland but feel a duty to the land and maintaining its productive integrity. Other options range from windmills to solar panels for green energy production. They also have development options, such as new homes, apartments, and Walmart. Another option is even selling their land to huge corporations and foreign investors and just walking away."

Helen continues to track the logic, "Pretty sure I'm following. Maybe. You mean that real farmers need to decide how much their land is worth to them and their families—and maybe even future generations. So, they need to decide what *business* decisions to make today while balancing moral concerns as well?"

Eric's eyes widen as Helen seems to understand. "Exactly. You see these windmills around here? Farmers get paid a lot of money to allow those to be built on their land. Same with solar panels. Did you know farmers get paid by the federal government for windmills about three times as much as they make farming? So, they need to decide today whether to stop farming their land and lease it out for the next thirty years. The math is about two hundred fifty dollars per acre of profits from farming, and that assumes a normal year with mild weather. They are paid about a thousand dollars per acre for solar panels with annual increases for inflation. Just some obvious questions, but if that ground isn't used for farming for thirty years, it won't be able to produce crops for at least five years afterward due to lack of nutrients, the sand from roads, topsoil erosion, etc., right? Why are we removing prime farmland from our overall supply for wind and solar farms in the breadbasket of America?"

"Well, about five years to return the ground to top-producing farmland, yes. Maybe even longer depending on what damage has been done to the soil." Helen energetically stirs her coffee again.

"That's right. And that's if those solar panels and chemicals used to protect the panels don't make it sterile. And some other questions: What happens to the windmills and solar panels after thirty years? The technology is obsolete in less than ten years, then the actual parts will be worthless and impossible to even procure. So, what happens to them? Do we take them down and chuck them into a landfill like the weekly trash?" Eric motions as if he's throwing out a bag of trash.

Helen seems more curious now. "I hadn't really thought about what happens next with these enormous investments in wind and solar. It's not like you just download a new software version or buy a new one. Back in China, we have these enormous cities that this company, Evergrande, built. They went bankrupt betting on future growth and more government subsidies. It wasn't really that hard to predict, looking back."

"Right, I've heard of them. They are called 'ghost cities,' right?" Eric asks, using air quotes.

"Yes, I remember that even back in early 2020, it was estimated that China still had thirty million unsold properties that could house eighty million people. That's the size of Germany," Helen confirms.

Eric thanks Virginia as she comes over with the check. "And another thing!" Eric smiles but continues, "My cousins, whom you've met, have had offers on their family farm for decades, like most farming families. The market price wasn't high enough for them to sell or stop leasing the twenty-five hundred acres they farm. They've even had offers for windmills and from global companies that want to buy it for commercial farming operations. But now, the solar panel industry is so subsidized by the US government that 'clean' energy companies can pay way above reasonable market prices for normal farming operations—all based on subsidies from taxpayers. Come to think of it, even the farm value today is based on federal crop insurance subsidies and forced ethanol uses."

"That *is* a whole lot of money, Eric," Helen agrees. Then she asks, "At what point does it make sense for them to sell then?"

Eric sees that Helen is following along. "Now, mull this over: what happens when a foreign entity—if they even know it is a foreign entity—wants to buy their farmland? We all know folks who have sold out for windmills and solar panels, and they, right or wrong, get branded as 'sellouts.' At what point does the math make sense to become a fellow sellout?"

Helen nods in agreement. "In China, your family is everything. Our ancestors are as important to us now as when they were alive and working hard. For me, I would question if your grandparents would want you to sell the farm or hold onto it. What's best for your current family—parents, siblings, and kids? My family back home would have some significant issues with these decisions."

"Correct. And what happens to the community even if your folks sell to a large conglomerate that doesn't have a real stake in helping other people, schools, sports teams, and churches, and then your family ultimately moves away from Central Illinois? We see that all the time, where kids who were born and raised here leave to find their opportunities elsewhere and don't come back at all."

Helen jokes, "You can't tell anyone I said this, and I'll deny it, but luckily, in China, we don't get these choices, and the government can just take the land if they want it anyway, so the stress is much less."

"Now, that's funny . . . and sad," laughs Eric.

Eric perks up even more. "But that's exactly right, Helen. Theoretically, what's the right answer? Where's the main duty? Are we, or my cousins in this example, responsible for holding onto the farmland our parents and grandparents have worked so hard to maintain, or do we ring the proverbial bell, sell it, and take that money somewhere that gets a much better return on our investment? Should they invest it in things that are more in line with what is in their best interest or the interest of their kids, the next generation? What happens if none of their kids want to farm? What about selling land at a premium to a foreign entity, like China, who may or may not intend to do harm to the area, the US, or even globally?"

Helen shifts in her seat again. "Well. These are good questions. I hadn't really thought about it from that point of view before. I guess I had only thought, primarily, that whatever the CCP wants me to do back in China, I just need to do it. And when it comes to my family, I'll do what's best for them and us after doing my main duty to my party."

Eric pauses for a few seconds and looks at Helen with concern. "I'm so sorry, Helen. I didn't even think about that for you. You have an obligation to a party, like Republicans or Democrats, but there's only one party, the Chinese Communist Party of China. Ugh, that stinks a bit, yes?"

"Well, I guess so. We just don't have many choices, and we're viewed much more as labor in the grand scheme of the CCP. That probably isn't going to change any time soon, but if I ever do anything that hurts you, you can know it was because the CCP made me do it." Helen flexes her biceps and playfully laughs.

Eric takes a final bite and looks a bit oddly at Helen. "You sure?" he asks with a mouthful of eggs and a funny look on his face.

Helen laughs and waves to the waitress for another cup of coffee. "Nobody is going to hurt you, especially me. I'll get another coffee too."

## DUTY TO PARTY

Eric holds up his index finger to make one last point. "Okay, let's finish up here, then go back to the lab and get some work done, but I'll leave you with this."

Helen leans in a bit to listen better as a rowdy group of college kids who look and smell like they have not been to bed yet come into the restaurant.

"Texas recently blocked a purchase of over a hundred thousand acres in southern Texas because it was being acquired by a Chinese corporation. The proposed owner was directly tied to the Chinese Communist Party, and the land was not too far from a military base. Remember that hot air balloon that we let float across the United States and didn't shoot down because we were told the communications had been knocked out? Well, guess what?" Eric sips his water.

"What's that?" Helen asks, although she seems to be tired from the conversation.

"It was transmitting data and imagery over normal cellular service. No clue how we let that happen, as it traveled over multiple military installations. Insanity, right?" explains Eric.

Eric sees Helen is done with the conversation and lays down thirty dollars to pay the bill. "Anyway, just something to consider because none of that seems like a good idea regardless of the profits to the actual landowners. So, I tend to think I'm coming down on the side of duty to country."

Helen nods in agreement but says with an ominous tone as she looks out the window, "I'm with country as well, but my country is defined by the party. And there are consequences if you choose otherwise."

Eric is taken aback by her comments but doesn't want to make her any more uncomfortable than she appears. "Agreed," says Eric. "Let's head back to work and see if Mitch is on to something."

Eric and Helen wave goodbye to their favorite waitress, Virginia, and hop into the minivan. They arrive back in the lab and both head to their respective work areas. After about an hour, Eric finishes documenting a critical stage in their testing of the small molecule pantaphos and its effects on brain cancer cells.

"Amazing!" Eric shouts across the lab to Helen. "Again, in a study of mice cells, pantaphos is breaking through the glioblastoma cell walls. I'm going to try more dosage variances, but if we can figure out how to inject this into brain cancer cells without it being toxic to the host, this could be a major breakthrough in a few years!"

"That's incredible, Eric! Congratulations. Keep it up!" Helen says with excitement.

"Will do, but how are your tests coming along with identifying pantaphos in onion, corn, and rice infections?" asks Eric.

"For all hybrids so far, I'm not detecting any pantaphos," explains Helen. "It's obviously a difficult molecule to isolate. So far, it appears that no current hybrid corn seeds are infected with pantaphos. Ultimately, we'll see the results in the yields to confirm our accuracy and yield projections, but it looks like we'll have a strong yield for corn this harvest. I'm also going to send these results over to microbiology to see if these results help their group create a new form of antifungal herbicide."

"Okay, I'm going to head home then. I'd say we've had a productive day. I'm exhausted." Eric shuts down his computer.

"Okay, I'm going to stick around and run some more tests, and then I'll wrap up as well." Helen barely peeks up from her microscope.

Eric is excited about the continued success of their research on pantaphos but is also still contemplating his breakfast with Helen that morning. He should have more conviction to answer a simple but challenging question like "When conflicts arise, how do you decide between your duty to your country and duty to your family?"

# CHAPTER 9
# CONSPIRACY OR REALITY

Back in his apartment after a solid nap, Eric gets ready to see some old friends at the best bar in Champaign, the Tumble Inn. He puts on his standard Saturday outfit: trendy Nike shoes, blue jeans, and a button-down long-sleeve shirt that's always tucked in. He wishes he could wear the exact same outfit every time he goes out, but he knows his buddies would constantly harass him, so he muddles through getting dressed. It's by far the worst part of his day.

Eric calls an Uber and heads over to Tumble Inn. It has been a local establishment for almost fifty years. The owner, Toby Herges, just passed away, so many locals are continuing to show their support, Eric's crew included. He walks in through the side entrance as he has so many times before and quickly sees his buddies already well on their way. His brother Cory is holding court, complaining about something; their great friend Johnny "Cubbies" Marquardt is in full agreement about sports atrocities, and Illini tailgate extraordinaire and cousin, Todd Osterbur, chimes in from time to time in his distinct voice that could easily be mistaken for "Deep Throat" from the Watergate audio recordings.

"Fellas!" says Eric. "How are we doing?"

"Doing great, Eric. Pull on up. We're solving all the world's problems right now. The small ones, like the stupid national debt, are handled. Now we're on to the difficult ones. Currently, 'how to get the Illini secondary to show up this season' is where we are getting stuck," Johnny says with all seriousness.

"You guys must have gotten past how to get the Cubbies to win another World Series, huh?" jokes Eric. "That's super important!"

Eric pulls up a chair. Almost instantly, the waitress, Charyn Ullrick (her folks used the "Ch" from her dad's name, Chuck, in a poor attempt at creativity for Karen), is ready to take Eric's drink order.

"Sharon!" jokes Eric.

"Karen!" Charyn retorts immediately, before Eric even finishes. "After all of these years, Eric, you need to come up with something better than how my parents can't spell."

"After all of these years, you still seem like you want to slice my tires," replies Eric.

"Well, you did date my sister and broke her heart, so there's that," says Charyn.

"Now, now, Sharon," says Eric, but he's ready to duck if a right hook were to come his way. "I did no such thing, and sometimes, things just don't work out when we're younger, you know. Maybe if she didn't scream at me so much, it could have lasted a lot longer," offers Eric, still very much ready to protect himself.

"You know she's going to kill you, right?" interjects Cory. "He'll take a beer, Charyn, and please remember which car is his and which is mine when you slash his tires tonight, k?"

"You got it, Cory, but I'm sure you'll give me a reason tonight to slash yours, too," Charyn throws back. "Full round of lattes, I'm assuming boys?"

"You know it!" the gang replies.

Charyn mumbles, "You guys are children." Then she heads off behind the bar, shaking her head with a big smile on her face.

"She loves us, I know it," says Johnny, the handsome but always single die-hard Cubs fan.

The boys talk about the usual suspects for about an hour and start to get a little tuned up, so they make their normal path, Cubs, Illini, and SJO football, and then move on to complain about liberals, not closing the southern border, and the national deficit, then back to what they will grill for tailgating and what games to bring along. Cornhole wins again over lawn darts.

Around the time the big decision of tailgating comes to a close, Christine walks up to the table and stands next to Eric.

"Oh no, she's arrived! How did that happen?" exclaims Cory as he gets up to give Christine an enormous hug and shoots a glaring smile at Eric. "Aren't you about an hour late?"

"Gents, this is Christine, my, um . . . friend," Eric says squeamishly.

"Friend, huh?" Johnny questions. "Cory's my friend too, but I ain't texting him for two hours every day for four months straight."

"She's not good with directions," shrugs Eric.

Christine jumps in, "It's true, guys. I'm fairly confident north, south, east, and west are all made up and meant to confuse people. I only understand forward, backward, left, and right for the most part. Sorry I'm late, but not really."

About that time, Charyn comes to Christine's side. "Sweetie, whatever choices you have made to be associated with this crew, you may want to seriously reconsider them. Whatcha drinkin'?"

"Whiskey sour with a splash of cherry," Christine quickly responds, like a lady who knows what she wants.

"A girl after my own heart!" Charyn looks impressed.

"Absolutely. Thank you so much." Christine nods to Charyn in appreciation.

"Don't worry about these guys; they are all harmless, but they talk way too much. Just walk away when you've had enough. If you become friends with them, though, they'll do anything for you." Charyn walks around to the back of the bar to start making the drinks.

"She's right, CP, you'll have no issues with these guys. In the very near future, they'll want to hang out with you more than they want to hang out with me." Eric looks over at Cory.

"I'm already there, Christine. Glad you made it. But CP? What's that all about?" asks Cory.

"Her last name is Pyle, so I call her CP . . . sort of how Mom calls you 'Oops.'" Eric stares at Cory, expressionless, until Cory finally shakes his head at the bad joke.

"Thanks, Cory. Always good to see you," Christine, still standing, says to Cory.

"You might as well sit down, CP," says Johnny. "It'll only get worse from here."

Christine sits down next to Eric and reaches into his lap to grab his hand. Eric quickly pulls away, hoping the guys didn't see it. Christine chuckles and flings her blonde hair back over her shoulder to further embarrass Eric. "Aw, I thought we'd hold hands in front of your buddies."

"No chance," says Eric with a grin. "I'd never hear the end of it. Plus, your hands always make mine so sweaty."

Charyn hustles back with the drinks and points outside. "The sun is going down, boys. What kind of night are we having?"

"Sun's down, time to go brown!" Todd rubs his hands together like he's planning a big night.

"Rules is rules!" says Johnny.

"Makers for me, Sharon!" says Eric.

"Makers it a round!" says Cory.

"BOOOOO," the table confirms the bad joke.

"Bro, you really need a new joke," Johnny says, shaking his head. "We even have a new guest tonight. Maybe give it a little extra effort."

"Johnny, have you even had a girlfriend since the turn of the century? Don't you still live with your mom?" Cory retorts. "Christine, if you have a friend who would take in a wounded, mid-twenties Cubbies fanatic, please send her Johnny's way."

"Yeah, sure." Christine looks around, seemingly already thinking about her pending exit. "You seem like a great guy, Johnny. I'll keep an eye out."

Christine leans over to Eric. "You sure it's okay that I'm here?"

"Heck yeah!" says Eric. "We've been hanging out all summer; it's time to introduce you to more people, I guess."

"You guess?" says Christine with a tinge of sarcasm.

"I know," laughs Eric. "I know it's time for you to meet more people. Maybe in a year or two, we can move into being boyfriend and girlfriend," Eric lays on the sarcasm.

"Let's not move too fast now," says Christine.

Charyn comes back with the round of Maker's whiskey.

"Thanks so much. Looks like I need to cancel my morning meetings." Eric is expecting a fun night with the fellas.

"Just wave me down. I don't have that much going on," Charyn shockingly says something nice to Eric.

"Let's go work on the jukebox for a bit, yeah?" Eric says to Christine.

Christine jumps up, ready for a change of scenery, and they head over to play some tunes. Christine slowly reads off the selections she's making, "Ryan Bingham, 'Bread and Water;' Shane Smith and The Saints, 'All I See is You;' hmm . . . Pat Green, 'Wave on Wave;' Uncle Lucius, 'Keep the Wolves Away;' and 'If We Were Vampires,' Jason Isbell and the 400 Unit."

"Wow, you know your stuff. Where did you learn Texas Country?"

"I was raised in Houston until I was about twelve years old and never lost the love of it." Christine keeps looking over the music options.

"That's right. I keep forgetting that. Very nice. Keep it up! Maybe a little Red Dirt while you're at it? CCR?"

"Sure thing. Cross Canadian Ragweed's 'Boys from Oklahoma' and Stoney LaRue's 'Oklahoma Breakdown?' You got it," Christine makes two more selections. "Okay, that should get us started, with a couple of surprises in there for you. Your buddies can play their Luke Bryan and Florida Georgia Line after this list plays," Christine says playfully.

"Let's grab another drink at the bar and give the guys a chance to calm down a bit." Eric grabs Christine by the hand and leads her to the bartender.

"Sounds good to me." Christine happily follows along and smiles a bit more as she looks down at Eric holding her hand.

Eric walks over to the bar and squeezes in next to a large man with super broad shoulders and very dark hair wearing cowboy boots and Wrangler jeans with a pearl snap shirt.

"Excuse me, partner," says Eric, "mind if I squeeze in here to grab a cocktail?"

"Not at all," says the man as he scootches his chair over a bit. "You need a seat for the lady? I'll get up," he says.

"No, no, that's okay. We're sitting at that table over there and just taking a break from my friends." Eric points to his buddies about fifteen feet away.

"Yup. I've been around here enough to know those guys are too much fun sometimes," says the middle-aged man. "What's your name?"

"I'm Eric, and this is Christine," says Eric as the man extends his enormous hand to Christine and then to Eric.

"Very nice to meet you, Eric and Christine. I'm Mark Samaan."

The bartender strolls over, and Eric asks Mark, "Would you like a drink, friend? It's on me."

"What are you having?" asks Mark.

"Well, been drinkin' Maker's Mark a bit. That work?" asks Eric.

"Hmm, let's do Weller 12, and I'll buy, then you can get the next one," says Mark.

"That's not how that was supposed to work exactly, but okay, fine," says Eric.

"Two Wellers, please, Carla, and whatever the lady is having too," says Mark.

"CP, Carla has been the head bartender at Tumble Inn for about thirty years, and everyone knows her. She's like Sam from *Cheers* at this point," Eric points out.

"You got it, Mark. What would you like, little lady?" asks Carla.

"I'm fine for now, Carla. I'm a lightweight, but thank you." Christine softly smiles at Carla.

"So, do you live around here?" asks Eric.

"I do," says Mark. "South Champaign, just down Neil Street a bit. I moved up here from Texas about a year ago and took a job with Busey Bank."

"I knew you looked familiar, but you're not in a suit tonight!" exclaims Christine.

"I'm sorry?" says Mark.

"I work at Busey Bank as well in the cybersecurity department and have seen you around the office before. You're not a hard man to miss," jokes Christine, referring to Mark's large stature.

"I could see that. I almost played football at Illinois out of high school but blew out a knee, so I just went to school here. Now it's just hard for me to fly coach," jokes Mark.

"I played football at Illinois, too. But I was more of a tackling dummy for guys that were your size. It hurts!" jokes Eric.

A man a chair away tries to slide over a bit but struggles. He leans in to introduce himself. "Excuse me, you guys, but I'm a huge fan of country music. Who played these tunes? I haven't heard Pat Green's 'Wave on Wave' for a while in a bar."

"I did," says Christine. "I was raised in Houston, so I like both kinds."

"Country *and* Western?" says the new friend, laughing but still struggling to move his chair a bit closer.

"Ah, I see you are a Blues Brothers fan too," laughs Eric, referring to the 1980 classic movie based in Chicago.

"Ok, but let's see how well you know your movies, too. My name is Richard Furr," says the stranger.

Eric pauses, thinking about the name, then blurts, "Dick Furr! What's a Dick Furr? It's for peeing, but that's not important right now. The movie is *Spies Like Us*!" laughs Eric.

"Well done, especially for your age. I like to get that joke out of the way, but, yes, my name is Dick. Nice to meet everyone," says their new friend. "I was raised in Prosper, Texas, myself. Small world."

"Excuse me, ma'am," Dick says to Carla. "Did I break this chair? Why is it so hard to move?"

"Well, that's Champ's old chair. Obviously, that's not his real name, but he was a regular here for thirty years back when I started here. That's where he sat before passing away about five years ago. Champ wore out the felt cushions on the legs of that chair, so the nails really stick into the floor. He wouldn't let us replace them, though. He used to say, 'I ain't going to move from here anyway; why spend the money?' But do you see those gashes in the wood floor?" Carla points down to the bar floor.

"Wow, some of these are deep."

Eric watches as Dick, with a curious look on his face, runs his shoe over the lines in the floor.

"Yup, that's from customers trying to move the chair like you are after Champ passed away. It's always fun to see new customers get frustrated with that chair. Champ would have loved it. Now, those chairs behind you," Carla points to the odd red chairs directly behind the group.

Eric, Christine, Mark, and Dick all turn around to look at the short, wide metal chairs.

Carla continues, "Now, those chairs were purchased from the Milwaukee County Fair a number of years ago by Mr. Herges. Champ would never sit in them because he wasn't sure he could get out." Carla laughs at the memory. "Champ was quite the interesting character, but we loved him. Nice to meet you, everyone." Carla heads off to serve another customer.

The group nods at their newfound knowledge then Mark continues, "I'm from Illinois mostly, but I do know Texas Country. I was down in Fort Worth for a couple of years and listened to 95.9 The Ranch religiously."

"Mark, why were you in Fort Worth? And what do you do for Busey?" Christine leans into Eric a bit more.

"After graduating with a political science degree from Illinois, I got a very, very low-paying job at a think tank in Fort Worth. I don't care where you graduate from, a political science degree isn't going to get you much."

"Think tank?" Dick asks quizzically. "Like those foundations that don't do anything but milk money from the federal government then lie to themselves that they really created something?"

Mark laughs. "Sort of, but I like where your head is. Believe it or not, this is more of a libertarian think tank, but I moved up here to help Busey's financial advisors grow their businesses. As Christine can probably tell you, regional banks have had some highs and lows over the past few years. But I'll also tell you, from my prior life, banks are constantly under cyberattacks. I'm sure Christine is very, very busy these days."

"Very true, Mark. The attacks just keep increasing in both amount and complexity, especially as AI continues to get more advanced," Christine confidently confirms.

"Yeah, um . . . maybe the Chinese have something to do with that," Mark says with a sly grin.

"No question that they do, and it's getting worse. Most people would completely freak out if they knew the level of attacks, espionage, and theft of intellectual property that is occurring." Christine looks at Eric to see if this has escalated a bit fast.

"Uh oh! We have a conspiracy theorist!!" Mark laughs as he points at Christine.

"It is what it is." Christine shrugs.

Eric leans over to Christine and gently says, "If you're having fun, then I'm having fun. But let's not get so worked up that I end up in trouble, okay? I think this guy would take me pretty quickly."

"It's a bit of a choice for me. Either I have another cocktail, and you get into trouble, or I continue chatting with Mark and stay calm . . . er." Christine shrugs again.

"Let's go with option B and remember that you'll see him again very soon at the bank," Eric cautions.

"Fair enough." Christine turns back to Mark and mouths "We're good" to him. Mark gives both Eric and Christine a thumbs up and a smile.

The jukebox changes to another country song.

"'Good Lord Lorrie' by Turnpike Troubadours?!" says Dick excitedly. "I sing this constantly to my wife, Lori. But I do have a question for you tin-hat conspiracy folk. You say that we'd freak out if we knew what was going on, but what's going on, again? I'm lost. And . . ." he gets Carla's attention, "I'd love another double Crown and Coke, please!"

Eric is confused at how this group is still discussing politics. "Well, I just wanted another whiskey, but sometimes this is just how evenings go at the Tumble Inn."

Mark says, "Well, let's make this a bit easier for us since, somehow, we have all become such great friends. I'll give a quick summary, then, Dick, you look it up and see if I'm making it up or not."

Dick pulls out his phone and says, smiling, "On it, Mark. The research department is at the ready!"

Mark turns to Dick with a wry smile. "Let's start out simple, then go from there. Anyone heard of Volt Typhoon?"

"Negative, but let's see what the Google machine has to say." Dick starts tapping on his phone.

"I'm very aware of those attacks," says Christine. "We updated our network off old routers many years ago, and it wasn't an issue for us."

"Okay," Dick jumps in. "Words, words, words. Got it. The Department of Justice and the FBI 'said on Wednesday they disrupted a sweeping Chinese cyber-spying operation that targeted critical American infrastructure entities and could be used against the United States in a future geopolitical crisis.' Okay, well, that doesn't seem like a good thing."

"That doesn't even scratch the surface," Christine stresses. "The Volt Typhoon CCP hackers infiltrated many areas of our infrastructure for several years."

"She's right," says Mark. "It took the FBI over seven years to figure out what the Chinese were doing, and it was Microsoft analysts, not the FBI, who figured it out. Then the FBI went through a court-ordered 'clean-up' process. They finally did what they could to shut down Volt Typhoon's access to small office and home office, or SOHO, routers and told the American public."

"So, it's all fixed now?" asks Dick.

Eric leans in, super curious about the answer but says, "We can just talk Illini sports." But everyone ignores him.

"Not even close," says Mark. "Imagine a bad guy wants to rob your house, but he has seven years to do what he wants to do, and you have no idea. You don't even know that he's in your home while you and your family are there. He can do all sorts of evil handyman projects, and you don't even hear or see him doing it."

"Okay, got it. Like a ninja-ghost-carpenter-type bad guy," Dick says with a laugh.

"That's extremely accurate, in a sense." Mark gives Dick a thumbs up. "So, now this bad guy has created all sorts of doors into and out of your house that you can't find or see, and only he knows which book to push to open up the trap doors. He's got rabbit ears on your TV, so he can change the channel or just turn it off if he wants. Now, apply this scenario to the water infrastructure for the entire United States."

"I don't really like where this is going," says Eric.

"Me neither," says Dick as he perks up to the new song. "But I do like 'A Country Boy Can Survive.' Maybe we have a fighting chance."

Mark continues, "So now, it's a few years down the road, and the Chinese still have access to the system that controls major water and wastewater utilities across the country. It's super simple: they disrupt the process, and we won't have a reliable source of drinking water. And we won't have faith in our water supply either. That's important, too—lack of trust."

"Ugh, this is an article from . . . March 19, 2024?!" Dick says, his tone escalating. " . . . hackers are pre-positioned inside IT environments . . . to enable disruptions across multiple critical infrastructure sectors . . . for as long as five years?!"

"Yup," says Mark. "And do you think the FBI and other agencies are going to tell the American public, much less the Chinese, what they really know or how vulnerable we are?" queries Mark.

"I can confirm they will not tell the truth, and I can also confirm they will punish, with jail time or the like, those of us who know more than we're allowed to say if we go public," says Christine. "And it's unnerving and not okay with me, but I also understand them trying to not incite total anarchy from the American public."

"Agreed," Mark concurs. "Let's save how much is too much for the public to know about threats to our country for another Friday night. Let's stick with actual confirmed projects for now."

"As you wish," says Christine. Then she squints at Eric to show she's a bit miffed that Mark blew her off but decides not to pick a fight.

"To summarize, operation Volt Typhoon is where the Chinese infiltrated to have full, unfettered access to most of our critical infrastructure programs for almost a decade. The FBI and NSA were years late in figuring it out, and the Chinese simply use outdated network gear that has been phased out by networking companies, like Cisco or Netgear. The government never upgrades these routers, and the CCP simply hacks into those networks to plant cyberattacks. These attacks could bring the US to its knees in days if not minutes. Do you remember how the US came to a screeching halt from 9/11? This would be exponentially worse, and we're sitting ducks across the country."

"Carla! Weller 12! Seems like you have a new sales guy here!" Eric points to his empty glass, then peeks over at his buddies, who are now playing darts. Johnny is stabbing a dart in between his fingers on the table to try to show off to the guys.

"Look over there, Christine," Eric nods toward the dart board. "I could be doing ninja-level bar tricks, too, instead of hanging out. You should be very happy I'm over here."

"Yes, yes, I'm very happy, and your sacrifice is duly noted," Christine says with immense sarcasm, shaking her head. "You guys never grow up, huh?"

"It would appear not." Eric can't stop laughing as Johnny stabs his hand with the dart, then cusses up a storm.

Dick has now tuned out a bit and is singing to "You've Got to Stand for Something" by Aaron Tippin. "This song may mean a whole lot more in the near future," says Dick, "but all this information is easy to find. Thanks, Mark. You opened my eyes a bit."

Christine turns back to Mark. "I'm well aware of operation Volt Typhoon, and you obviously are as well. What else is out there?"

"Well, we could chat about the food supply inside the US or the food supply outside the US. We could talk about energy, such as liquified natural gas logistics, and how much that depends on its own digital network, which has no doubt been hacked. Maybe some bioterrorism, shutting down nuclear facilities, or maintaining our current energy independence if we're smart enough to hold onto it. How about something that may have impacted you guys recently?" asks Mark.

"What's that?" asks Dick.

"The multiple AT&T cellular tower 'outages,'" Mark says, using air quotes.

"Ugh! What do you mean? I thought AT&T said that was a software glitch or something." Dick seems a bit bewildered.

"Okay, what about given what you now know about Volt Typhoon," Mark continues his education of the group, "and how long it took for the government to figure it out? The government finally told the American people about that issue because the hack went to court, and details were revealed. Do you really believe the outage was an issue with rolling out a system upgrade for a company that size? No chance."

Dick takes another swig. Mark laughs at Dick but continues, "Did you know almost all military phones were impacted and did not work when that 'outage' occurred? Verizon, an unrelated company, had issues too. A month later, AT&T tells us it was hacked, and millions of customers' social security numbers were stolen. No chance we're not being lied to about the true cause, but the majority of the country either believes it or doesn't care. The larger issue is that it confirms our wireless communications are compromised and vulnerable. Want to layer on no drinking water, no communications, and our military being in the dark too? Tom Clancy would be proud," explains Mark as he watches Dick's eyes widen with concern.

"Okay, I'll do one last research project for you here, Mark." Dick picks up his phone again and starts to type. "Here's what I'm seeing for the AT&T outage. We were told it was a technical glitch, but we'll never know. US Senator Rubio thinks it was a glitch as well because a real Chinese cyberattack would be 'one hundred times' worse."

Dick continues to quickly read, then pauses a bit. "Well, this isn't good at all. This is from the director of the FBI:

"'... FBI director, Christopher Wray, has also expressed concern about China's cyberattacks against the US and its allies, saying they are reaching a "fever pitch."

"'You might find your companies harassed and hacked, targeted by a web of corporate CCP proxies. You might also find PRC (People's Republic of China) hackers lurking in your power stations, your phone companies, and other infrastructure, poised to take them down when they decide you stepped too far out of line and that hurting your civilian population suits the CCP.

"'China-sponsored hackers pre-positioned for potential cyberattacks against US oil and natural gas companies way back in 2011, but these days, it's reached something closer to a fever pitch,'" he continued. "'What we're seeing now is China's increasing build-out of offensive weapons within our critical infrastructure, poised to attack whenever Beijing decides the time is right.'"

"Okay, I've had enough espionage fun for one night, and I want to go back to my 'head in the sand' crew and remain blissfully ignorant. Very nice to meet y'all!" says Dick as he picks up his chair to slide down the bar again while softly singing "If We Were Vampires" by Jason Isbell and the 400 Unit.
"I think I really like this song," says Christine as she gives Eric a kiss on the cheek, then points to Johnny and Charyn doing some version of the Texas two-step by the jukebox, Johnny stepping all over Charyn's feet.
"I think I do, too," says Eric as he gives her a big hug. Then he turns to Mark. "Mark, very nice to meet you, new friend. We're going to say good night to our buddies over there, then head home."

"Very nice to meet you too, Eric. And Christine, I guess I'll see you in the office. If you need anything at all, just let me know." Mark salutes them goodbye.

"Absolutely. I'll be in the lab again next week and will be happy to put my blinders back on about how the CCP is going to take down our communications." Eric shakes Mark's hand.

"Eric, the comms are only the beginning and the easiest to see. Keep digging, and you may find things you don't want to see in our food supply," Marks warns ominously. "And if you are curious about how the CCP is using students from the University of Michigan and the EV battery maker Gotion as a launching off point for military espionage, you'll be interested to see how they bribed city council members, including allegedly paying a farmer eleven times the market value for his land. That should help keep you up at night as well, but keep fighting the good fight."

"Sheesh, Mark, you read a lot of things that I don't, but I need to be better here. Have a great night." Eric and Christine walk out of earshot of their new friends, holding hands.

"I really don't like hearing about how exposed we are as a country. What do you think?" Eric asks Christine.

"I think you need to read a bit more and pay attention to what's going on around us," Christine says, implying Eric needs to stop being so naïve. "I didn't find anything he said surprising in the slightest. We all need a plan for when, not if, we lose the things that make life's necessities easy to obtain, from cell phones to food at the grocery store."

"I can see that, and I've made a mental note that my head is up my can a bit. Should we say goodnight to the guys or just Casper?" Eric points to his buddies playing Euchre. Charyn is now sitting at their table hanging out since most of the customers have gone home. "I'll warn you, if I go back over there, it may turn into another hour or more."

"Charyn looks like she has them under control. Let's just leave them alone," Christine offers. "I'm beat anyway. Are we still doing lunch tomorrow?"

"Oh yeah, lunch, of course." Eric works to hide that he forgot. "We'll hit up that restaurant Helen recommended, but I do want to go into the lab for a bit in the morning. Our buddy Mark here has given me some ideas."

# CHAPTER 10
# YOU'VE BEEN WARNED

"**H**E's here! Everyone be perfect today!" David hears the owner of Shiquan Wonton say in Mandarin to the back kitchen staff. David and Helen Chan wait at the hostess stand as the owner, Tsue Wong, hurriedly walks over to greet them.

Shiquan Wonton has been on the campus of the University of Illinois for over twenty years. Mr. Wong immigrated from rural China over thirty years ago with his family and took a job at a local liquor store while his wife worked double shifts at a donut shop and cleaned local office buildings most evenings. About twenty-five years ago, a stoic middle-aged Chinese official who was working undercover inside the United States approached Mr. Wong at the liquor store with a proposition. Mr. Wong would be put on a salary, take a paltry commission for all sales through his store in exchange for rudimentary bookkeeping, and be involved in the Chinese drug trade throughout the Midwest. There were no questions posed, nor opinions accepted, but now, he and his family operate one of the busiest Chinese restaurants in Champaign County, inside the restaurant and out.

"Mr. Lee. Very nice to see you for lunch this afternoon. Please come sit at our best table," Mr. Wong says in Mandarin while bowing to both David and Helen as they nod in return. For a Sunday, the restaurant is rather busy, but Mr. Wong does give them the best table since Helen made a reservation two days prior.

"Thank you, Mr. Wong. We'll just have two of your specials today and would prefer our privacy, please." The pair sit down in a corner booth as the workers in the back work hard to get a good look at the famous espionage director David Lee. He can see them but keeps his head low.

"As you wish, Mr. Lee." Mr. Wong scurries off, directing his staff to get back to work.

"Mr. Wong helps us out quite a bit with couriers, but I really wish he made better wonton soup," David says dryly.

"Okay, please update me on your projects." David quickly switches to a more serious tone.

"Yes, Uncle." Helen addresses David as "Uncle" in the traditional but informal Chinese fashion for elders. This shows respect to people they have known for some time, even though there is no familial connection. All other student agents refer to David Lee as "sir," but Helen has known David her whole life. "Let me know if you want more details, but I'll keep it nontechnical if you would like," Helen replies.

"Understood. I'll ask as needed," David says curtly, letting Helen know he's not in a good mood. Criticisms of her will come soon enough. They pause to allow Mr. Wong to deliver egg drop soup to their table and then shuffle out of earshot.

"Egg drop, much better than their wonton," David confirms.

"Regarding the pantaphos lab tests, manipulating the results is always done after hours. Covering it up is getting more challenging because of other students testing brain cancer treatments in the lab late at night as well. I currently switch the results from non-Elevation Seed hybrids, such as Beck's and Wyffels, when they show corn rot due to the pantaphos that is being inflicted on the crops in the fields. I don't believe I'm under any suspicion there, but that might be an issue if I were to get assigned to another project in the future."

"So don't allow yourself to be reassigned," David says firmly, then takes a quick sip of his soup.

"Yes. I will try my hardest," Helen quickly says, then also slurps some of her soup. "You're right; this is good egg drop."

"Okay," David focuses, "but concealing positive corn rot is critical to masking our projects in the fields. Let me know if you see any issues arising, and we'll work to help you take care of it." David finishes the rest of his soup and listens to Helen.

"Understood, Uncle. But please remember that the biomedical students and staff are also running their own tests at Morrow Plots for other uses and applications," Helen explains. "I haven't seen that pantaphos tests are part of their curriculum, but it's something our analysts over there should watch carefully."

They both pause as Mr. Wong shuffles over and delivers egg rolls to their table, then scampers away again in silence.

"We have four students who are working inside that lab, and they are aware of the risks as well. We have a mitigating plan in place. I do not have concerns about them," David says in an even firmer tone to continue to send a message to Helen that he is not pleased with her results. "Have you identified seeds that we need to export back home?" David takes a bite of a crunchy egg roll.

Helen's face stiffens as shegrasps his displeasure, then concurs, "I do have the soil report from our partners in Hong Kong regarding the struggling farmland outside of town. Due to the high quality of the soil here in Central Illinois, the crossover of hybrid seeds to Chinese locations is a challenge. We are looking closely at yields from the worst soils in this area that have similar compositions to China."

"Very good, that's critical to us with the Ukrainians not able to export as much corn. It will be even more important after we diminish corn production here in the United States. We must be able to grow our own food supply," David commands.

"Yes, Mr. Lee." Helen has finally grasped the seriousness of the situation and reverts to formally addressing David. "I am aware of and committed to the long game. But please understand there are better geographies from which to steal corn and other seeds within the United States that better reflect our soils in China."

"I am aware. We have other students like you in many universities with similar goals, but to be candid, they are not as talented as you are." David pays Helen a rare compliment.

They pause as Mr. Wong brings two hot plates of Szechuan chicken. "Mr. Lee, this is your plate. I know you like your food a bit spicier."

"Excellent, Mr. Wong. Thank you so much. The soup and egg rolls were excellent. I'm sure this will be just the same." David feels weird paying a second compliment as Mr. Wong backpedals away.

Helen picks up on the compliment then focuses back on the program. "Well, thank you, sir. I'm being trained very well by the Americans. How is the nematode project? Do you need any help with the seed treatments?" Helen takes the opportunity to quickly eat her last bites of egg roll.

"Currently, that project is working well at the Shafer Chemicals treatment plant. We have the lab and the processing facility under tight regulations to avoid detection from any government agency. The USDA is nowhere near detecting we have two variants of seed treatments, one for Elevation Seeds and another for the competitors' seeds. It is impressive how relaxed the USDA technicians are regarding their annual inspections. I do not believe they even have the testing equipment available to identify the variants."

David notices a familiar face delivering fortune cookies to their table.

"Mr. Lee," says the young man in Mandarin with a very deep and pronounced bow.

"Ming," says David in Mandarin with a slight lowering of his head. "Very nice to see you. How was your trip to Los Angeles? I trust there were no issues?"

"No, sir," says Ming with pride in his voice. "No issues whatsoever. I'm always here to help in any way possible."

"Very good, Ming. I'll be calling on you soon for a larger project in Chicago's Chinatown. I'm assuming you are okay with interacting with the cartel to continue delivery services," David says more as a statement than a question.

"Of course, Mr. Lee. Anything you wish," says Ming.

"Very good. You have cooked a wonderful meal for us. I will call you to the Union in the near future," David says, obviously dismissing Ming.

"Thank you, Mr. Lee," Ming rushes back to the kitchen.

As Ming departs, David notices two new patrons have arrived tableside: a large white male with a big smile and a beautiful blonde woman by his side.

"Helen!" exclaims Eric. "How are you? You remember Christine."

David has heard about Eric and is immediately concerned but quickly changes his demeanor. He dons a smile and looks deeply interested, which is effortless for him, given his many years as an undercover agent.

"Oh my goodness, Eric, what are you doing here?" asks a shocked Helen. Helen does not slide into her cover story as effortlessly as David does.

"You recommended this restaurant before, so Christine and I ordered some takeout, and we're picking it up. I don't speak Mandarin at all, but it sounds like you may be going to the Union? Are you guys going to play some pool?" Eric asks with a chuckle.

David stands to greet Eric and Christine in excellent English. "Um . . . no. No pool for us. We're Asian. We don't swim," says David with a laugh as he makes fun of the stereotype that Asians can't swim very well. He has a planned cover story for instances like this one. "My name is David Lee, and I'm Helen's cousin from China. I am traveling the US for about six months to see your beautiful country."

"Very nice to meet you, David. Have we met before? And that's very funny about swimming. I guess you don't play in the Union pool hall, huh?" replies Eric.

"Um, no. No pool for us," David says confidently, although he is fully confused. "I don't believe we have met at all before." David guards his concern that Eric has recognized him from the high school football game.

"And this is Christine. Helen knows her," says Eric as David and Christine shake hands.

"Very nice to meet you too, Kristin." David softly bows.

"It's Christine, but very nice to meet you too, David," Christine says with a warm smile.

"How are you doing, Helen? Beautiful Sunday out there today," says Christine.

"Yes, yes, very nice. David and I are going to go for a walk here in a bit and check out the campus," Helen says with a smile.

"Okay! Great to see you guys," says Eric as he walks over to the counter to grab their lunch and head out the door. "See you soon, Helen! I'm going back into the lab today to run some more tests!" Eric calls out as they leave the restaurant.

Helen and David sit back down quickly, and the smiles quickly disappear from their faces.

David stares at Helen for a few seconds, trying to read her. "He may be a problem, Helen."

David waves over Mr. Wong, then sternly says to Helen, "Let's go for that walk."

"Yes, Mr. Lee?" says Mr. Wong.

"Very good as always, Mr. Wong. We are ready to leave," says David.

"Thank you very much, Mr. Lee. As always, there is no charge. Please enjoy your day." Mr. Wong waves a worker over to clean up the table.

"Very nice to see you again. I shall be reaching out to you and your team soon. We need to increase the flow of funds through the restaurant, as we are taking on more business from Chinatown and our Mexican friends." David and Helen stand up to leave.

"Of course, Mr. Lee. As you wish," says Mr. Wong as David and Helen exit the restaurant.

David and Helen then head east on Green Street and begin the necessary constant student dodging as they walk down the sidewalk. David gets frustrated with the foot traffic. "This is like walking in Times Square. Incredibly annoying." They walk in silence for another couple of minutes as David builds up the tension for Helen.

David finally breaks the silence, "Helen, I have hope that you will be a great asset to our party. Your Uncle Houbin is a great leader on the mainland and has been a mentor to me for almost twenty years." David lowers his voice. "But I do have great concerns about your relationship with Eric, your commitment to the CCP, and your overall inexperience to execute our projects inside the United States."

"You do not need to be concerned," Helen says anxiously. "You have known me since I was a little girl. What have I done to cause doubt?"

David and Helen cross over Wright Street. David is curious about the actual campus more than usual. "Helen, what is this statue here?"

"That is the Alma Mater," replies Helen. "Why do you ask?"

"We call home base 'the Union' in order to blend in, but I didn't know what Eric was referring to in terms of the pool, and I felt exposed. Is there a pool in the Union?" David questions.

"No. The student Union, the name we chose, is right there," she says as they continue to walk down Green Street. "It's a place for students to study and have meetings, and there are a lot of games—such as pool, or billiards—inside. I do assume that was confusing for Eric and may have given him some pause or second thoughts."

"Understood. But back to my concerns around you and Eric. I have been told you two are becoming friends." David returns to a demanding tone.

"As you know, this role is challenging because I need to gain his trust. I also learn from him and the other analysts in the lab. I will take that knowledge back with me to China and truly improve the food supply on the mainland. I also need his approval to run separate tests that we use to cause disruptions in the corn seed supply in this area," explains Helen, but not defensively.

"I understand that, Helen. My concern is that you focus on our mission and that your allegiance to the party is never in doubt. As you know, if we cannot fully trust our associates, then changes are made. You have seen that before," David says in a very ominous and threatening tone. "And how did you handle that analyst, Steve Smith, who was questioning your results?"

"He stopped asking questions after I told him I would rerun the labs and thanked him for helping me to learn. I blamed it on my inexperience with the new equipment." Helen grows somber and quiet, then puts her head down as they walk. David sees that Helen understands he is threatening the lives of her and her family. "Did you kill him?"

David is not concerned about hurting Helen's feelings in the slightest and lets her stew with her thoughts for about a block. He never answers her question.

"What is that over here?" David finally breaks the silence.

"What?" asks Helen as she is jolted from her thoughts about Steve being murdered.

"This area here looks different than other places," David points out. "The other buildings were older and had more stone, but these seem modern with more glass."

"This is the engineering campus. It's newer than many buildings around the university. It's very nice. We have over twenty student associates who work inside those laboratories for us," Helen confirms.

"Very nice buildings, and yes, we have more than that now inside the different colleges, especially chemical and electrical engineering, and a group that is studying artificial intelligence," David says.

"We have leveraged the Small Business Innovation Research, or SBIR, and Small Business Technology Transfer, or STTR, from the US Department of Education with an incredible level of success. However, I do need to get back to *our* Union. How do we get back to our cars?"

Helen suggests, "Let's cut through the Quad."

They head south through the student Union and see college kids fully embracing the carefree world of college life, but David is still confused about what the Quad is. They walk out of the Union, and a large open field of grass is revealed. He realizes he's now standing at the Quad.

"Ahhh . . . the Quad. Very nice. What is this, about five acres?" David comments as Helen forces herself to stay engaged. "There's lots of area to land drones if needed."

"Yes, that's probably correct. There are many buildings, about fifteen, and classrooms surrounding the Quad. Foellinger Auditorium, right there," Helen points to the regal-looking building at the end of the grass, "is where I've had some very large classes. The Quad is a nice place to study outside, too. A little-known fact someone once told me is that the sidewalks crisscross the lawn, but they let the students trample down the grass first to see where they would like to walk, then laid down the sidewalks. I thought that was clever." Helen struggles to sound positive.

"Fair enough, Helen. I can find my car now," says David. "To be clear, I know you are trying your hardest, and you are doing a respectable job. Keep pushing toward our specific goals of damaging the US food supply and exporting seed technology to China. Do not let the US do the same to us. And do not let your friendship with Eric get in the way of us accomplishing those goals."

"I understand, Mr. Lee. I promise." Helen continues to avert her eyes.

"We won't discuss this again." David walks intently across the Quad, leaving Helen alone with her thoughts.

# CHAPTER 11
# DUTY TO GOD

"So, your dad told you *not* to get into the grain business?" Christine asks Eric as they cruise down County Road 2150 in his F-150 toward his hometown of Royal to go to church.

Eric has been spending more time with Christine recently, but it's a large step to take her to church with him. Even though they had been working like farmers in the fall, they still made enough time to develop their relationship. Christine is intelligent and hardworking but also kindhearted. She has a very stubborn streak that gets a bit on his nerves from time to time, but that trait translates to being driven and appreciated at work. She recently got a promotion this fall to Director of Cybersecurity at Busey Bank, which brought a nice raise for her. She promptly bought a new designer purse and Jimmy Choo shoes, whatever those are. Christine also keeps Eric in line when he starts to work too much, so she requires weekly lunches, like the one last week when they ran into Helen.

"Pretty much. He and Grandpa Buchanan had enough, I guess," Eric says with a smile. "We had the conversation when I was in eighth grade and working on an international currency paper. I got to talking to Dad about what I should do when I grew up. I get it, though; running companies in small towns has all sorts of challenges."

"International currency in eighth grade? You're not *that* smart, Eric," Christine says with a very skeptical wry smile.

"Not at all. I still don't understand it, not even close. But I did get an A because the teacher, Mrs. Schmidt, didn't understand it either and I guess wasn't in the mood to figure it out." Eric shrugs while trying to hold in a laugh.

"So, this is the 'good' side of the tracks." Eric uses air quotes as they enter the west side of town. "I'm from the other side of the tracks, though." Eric smirks, then continues to explain, "Over there are the newer homes, and, no joke, one of those streets, that one right there, is named Kristie Street after Farmer Behrens's granddaughter. He broke up some farmland and sold the lots to build new homes. The town is basically landlocked because of farmers who won't let their land turn into anything other than crops."

"Super interesting. Because this town is so neat, you would think lots of people would want to live here," Christine says as she points to an updated two-story house.

"I agree. Great people. Great schools," says Eric. "That house you're pointing to was Ben Frerich's old house. He moved further out into the country but fixed it up inside. It's looking great now. He's also good friends with Cory. This does go back a bit to what Helen and I spoke about at Merry Ann's diner the morning after the SJO football game."

"What's that about? I don't remember you telling me," asks Christine. "And why are we going so slow?"

"My mom gets so mad when I speed through here, and I know she's watching from somewhere." Eric looks around jokingly. "And those cars in front of us are surely going to church as well, and they'll snitch on me, no doubt."

"Anywho, we were in the lab, and I was starving, so we ran for breakfast yesterday morning at Merry Ann's." Eric takes a peek at Christine to make sure she's still listening. "We got into a philosophical discussion about our duty to country versus our duty to family. 'Our,' meaning you and me as Americans and the farmers around here too. Helen brought up duty to party. I thought it was a little interesting that 'party' could be a priority, but the main point is similar to Farmer Behrens's conundrum."

"How's that? Seems like Farmer Behrens just sold his land to make some money," Christine asks quizzically.

# DUTY TO GOD

"Well, I guess that embodies the whole argument right there," Eric shrugs again. "Should Farmer Behrens have kept his land intact and handed it down to future farmers, sold it for home lots and made some more money in the short term, or a combination of both? I'll also make it a bit more confusing: there are some folks who believe some of these farmers should sell their land that is right next to town. Then the town can expand and promote more economic growth."

"That is an interesting dilemma. From what I've picked up on in my short time here, there's a bit of division when it comes to people's opinions." Christine rubs her chin. "I don't see this as an overly open, public discussion either. However, I can tell you from my time chatting with Katie that she thinks about farming much differently than her parents, Mitch and Marsha."

"And she doesn't live in Royal any longer either, to your point," Eric agrees.

"And neither do you. You already moved on from a family business, and it sounds like you were steered away by your dad at an early age," Christine says.

"Yeah, that's fair. Maybe it's the same for most kids around here, but the reality is that farming can only support so many people these days." Eric points to the corn and bean fields that seem to go on forever. "Families used to have so many kids because they needed the cheap labor to farm all of that ground," Eric explains. Then he says with excitement, "Speaking of cheap labor, the Community Building is coming up on the right. That's where we met and where I cleaned those bricks as a kid!"

Christine's quizzical expression gives Eric pause, and he gets a bit more serious. "I didn't mean cheap labor in a mean way. I'm just saying that families needed to come together to help with the farm, and then as those kids grew up, they had a stronger connection to farming. But as farms continue running on technology and impressive farm equipment, more can be done with fewer people. Then, fewer people are needed to farm . . . and there's less of a connection to the farm and less farming skill sets, and the kids move to new careers."

"No, I get it and didn't think anything of it. It's interesting that the connection to a family farm can be lost rather quickly. Like, inside one generation." Christine pauses, contemplating her theory. "Katie knows very little about farming and probably doesn't have much of a desire to learn. You have a connection to technology through biochemistry that supports farming, but it's not traditional farming at all. And I don't think you know that much about farming either."

Eric sees that Christine is understanding and asks, "Exactly, CP. Do people who support the industry, like me, for example, care slightly less about who owns the farmland and more about a thriving industry instead? Also, do they care less about sovereignty, or . . .," Eric pauses to stress the point, "duty to country, than their careers that support their family, or their . . ." Eric pauses again, "duty to family?"

Eric and Christine drive by Little Roch's Bar and Freeman's Tavern, and Christine ducks her head down to look through the windshield and get a full view of the large white grain elevator to her left.

"It's tall, isn't it?" asks Eric, also looking up.

"Still, I'm amazed at how much grain this elevator can hold," says Christine. "How tall is that again?"

"The concrete elevator right there," Eric points to the largest concrete grain silo directly to the left of the car, "is about two hundred feet tall, and most of those wider grain bins over there . . ." Eric trails off and points just to the right of the concrete elevator.

"Yes, okay, I see them, behind the town's orange and blue water tower in Illini colors, nice," replies Christine, still leaning forward and trying to take in all the structures.

"Yes, those. They are about a hundred feet high, but also much wider, and hold even more corn than the concrete elevator. That structure now mainly acts as the heart of the conveyors moving corn and beans all around this place. It's truly impressive. It starts with trucks bringing crops in from the fields, then storage over the winter, drying to around 15 percent moisture, back to storage, and finally to the trains that load up a hundred freight cars before they keep heading south."

As they cross the train tracks, smoothed out by wood in between the tracks to allow for cars to pass, Eric points to the south at the secondary track to the side of the main rail line. "There are even a few trains that run through here during the fall harvest to make room for all the corn coming into town from around the area, and they are parked down that line of rail down there. Some crops are temporarily dumped onto overflow ground storage over there before the trains create more space inside the bins. As a kid, the piles were so high we would surf down them, but most of the grain is kept here after harvest and over the winter to let it dry out. Then it ships lighter and is more useful to the chicken plants down in Arkansas or the feed lots in Texas," Eric continues explaining.

"Okay, last question before we get to church: is that a lot of grain or not a lot of grain?" Christine asks, staring back at Eric.

"Well, about twenty million bushels of grain run through this elevator every year, and the US produces over fifteen billion bushels of corn a year. But!" Eric pauses and stresses, "Central Illinois produces about 10 percent of all the corn in the US, which is about the same as Ukraine. Now, granted, that number varies a whole lot based on weather . . . and wars, I guess."

"Okay, that does seem like a lot, but I'm also saying those are some tall buildings." Christine giggles.

"Yes, they are. I've only been to the top of the concrete elevator a few times as a kid, but it'll get your attention. Not a whole lot of reasons to go up there, but I'm happy to take you if you want," Eric offers with a wink and a smile.

"I'm good. So, who are we meeting at church this morning?"

Eric takes a right onto Church Street about two blocks away from the train tracks.

"I still can't believe how close you lived to your whole family growing up," she adds.

"I know. That is Grandpa Buchanan's old house on the corner. Mowed that lawn quite a few hundred times. I would expect quite a few people to be here since it's the 10 a.m. service. Eric can't help but blush. "It will mean a lot to Mom that you showed up and she gets to show you off to her friends."

"I'm very happy to be here, but does she know I'm not overly churchy?" Christine calmly asks.

"Not really, but you were raised Lutheran, so you'll be fine." Eric rubs her arm. "It just makes her feel better with us dating that we have some spirituality in our lives. I'm terrible about going to church, too, and need to get better. But like you know, my church is more the outdoors. Just smile, wave, and keep moving until you get to Mom and Dad.."

"Okay, I can do that. Is that their car parked over there? They are always so early. Can we park over by them?" Christine asks as Eric pulls into the side parking lot, clearly missing the hint that she already has an ideal parking spot in mind.

"No, no, not here. There," Christine emphatically points out. "You always miss the good parking spots!"

Eric shakes his head, as he can now sense the 'parking space judgment' coming from Christine, and backs up, then pulls into the other parking spot. "Not sure I've seen anyone get so emotional about parking. I just hope the real Judgment Day isn't as judgmental as finding a parking space."

"Well, just do better next time," Christine says sarcastically.

# DUTY TO GOD

The St. John Lutheran Church of Royal was built in 1910 and has had a few renovations over the years. In a three-acre open space to the west, kids are screaming and running outside with their chaperones. The older patrons are flowing through the front door in their suits that they have owned for thirty years while exchanging pleasantries with their friends and neighbors. The younger crew wears much more casual clothes. They high-five each other, celebrating their Gen Z inside jokes that make no sense. The parking lot is full, with about fifty cars, and a few more families that live within walking distance hustle down the sidewalks.

Eric gets out of the car, then slowly walks with Christine, trying to enjoy the beautiful day with the sun making its way across the blue sky and vibrant green crops in the distance. The temperature is in the mid-seventies and will quickly turn into a balmy and humid eighty-eight degrees. The corn is just starting to wither from its peak height of about seven feet, and the soybeans are in full green bloom in a lush green carpet that extends for miles.

"Hey, Mom. Hey, Dad," Eric says as they find his folks waiting on the sidewalk next to the church's side door.

"Hello, Mr. and Mrs. Buchanan," Christine says with a big smile, wrapping Sheila in a hug.

"We always like to sneak in and out of the side door," Sheila says. She's wearing a new flowery dress that highlights the season.

"It depends on what sports are on and how fast we need to get home," Les says sincerely.

"Well, we are meeting at Aunt Lisa's at 11:30 a.m., so we'll need to make a quick exit today," Sheila says. "My pecan pie and sweet potatoes are ready to go, so we should be on time."

"Eric didn't tell me to bring anything. I'm so sorry!" Christine says with concern and quickly slaps Eric's arm.

"Don't worry about it at all." Sheila looks at Eric with disappointment. "I assumed he would forget to let you know, so I made a salad that you can take in."

139

"Thanks so much, Mrs. Buchanan," says Christine as relief returns to her face. Then she scowls at Eric.

"My fault . . . again. I'm a dude. We can't be expected to remember details. If it isn't in my calendar, just assume it isn't going to happen, please," says Eric as he turns his back on them to enter the church.

Eric walks into St. John Lutheran Church, which has several levels and resembles most country churches in size, structure, and design. Colorful scenes of Jesus surround the congregation as sunlight pours through the stained glass. The church holds about 250 people between the main level and the upper balcony. The upper level is typically reserved for the choir on Sundays. The lower level is about 75 percent filled, and the Buchanan family slides into their normal seats in the back right corner.

Eric explains to Christine, "That is Pastor Wissmann about to speak. He's been our pastor here for quite a while and is the dad of my good buddy Luke. They moved here from Bismarck, North Dakota, when we were in eighth grade."

"Well, that's interesting," says Christine as Sheila looks over at Eric with a glare that says "Quiet!" Eric's mom screams with her eyes.

"I'm almost thirty years old and Mom still does that. Classic," says Eric with a chuckle. "Time to be quiet and stay out of trouble, or she'll make me mow the lawn."

The church service continues in the same manner Eric has seen for most of his life. Christine joins the family for communion and seems to enjoy Pastor Wissmann's sermon about duty to God and family. After about twenty minutes, Eric starts shifting in his seat. His right knee begins to rapidly bounce up and down, and he fidgets with the bulletin, trying to calculate how much longer the service will last. The Buchanan "jimmy leg" strikes again. Finally, the service ends, and Pastor Wissmann walks down the main aisle, followed by the ushers, who motion to dismiss the patrons starting from the front and continuing to the back.

Finally, it's their turn to head out of the church and say goodbye to Pastor Wissmann.

"Hi, Eric. And who is this?"

"This is Christine," says Eric. "She's a friend of mine from Champaign."

"Very nice to meet you," says Pastor Wissmann, standing with his long white robe highlighted by a red stole. "I hope to see you here again."

"Very nice service, Pastor Wissmann. I hope to be back here soon, too," says Christine with a warm smile as she shakes the pastor's hand.

Christine looks at Eric with an exaggerated and loving, but sarcastic, look. "You know, I bet they hold weddings here too."

Pastor Wissmann says with a good sense of humor, "Yeah, Eric, you just let me know when you want to tie the knot, okay?"

"I need to go eat lunch," says Eric as his face quickly turns beet red. "Great to see you again, Pastor, and I'll text Luke that you're looking for someone to marry."

"Just giving you a hard time, Eric," Christine laughs with Pastor Wissmann. "It's just fun to see you squirm."

Eric says loudly to change the subject, "Mom, want us to help take the food to the farm?"

"No, we'll get it. You guys head over. The Harms's went to the early service at the Flatville church, so we're running a bit late already."

"Gotcha. See you there." Eric and Christine walk the short distance to the truck holding hands. Eric opens the door for Christine, then slowly walks around to the driver's side. They start to head out of the parking lot.

"I have to admit I was thinking about Pastor Wissmann's message around duty to God and your chat with Helen about duty to party and country," Christine quickly slides back into their philosophical discussion. "It really isn't that clear to me what my own priorities are regarding my duties. Frankly, I do not like that my priorities often don't feel aligned with my personal goals, or even my beliefs, for that matter." Christine thinks for a second as Eric waves several town elders to proceed slowly crossing the street to the parking lot.

Eric sneaks a side look at Christine. "I'm not really sure what you are saying."

Christine pauses. "For me, duty to family always seemed like the priority. I'm still convinced that's the right answer, but duty to God is interesting too. Since I'm not overly religious, I take it to mean duty to community. But how do you define that, and where does it start and stop?"

Eric thinks for a second, then responds, "Very good questions. We have a wonderful community here, and serving the town should be a priority, but not over duty to family. And duty to a party, whatever that means, doesn't make any sense. I'm trying to think back to my philosophy classes at the U of I. This was discussed at some point, but the reality is that I didn't have enough life experience in college to comprehend those choices and my priorities. I would even say that some folks never get to the point of making a clear decision in their entire lives. That seems sad to me."

As they continue to chat, Eric navigates the crowded parking lot and sneaks out the back exit to the country roads. He continues to drive slowly down the paved roads while kicking up gravel from time to time. He cautiously rolls through the rare stop sign. Since it's harvesting time, he can't see who is coming or going because of the tall corn blocking the view, and people are known to drive very fast on these country roads sometimes. Thankfully, the farmers often remove the tops from the corn stalks on the corners to increase visibility at the stop signs.

Christine puts her window down and sticks her hand outside. "It really is a beautiful morning. Well, we do sound like some rather weak philosophers, far from Socrates and Aristotle, but the questions are important ones. Especially for people in farming communities or anyone who has a business around here. They need to openly plan handing it down to the next generation. People like your cousins will need to consider all of these things. What are people's priorities among their duties? God, community, country, family, and maybe even party, if that's important to them?"

Eric drives past Farmer Behrens's old farm in the country and turns to head to the farm where his Aunt Lisa and Uncle Skeeter have lived for decades. "If I had to make a decision, I'm still putting my duty to family over everything else. Then my duty to my community, or God. But, to me, that's also doing the right thing when nobody is looking. I'm trying to figure out where spirituality fits into that. I do know my soul feels better when I've been hiking or fishing or just being outside in nature. Does that count?"

"I'll give you credit there, Eric," Christine says with a kind smile as she moves her hand up and down with the wind. "I feel calmer already just opening this window. You're onto something, I'm sure."

"Whew." Eric smiles back. "Then I would go with my duty to my country, but I would like to reserve the right to adjust the order a bit. This is Harms Farm right in front of us."

"Fine by me; adjust as you see fit," Christine says, then gets nervous as they start to cross over the cattle guard to enter the Harms Farm's driveway.

"Don't worry, these things have been here for decades and hold up semis," says Eric. "Those rods are made of steel and easily hold up tractors that weigh twenty-five tons."

"Okay, good. So weird to me to have that as an entrance," Christine says in a more serious tone. "I'm assuming we're going to pause this discussion around the rest of the family?"

"Let's hope so, but we'll see how many glasses of wine you have, too," Eric says, questioning a bit.

"Good point," Christine says with deep sarcasm. "I'll just remember to only bring up politics and religion like I was taught."

# CHAPTER 12
# LABOR DAY ON THE FARM

"I MAY be old, but I'm not crazy!" Aunt Lisa shouts at her kids while sipping lemonade at her outdoor metal table, briefly taking a quick break from furiously working in the kitchen for a Labor Day family lunch.

Eric, and especially Christine, are not sure what is going on and are contemplating getting back into Eric's truck and finding a new place for lunch. Eric quickly appreciates the classic rural scenery. The sprawling farm has grain silos and that gravel entrance that begins with the round metal cattle grate that made Christine so nervous. The sun continues to shine bright in the sky, and the crops literally go on for miles and miles. A couple of cows graze in the pen by the old wooden shed. The aging donkey, Ruth, is watching the commotion, but she is getting a bit uneasy, her tail swishing and ears perked up.

"Lisa, I'm not saying you're crazy," teases her oldest daughter, Anna Meier. "I'm just saying your hearing may be off a bit from being on the farm for so long." She smiles at her younger sister, Tina Brown.

Tina shakes her head at Anna for being so ornery, "Clean it up, Anna." Tina is extremely sweet, but decades of farming and parenting three boys have removed some of the sweetness and converted it into verbal efficiency.

"Eric, tell these kids that my hearing is fine. I have listened to their BS for decades, and nobody questioned my hearing all those years!" An agitated Aunt Lisa says over the laughter of her family.

"Aunt Lisa, I'm sure they are making this all up, and you're fine. Plus, you're barely pushing fifty-nine anyway, so who cares?" Eric tries to calm her down by giving her a big hug.

"Get away from me. Fifty-nine? Try eighty. I've been around here longer than any of you have been driving, and I know what I'm hearing!" Aunt Lisa persists.

Eric laughs while looking toward Christine and shrugs, having no clue what the argument is about. He then turns his attention to Tina, who is sitting next to Aunt Lisa, for some guidance.

"She's claiming she can hear buzzing in the middle of the night, Eric," Tina says curtly, gently tapping her glass of iced tea. "We're saying it's power lines, planes going into Willard Airport, or maybe even just the peaceful sounds of dementia."

Christine quickly turns away from Aunt Lisa to hide her laughter as Eric doubles over laughing.

"You guys are so mean," says Eric.

"Only on certain nights!" Aunt Lisa corrects the record. "And it seems like it's when it's really dark out. That's what I'm saying, Tina."

"Lisa, don't worry about nothin'. At your age, it's all gravy, and you'll outlive the rest of us anyway. Then, you'll really have the last laugh," cracks Eric.

"Oh, just shut it, Eric. You're no help either," Aunt Lisa says and storms back into her large one-story ranch home.

Eric laughs, then takes a longer gander around Harms Farm, where his cousins were born and raised and Aunt Lisa has lived for almost sixty years. His Uncle Skeeter passed away about five years ago and was a character himself. Scattered around the farm are Uncle Skeeter's toys, countless functioning and nonfunctioning antique tractors that were his pride and joy. And those are just the toys that are in sight. As the saying goes, the difference between the men and the boys is the price of the toys.

"Where did Ruth go?" Eric asks Anna as he pets their trusted guard dog, Ricky Bobby. Ricky Bobby is much calmer than their old dog, Jodi, who would literally bite through tires as they rolled into and out of the farm. She even popped semi tires, which still seems impossible but also terrifying for little kids.

"Oh, some of the kids were pestering Ruth too much, so she walked back into the barn. She'd had enough," Anna says, pointing to the livestock barn.

"Well, Christine, sorry for the delay, but the girls just kept picking on Aunt Lisa. I don't believe you have met my cousins, Anna and Tina. You met their brothers, Danny and Jeff, during Royal Days." Eric says as Christine extends her hand out toward the sisters.

"No, ma'am! We hug around here!" says Tina, pulling Christine in. Then Anna, begrudgingly, as she is not a huge fan of hugs, does the same. "We've heard that Eric has had a girlfriend for a minute. Very nice to meet you."

"Girlfriend, huh?" says Anna. "I thought you were allergic to those."

"Easy, Anna, easy!" says Eric as his face gets red again and Christine laughs at his nervousness.

"He's trying his hardest and doing fine most of the time, ladies, but he still needs some major help." Christine gives Eric a shove.

Christine's shoulders relax, and she leans into Eric. "Very nice to meet you two. Where are the boys?"

Anna points southwest. "They are working in a field with Jeff's boy, Brandon, a few miles that way. They should be here soon for lunch, then they'll head back to the fields."

"Ok, I'll take her into the house to see if we can help." Eric forces himself to grab Christine's hand and overcome his disdain for all things PDA, then leads her up the rest of the driveway and through the double-car garage to go inside the house. One side has Lisa's red SUV with a license plate that simply reads "Lisa" and a cherry red golf cart that is made to look like a Case IH tractor.

Inside, Aunt Lisa takes the sliced turkey over to the main island where the rest of the fixings are, and Christine starts to move the rest of the sides over to the island as well. Eric hears the sound of diesel engines coming toward the farm and confirms, "Sounds like the boys are here, Aunt Lisa."

"Looks like it," says Christine as she watches two semis pull into the driveway. "How old is that kid driving one of those semis?" Christine peers intently through the window.

"Oh, don't worry about that. That's Brandon, and he's probably been driving a semi since he turned fourteen last year. Same as his dad," Eric explains.

"What else is going on, Lisa?" asks Eric. "Feeling good?"

"I'm feeling pretty good, Eric. Thanks for asking. Well, the girls and I are having fun playing Euchre every Thursday. Berniece is still a cheater, but I've learned to let that go, as I'm a calm and forgiving person," Lisa lays on the sarcasm. "I did run into Keith Sjuts the other day at the IGA. That was a bit interesting and made me think of you, Eric," Aunt Lisa says as she continues to stir the side items and make sure there's enough butter in the mashed potatoes.

"Oh yeah, is he still driving for Shafer Chemicals?" Eric grabs a side dish to take to the kitchen island.

"Well, yes, he is. I mentioned to him that you are still involved in some sort of seed research, analysis, or something. I never really understood what you do, Eric, to be honest." Lisa shakes her head in confusion. "Anyway, he said he's been trucking for Shafer for years, and there are two loading areas for the chemicals. I asked him why, and he said he didn't know. He wanted me to ask you." Aunt Lisa looks out the window to make sure the boys come straight in after parking the semis by the barn.

"Really? I guess I have no idea." Eric considers potential options. "As I understand it, old man Shafer sold his company to someone a while back when he was retiring. Now, who was that?" Eric pauses to find the information way back in his brain.

"That's right;" Eric looks toward the ceiling to keep his train of thought, "the company that bought him out was a bit of an odd story." "One of the nephews of the founder of Archer-Daniels-Midland Company, the large agriculture conglomerate out of Decatur, took some of his inherited money and started his own company, CO Daniels. They were around for a very long time, since like the early 1940s or something. CO Daniels bought Shafer Group, but CO Daniels is now owned by a new company, I believe. It's a bit complicated."

Eric hears the back screen door open and bang close. "There are the boys. I bet they know more since they are closer to the ground than I am."

Danny walks into the kitchen, and Eric shouts at him, "Danny, do you remember who owns CO Daniels these days?"

Danny is confused. "Well, hi. Good to see you again, Christine." He gives her a hug. "What was that again, Eric?"

"Sorry, Danny," Eric apologizes. "Your mom and I were talking about how CO Daniels acquired Shafer Chemicals. I think C.O.'s is owned by a holding company that controls a few ag companies. I'm pretty sure they even own Elevation Seeds too. Who would that be?"

"Oh, that's WH Group. They are out of China or something but were originally Walter Herzog, Inc. out of St. Louis. They were acquired by a Chinese company. That's my limited understanding, at least. Why, what's up?" Danny asks as Jeff walks into the kitchen with his son, Brandon.

"Hi again, Christine." Jeff gives Christine a classic "country" side hug. "This is my son, Brandon."

"You drive that semi like a pro. That's super impressive," Christine says. Brandon blushes at the compliment. "I think this entire family turns red when someone says something nice," Christine jokes.

"Yeah, that's about right. We like to lay low around here," laughs Jeff. "Speaking of laying low, Eric, that analyst of yours from the lab was over at Hans Pein's old farm the other day."

"Was that who that was?" asks Danny. "Helen, was it? We met her at the SJO football game, right?"

"I don't see many Asian ladies around here, so I'm fairly confident," confirms Jeff. "Does she drive a gray minivan? A Honda Odyssey or something like that, Eric?"

"The old farm about a mile away from here?" Eric is confused. "Well, that's odd. What was she doing over there? Helen does drive a minivan to transport lab equipment and bring samples in from the fields." Eric furrows his brow, trying to think of a good reason.

"No clue. We just saw her as we were rolling down to a field, but it looked like her pulling into the driveway," says Jeff as Eric's parents walk through the door with his mom's famous pecan pie. Sheila smoothly hands Christine a salad, so she can lay it on the table as well as her contribution, then wink at each other.

Eric turns to Christine, shaking his head in doubt. "That's really odd. I'm guessing it was someone else, and the boys got confused." Eric turns back to his cousins. "Gents, if you see her again, would you mind taking a picture so I can be sure? I'll ask her on Monday as well. So strange, though."

Eric walks over to give his mom a hug. "Fancy seeing you here," Eric says. "Traffic tough, and that's why you're late?"

"Cubs," says Eric's mom with a sour face.

"Bases loaded, nobody out. We need to trade Happ," scowls Eric's dad as Eric shakes his head at the many, many times he's heard his dad complain about Ian Happ.

"You just need to become a Cards fan, and you'll know what winning feels like!" jokes Danny, giving Les a hard time about being a Chicago Cubs fan over his St. Louis Cardinals.

"Okay, everyone. Get moving! This food isn't going to stay warm forever, and this kitchen ain't staying open forever either!" Aunt Lisa rings the figurative dinner bell.

The Harms, Buchanan, Meier, and Brown families, who all started with Grandpa and Grandma Buchanan, raid the food on the kitchen island. They then form their respective troops of kids, grandkids, and the three remaining grandparents around the dining room and kitchen table. The parents quickly send the younger children down to the basement. Eric misses his brothers, Jason, Joel, and Cory, but knows that their wives are in charge, and they can't make it this time. He slides onto the mahogany wooden bench with his cousins in the dining room with an overflowing plate of food.

Christine scootches in next to Eric to join the crew. Eric knows that things are progressing with Christine, and he finds his heart warming up as she engages with his extended family like an old friend. He needs to figure this out *pronto*. Is it time to run like usual? Engage the old early-and-often rule? Probably.

"Anna, we were just chatting with Aunt Lisa about old man Shafer selling his company a while back. Didn't he have someone who could run it for him, like a kid or something?"

"He had a daughter who was involved for a while, and he was grooming her to take over the company, but then he passed away, and she sold it for a really good price to CO Daniels. She's retired now and dabbles in this or that," explains Anna as she takes a bite of her turkey sandwich smothered in homemade gravy.

"Interesting," Eric says thoughtfully. "I guess the same could be said for this farm, but the boys—and even you and Tina—have done a great job of taking it over and keeping it in the family. Have you ever thought about selling it?"

The boys look at each other and shrug, then look back at Eric.

Jeff finally says, "We've had big corporate farmers, like WH Group and others, look to buy the farm for many, many years. Prices for farmland are higher than I've ever seen, but we love it and can't imagine handing it over to anyone else. We would never allow those silly wind farms to destroy our landscape nor those 'environmentally friendly' solar panels."

"Jeff's right, Eric," Danny nods in agreement with his brother's opinion. "We could sell the land for a pretty penny, but this farmland is worth more to us than just the money that it brings in. It's a way of life for us, our kids, and our friends, and I just don't think that Dad would have wanted us to work as hard as we all have just for us to walk away from it. So, we don't." Danny shrugs again, confirming it is just that simple.

Tina jumps in, "Out in Western Illinois, plenty of farmers sell out and, ultimately, they seem to lose their way. There are a few that find new things to do and are mildly successful, but I just don't think it's a good idea. Another critical component is who the buyer is."

Christine swiftly reaches across Eric to grab the wine, then asks, "I'm out of my league here, but what do you mean by 'who the buyer is,' Tina?"

Eric looks at Christine and gives her an approving glance for jumping into the fray. *Okay, fine; maybe I'll stick this out a bit longer*, he thinks to himself.

Tina continues, "Well, WH Group is a Chinese holding company. They buy local companies, like Smithfield Foods, and run those companies like normal. It all seems on the up and up on the face of it, but we have no clue what's going on behind the scenes. Nobody I've talked to understands their US operations. CO Daniels is about the same since they own Elevation Seeds and Shafer Chemicals. Their CEO is from China but lives in Springfield and is constantly with politicians down there. It's also very strange how much farmland gets purchased by foreign companies, many of which are Chinese. And I know many are hidden under corporate structures that are almost impossible to trace."

"Thao Te is the CEO of CO Daniels. I met her at the Spring Royal

Days. She seems nice enough to me," says Eric.

"I'm sure she is," Anna jumps in. "But who back in China is telling her what to do here in Illinois? Who's funding all of this? What are they trying to accomplish by buying farmland, seed companies, and even a chemical company? Again, I see too many interactions between the University of Illinois and the Chinese Communist Party—the Ministry of Education specifically—from my audits at Illinois."

"I'm sorry, Anna, but what do you do for the university?" asks Christine as she takes another sip of wine.

"It's a bit boring, but I'm an ex-accountant, and I audit all of the various departments under the University of Illinois's primary limited liability companies, or LLCs. There are probably over a thousand departments," Anna explains. "But I only audit a handful of them."

"A thousand?!" exclaims Danny. "I had no idea! How does a university have that many departments?"

Anna continues, "Very good question, Danny. The school has interests in all sorts of joint ventures, charities, tax-friendly foundations, and investments in research. Some of their departments have licensed their patents to start-up companies and made them many millions of dollars. But I will tell you this for certain: I do not ever want to see farms—especially this farm—sold to an international company, ever. We should never be selling our food supply to non-Americans. That's insanity." Anna pours Christine more wine, seeing her furrowed brow as she tries to piece all of this together.

Eric agrees, "Cory works for the University of Illinois Foundation, and they just raise funds but are technically a separate entity from the University of Illinois. We have a separate entity for the lab as well, so we can get special grants from around the world. We get grants from the Small Business Innovation Research, or SBIR, and Small Business Technology Transfer, or STTR, programs.

Every university does it, and that's just how it works for so many of our departments. The good thing is the federal government doesn't track the funds too closely, so I get to use them as we see fit."

Eric then continues, "We're probably a bit off track, though. My main question was around, well, what I would call duty. I've actually had this chat with our analyst, Helen, who you saw at that farm next door, about duty. We ended up talking about duty to country and family. She took it a step further from duty to party, meaning the Chinese Communist Party, or CCP. Like you said, Danny, Uncle Skeeter would not be happy about selling the farm. I guess you would fall on the duty to family side?"

Danny looks at Jeff, "Um . . . I guess. We don't really think about it that way, but yeah. Duty to Mom and Dad, even Grandpa and Grandma Buchanan, and Opa and Oma Harms."

Eric leans toward Christine. "Opa and Oma are German for Grandpa and Grandma."

"I know what that means. My family is about half German Lutheran too. I'm in my element here!" Christine says to the amusement of the rest of the family.

Eric poses a question: "Okay, how much would it take for you to sell the farm? I know you'd sell at a certain number. Call it, for giggles, one billion dollars. Are you a seller there?"

Danny and Jeff both chime in, "Yeah, we're sellers for a billion."

Eric continues, "Yeah, that would get your attention, but now, how about if it's a CCP-controlled company?"

Jeff says, "No way I'm selling our farm to China."

Eric prods, "Danny, feeling the same way?"

"I see the point here, but I'm not selling our farmland to China either." Danny bristles at the thought. "But I do know many farmers who would never give it a second thought, selling their farms to the Chinese. Heck, many of these sellouts around here have already installed Chinese wind and solar farms since most are manufactured in China with US dollars. I'm not a fan at all, and frankly, those farmers are looked at differently these days because of it. I get the money part of it, but they still seem like sellouts to me. They don't understand what it truly means to sell our land to countries that despise our way of life." Danny's face turns flush from his frustration.

Eric keeps pressing the issue. "Okay, just something to consider: at some point, if your duty is to your family, is there not a price where selling the farm is in the best interest of the family?" Eric asks calmly. "In theory, it could happen, and you would have to then be concerned about your farmer's tan coming from Central Illinois or a resort in Mexico."

Jeff wraps it up succinctly. "No, I get it. We don't really have that issue today, but maybe we will down the road. Do we want to leave that much money on the table to protect our current lifestyle? I guess it also depends on what our kids want to do."

Eric looks at Anna. "Agreed. That's my point with Shafer Chemicals and his daughter. I'm not sure she's overly excited about selling to the Chinese either, but whose job is that really, hers or the federal government's? Who's in charge of keeping bad actors from buying up America's resources?"

Anna is getting mad now. "I still don't care. We're not selling this farm to any international company, regardless of the price, and that's that. I just read an article in the *New York Post* that showed all the farmland the Chinese have bought around our military installations. It's crazy! And oh, by the way, Eric, you know those SBIR and STTR grants that you like so much because of the freedom you have?"

"Um, yeah?" Eric is taken aback by the question.

"Well," Anna is going to school Eric again. "There are hundreds of department heads who use those funds to recruit and maintain students and support staff as CCP agents across the country, monitoring our education system, military installations, and infrastructure. You need to do more research into foreign influence in our universities, especially around the CCP."

Christine hits Eric's arm. "Our new friend Mark was talking about this the other night, Eric!"

Tina laughs with the boys, trying to tame the mood. "It's okay, Anna; this is just a hypothetical . . . for now. But if it becomes a real thing, then we'll make sure you have the final say on walking away from millions."

Christine pours herself another glass of wine. "This lunch reminds me of my family's lunches, except they would just be fighting about the Chicago Bears being terrible."

Anna gets the last word: "I'm just saying, there are some alarming things around here, and everyone had better start paying more attention. The Chinese are already buying up farmland in Manteno under that Gotion company. That company's corporate charter specifically calls for allegiance to the Chinese Communist Party!"

As Anna completes her rant, Eric recalls the concerns Mitch and Tumble Inn Mark shared and some of his conversations with Helen. *Maybe I need to wake up and start asking more questions about what's really going on around here.*

# CHAPTER 13
# SCORCHED EARTH

"Yes, sir. We can use the drones to spray mustard gas on any open-air venue, including Memorial Stadium, within four hours," says Tom. He is recalculating his math and reviewing his documents, which are spread over the main conference room table at their clandestine HQ, the Union, in the cornfields.

David has called his team leaders together in the glass conference room to update him on their various projects but also to finalize details should the group need—or get ordered by Beijing—to use their programs to essentially start World War III. David's "you don't have to get ready if you're always ready" attitude consistently keeps Tom, Chinaloa, and Z on their toes as he moves from normal protocol to worst-case-scenario planning. This meeting is a worst-case-scenario planning session.

"Very good, Tom. Walk us through those details," David commands while standing behind Tom, trying to get a peek. David then slowly paces around the table. His team's faces are more attentive than usual. He notices everyone is dressed in more formal business casual than on a normal day and finds some satisfaction knowing his team is taking this seriously.

"Yes, sir. We have the T40 drones that are currently kitted with the Shafer Chemicals pantaphos herbicide," Tom continues in an uncharacteristically serious tone. "As you know, we use that herbicide to spray the non-Elevation seeds at night in order for those cornfields to experience much higher rates of corn rot. We would need to clean out those containers and prepare the Mustargen and water solution. Then we would add on the high-pressure sprayers that create the actual mustard gas so they can spray from the T40 drones. Those are obviously not actual T40 drones but the drones we created after stealing the manufacturing specifications. We added on night vision in case we need to covertly attack almost anywhere in the Champaign-Urbana area, but mainly, the campus is where we have a very high concentration of targets," explains Tom.

Helen steps in to provide further details. "In addition, our lab confirms all the results for various seed providers. We have also modified them to coincide with expectations from seed providers. I have created a process to remove the pantaphos molecule easily from all samples, but generally, I just modify the results in the database without needing to change the actual samples to save time. Manipulating their samples also comes with additional risks based on the level of variances we would expect to see in the laboratory."

"I'm following. How is the supply of Mustargen currently?" David asks.

Tom points to the twenty fifty-gallon blue drums sitting inside the highly secure warehouse located at the Union. Three large guards stand at attention like they are protecting Buckingham Palace and don't move in the slightest.

David calmly interjects, "And the issue we had with the junior lab analyst, Steve Smith, who was asking too many questions has been handled." Tom knowingly nods in approval while Helen goes ghost white.

"Please continue, Tom," says David.

"Yes, sir," Tom focuses their attention on the chemical drums. "We only have enough for one very specific attack. Of these twenty drums, two are full of Mustargen that our techs ordered, stole, and then changed the inventory count for inside the biomedical lab at Illinois. The other eighteen are water-soluble saline solutions that allow the Mustargen to turn into mustard gas under high pressure. However, it still has a low enough viscosity to work with the high-pressure spraying systems of the drones. That same spraying apparatus is what we use to spray the pantaphos herbicide. For something so simple, it's quite complicated."

Tom continues to navigate around the mechanics of the drones. "In addition, the battery life of the drones is only about two hours, so we will need them to complete the mission, then ditch them off campus to try to create a separation from the actual event. The other option is to station our techs close enough to the strike point so they can reload the mustard gas and swap out batteries for multiple attacks. That is much riskier, and we would need to acquire more Mustargen."

"I understand, and again, this is a last resort option should any of the federal agencies get too close to us. If that happens, we will move our gray zone invasion to a true invasion that risks direct war with the United States." David inspects the night vision cameras. "So, we don't need the night vision cameras at all, even if we don't have all the farms' GPS coordinates?"

Tom answers in a technical tone, "No, sir. Our engineering analysts extracted almost all the geofencing data needed for this entire area, including farms and their ownership boundaries. In addition, we captured information on obstructions for flying the drones from the FAA, power and light poles from the energy company, and homes where people may see or hear the drones from each municipality's records."

David nods in approval. "So how do you control these things, then?"

Tom points to their server room. "The GPS data for each drone is stored on our highly encrypted server here at the Union, which is connected to the drone controller. I can also use my iPhone if needed, and we can simply push 'Go' from the drone app for a pre-planned trip, and that exact flight pattern will be followed perfectly using those GPS coordinates. If we need to take over the drone, we can easily do that as well and upload a new set of instructions. The drones will fly that course as long as there's enough battery life."

"Impressive, Tom. What are the farmers doing with their GPS coordinates? It seems odd that they need that level of detail." queries David.

"Sir, their tractors, combines, and even some of the plows have GPS reporting and tracking capabilities. The farmers measure soil composition and elevation to determine low spots where water will pool and cause crop loss. The main analysis tracks the yield in their fields so they can identify which seeds are producing the best and which are not. There is a lot more data than that, and we are working to put it to use, but with their geofencing and Elevation Seeds knowing who is using which seeds, we can isolate their crops rather easily. Our initial results show at least a 10 to 15 percent reduction in corn yields between Elevation Seeds and our competition."

"Correct me if I'm wrong here," directs David, "but essentially, Shafer Chemicals provides seed treatment chemicals to almost all seed providers as we have pushed out Corteva. Shafer has two versions of each chemical that goes into the seed treatment process. The one for Elevation Seeds contains an herbicide for microworms, or nematodes. The worms reduce yields but are not that easy to spot because they leech off the corn stalk roots."

"Yes, sir," replies Helen with a forced businesslike tone. "Nematodes are very hard to detect unless you are looking for them, and most people do not pull up their stalks to look for them, as they assume the herbicides will control them. Like the pantaphos experiments, hiding the nematode results is rather simple. It's even easier due to the nematode worm not being a likely culprit in reduced yields, so most tests are not looking for nematodes."

"And you have the truck drivers fill up their storage containers at two separate locations at Shafer Chemicals, one for Elevation Seeds and the other for their competitors?" asks David.

Tom continues since this is his domain, "That's correct, sir. There's an innocuous step inside the manufacturing process where these chemicals are essentially baked onto the seeds by things called seed treaters as the seeds work their way through the manufacturing process. It's not overly complicated, but it's also very hard to detect. Essentially, at that phase of production, the seed providers assume the chemicals we provide are consistent with our material safety data sheets, or MSDS, and there's not a good way to confirm it one way or another," Tom explains. "For whatever it's worth, this is why we are fully vertically integrated with heavy controls and security in place back home to ensure our enemies are not working to damage or control our food supply."

"Genius, Tom. So, we're using our CCP analysts planted inside the university and their specific research into curing cancer using both Mustargen and pantaphos, then stealing their technology and leveraging our ability to purchase US companies that are directly tied to their food supply. Very good. What else is there?" David looks around at his leadership group.

"Well, you are understanding the details, but I'm assuming the CCP's connections inside federal agencies are aware that we have some very 'scorched earth' options?" asks Tom.

"Tom, let's keep our projects in the appropriate silo, but generally, yes." David starts to walk toward the only entrance and exit, which is guarded by two heavily armed Chinese men, Chen and Davuth. "The CIA, DEA, and FBI understand that if they want to crack down too much on the drug trafficking from the cartels, fentanyl especially, we have some major financial levers we'll pull, heavily damaging both countries. And if needed, we have contingency plans in place that will kill thousands of Americans. They don't want to play chicken with us, but let's stay prepared and ready to move quickly if needed."

"Always, sir. Good to see you again today." Tom bows.

Helen walks out with David, leaving Tom inside the barn.

"David, would we really go, well, scorched earth on the university?" asks Helen.

"Are you questioning the decisions of the party, Helen? That's not a good idea either," David says sternly.

"Absolutely not, Uncle. I'm sorry for asking," Helen says as she lowers her head in embarrassment.

"Helen, we are here in America to further our party's objectives, to provide leverage to our leadership to continue our plans for the ultimate domination of the world so that our future, and our children's futures, are under the CCP's umbrella and not under the umbrella of an imperialistic country halfway around the world," David says in a much sterner tone. "We need all soldiers and patriots to understand what we are working toward. This is a decades-long struggle, and we will hand off our work to the next group, who will have the same exact goals we do. We will never give up until the Chinese people, and the Chinese people alone," David shakes his fist aggressively, "determine our own destiny. We will all make sacrifices for our goals. And Americans may need to be sacrificed. If you are not completely committed to our projects, then we need to have a very serious discussion about your future and your family's future in Hong Kong. Do I make myself clear?"

Helen snaps back to attention, as she comprehends the direct threat he is making. "I fully understand, sir. And I will do whatever I need to do to keep our success moving forward. Eric is at a farm not too far from here, and I will return to the lab to continue my work."

David sees Chinaloa briskly walking from the maintenance shed to the main house and calls her over. "Chinaloa, can you chat with us, please?"

Chinaloa perks up and comes over to David and Helen. "Yes, David? What's going on?" She puts her arm around Helen's shoulders and gives her a squeeze. David has been discussing with

Chinaloa that he'll need her help to give Helen some moral support. He's been the exclusive bad cop, and now it's probably time to bring in a good cop.

Helen softly leans on Chinaloa, and both melt into each other as Chinaloa is almost a foot taller than Helen due to height and heels. David hasn't seen a motherly side of Chinaloa like this before, but he can see from Helen's response that she's needed it for some time.

"You'll remember some of the conversations between you and me and even some of our mentors from many years ago, but Helen is struggling with our projects, our goals, and even following the rules of the CCP." David continues his bad cop approach.

"I see." Chinaloa gently extends her arms and straightens Helen's hair around her solemn face. "How are you doing, Helen?" Chinaloa looks into Helen's dark eyes.

"I'm fine, Chinaloa." Helen shakes off tears, which never appear. "I just need to get back to the lab to keep my projects on track."

"I understand. Can I tell you something? When I was about your age, David and I were coming up through the Ministry of State Security," Chinaloa says calmly.

"Yes, ma'am. I've only heard things here and there." Helen stands back to listen as a forklift scoots around near the barn, shuffling chemical containers.

"David and I have known each other for almost three decades now." Chinaloa straightens her dress. "As you know, we agents get picked at rather young ages and are then groomed for our service. That's why we can blend into America so easily with our looks, our Midwest English, and our knowledge of the American way of life. You are no different and fit into the United States with greater ease than most Chinese would ever be able to do, and that is what makes us so dangerous—and valuable. However, there are times when we get lulled into the American way of life and start to ask questions. Does that happen to you?"

Helen sneaks a peek at David for any potential cues. "Not really. I just want to do my job and serve the party."

David stays firm, but Chinaloa kindly exhales at Helen's attempt at staying noble to the cause and winks at David. "It's okay, Helen. David and I have had this conversation over the years. It's a natural part of the process."

Helen lifts her head and looks at David for more guidance. He nods to her and then to Chinaloa, indicating it's okay to open up a bit about her feelings. Helen looks back into Chinaloa's caring eyes, paying attention again and standing up straighter.

"Good. Again, David and I have talked about this for an exceptionally long time." Chinaloa softly clasps her hands in front of her thin waist as she looks down at Helen. "The roles we play are not easy ones. The jobs we do are dangerous, and we are very much lone wolves when it comes to our daily activities. You have been in that lab for over a year now with no supervision and limited guidance from us. It seems your American director, Eric, treats you very well. All of that is difficult and confusing. And we know the Chinese way is, oftentimes, not overly kind, gentle, or caring." Chinaloa rubs Helen's arm. Helen nods in agreement.

Chinaloa continues, "And to be honest, the majority of our leaders are chauvinistic jerks. I genuinely don't like most of them. David is hard on his team because we are doing important work for the party, but he's a good boss. A fair boss. I know what to expect from him, and he knows what to expect from me. We are lucky to all be working together, and hopefully, you see that."

Helen looks over at David and smiles at him. "I see that, but why . . ." Helen stops speaking. "I see that."

"Why do we threaten your family back home?" Chinaloa notices Helen's concern.

"I guess," Helen softly responds.

"Sweetie, the CCP will always have contingency plans. You know that," Chinaloa says firmly. "The men back in Beijing are there because they are loyal to President Xi, and they have seen other men in their roles be thrown in jail, tortured, killed, and lose their families, and they know it can happen to them. They need to make sure we are under their control as well. That includes everyone from you up to, and including, David. They do this to protect themselves and their way of life. General Houbin has his job because his predecessor was jailed for 'corruption,' but we know it was because he was gaining too much power and was a threat to his supervisors.

"As I was growing up in the MSS, I figured out something very important. This whole group at the Union has," Chinaloa says mysteriously.

"What's that?" Helen focuses intently on Chinaloa's next words.

"We can make a lot of money." Chinaloa holds her gaze as David quietly nods.

"That's right, Helen." Chinaloa stands up even taller. "These shoes, this dress, this hair, Z's cars, Tom's pizza bill . . . it all costs a lot of money. We have an incredible amount of autonomy out here, and millions flow through our operations at the Union. I'm all for supporting the party and not having myself or my family killed." Chinaloa pauses. "Ultimately, I'm trying to take down the US and bring China back to the forefront of global power, but I'm also making a lot of money. David is as well, more than all of us, but he invests his money and wields his power around the US, Central America, Hong Kong, and back home in Beijing."

"So, you do this for the money, Chinaloa?" Helen tilts her head in confusion.

"Helen, there are many reasons why we do what we do." Chinaloa looks directly into Helen's eyes. "Fear of repercussions is an enormous motivator. Dedication to the People's Republic of China is an enormous motivator. Never let those two things fall away, or you will find yourself in a very bad situation. Clearly, David is warning you of this, but . . ." Chinaloa pauses. "You are a smart girl. If you can get past your moral trepidation, you'll see that you can accomplish the CCP's goals. You'll also make a lot more money here than if you worked back in China, where people closely watch you and keep putting their hands in your pocket. The reality is, it's much easier here in America than back home for us. Women simply have more freedoms here. You are so smart and beautiful, so take advantage of that."

Helen nods. "I understand. Thank you, Chinaloa. I'll go to the lab now."

"Very good, Helen. You'll figure things out. I promise." Chinaloa pats Helen on the back as she walks to her minivan.

David watches Helen slowly drive down the driveway, then he turns back to Chinaloa. "What are you thinking?"

"Honestly, David." Chinaloa scrunches her nose. "When we were her age, we were more ruthless. More jaded from our childhoods. More trained."

"Brainwashed, you mean," David concurs.

"Yes. We were hardened by twenty-five. You had killed many dissidents by that time and were leading warriors. I was deep undercover in Central America creating our money laundering program. This girl? She's soft. She's not cynical, greedy, or even a narcissist. Without those traits, which we all have in spades, she has no chance of being successful in this life. I'm fairly confident this is not going to end up well for her."

# CHAPTER 14
# A WOMAN'S INTUITION

"Eric, sorry to bother you on the weekend," Mitch says, sounding worried. "I wanted to chat with you about my concerns that something isn't quite right about Elevation Seeds. I've been tracking yields and talking to a number of farmers. I'm a bit stuck, and I need your help."

"This doesn't sound good. Do you want to come over to chat about it?" Eric asks as he puts Mitch on speakerphone so Christine can hear him as well.

"No, I'll tell you what I know and send you my spreadsheet, but you need to do some more lab work is my guess," explains Mitch. "I've surveyed thirty fields so far and about two hundred different samples."

"Oh my goodness, Mitch, that's a ton of work," Eric says with surprise.

"Yeah, that took some time to do," Mitch agrees, "but it should help you see the results that I'm seeing."

"Okay, can you email the results over to me, and I'll take a look?" asks Eric.

"Already in your inbox, Eric. I walked into all of those fields and took GPS locations of the ears that I pulled from various corn stalks. I also pulled out a few of the stalks—not too many because they aren't my fields, obviously—to take a look at them," explains Mitch.

"Okay, so what did you find?" asks Eric, still concerned but a bit confused.

"A few things. First, there's a sizable yield difference that I'm seeing with Elevation Seeds hybrids compared to the others, such as Beck's, Wyffels, and Pioneer," Mitch continues. "I'm talking like twenty-five bushels per acre different, and there's just no way that Elevation Seeds is that high. The numbers are also in line with a better-than-average harvest, which probably has to do with the great weather we've had. So, it got me thinking, 'Why would the other yields be lower?'"

"Great question." Eric is intrigued.

"Now, here's the odd thing." Mitch pauses and takes a deep breath. "If you map the GPS points and the projected yields, the higher yields are closer to the roads and the lower yields are more toward the center of the fields."

"Okay, but that could be due to water drainage, low points in the fields, heat, or a couple of other reasons, like pests or disease," says Eric, a confused look on his face.

"I agree, but get this: the lower yields oddly almost make a circle. Then the rest of the yields are a bit higher, but still not as high as Elevation," says Mitch. "Meaning, Elevation Seeds produces around 250 bushels an acre, and others are producing about 235. The yields in these circles are closer to 225 an acre. And here's another odd thing: the center of the circle isn't too far from your Aunt Lisa's Farm."

"That's so weird. How big is the circle?" asks Eric.

"It's about five to seven miles in diameter, give or take," says Mitch. "But there are a few other circles with similar patterns in the area too."

"Come on, Mitch, you sound like a crop circle wacko right now!" laughs Eric.

"I'm well aware, but these aren't crop circles at all. They seem to only impact yields," Mitch continues. "But what's the question you're actually missing?"

Eric pauses and looks at Christine, shrugging. Christine mouths "How would I know?"

Eric finally says, "I don't know, Mitch. I give up."

Mitch calmly continues, "The biggest question is why? So, I studied and tracked the locations and corn hybrids at home. I found the main cause isn't driven by a difference in the kernels or even the number of husks per plant, which really drives the total yield. But the husks inside the circles showed higher amounts of corn rot—not a ton, but I could track the pattern."

"Well, that is interesting," says Eric. "Anything else?"

"Yup," says Mitch. "I looked at the actual roots of the corn stalks and found there are signs of worms, or nematodes, on the non-Elevation Seeds stalks. Again, nothing crazy, but those worms are nullified by the seed treatments. Lumialza has been the nematicide seed treatment of choice for years, and we've never had a worm issue."

"Okay, I'm following, but we have tested for all of these things in our lab, and none of this makes any sense to me," explains Eric. "Are you sure your data is correct?"

"Again, buddy, you have all of my data in your inbox, and to your point, I'm mainly a seed salesman and a farmer, so you need to do some more research and digging on your end to see if I'm close, or maybe I've finally lost my mind. Marsha is convinced I lost it a long time ago," Mitch thinks he's funny.

"Well, maybe she's right, and maybe she's wrong, but this is very weird. I'll look into this ASAP at the lab. I've got some time tonight," says Eric as Christine shakes her head no and mouths "We're watching a movie." Then she jokingly smiles and waves her approval to him.

"Okay, but again, Eric, you need to tread very carefully here," Mitch warns. "We're talking about a lot of farmers and all the people that work for Elevation too. Let's make sure this is thought through."

"I understand, Mitch. Just between us for now. Only if we find hard evidence will I take this any further," says Eric. "Thanks again. I'll head over to the lab."

"Have a great afternoon and evening, and let me know if you need anything at all," says Mitch. "I'm happy to go get more samples too."

"I appreciate that, as always. I'll keep you posted." Eric hangs up.

Eric looks at Christine. "Well, that's just the oddest thing I've heard in a while. None of it really makes any sense."

Christine looks at Eric with a slight squint and furrowed eyebrows.

"What?" asks Eric, trying to read what Christine is thinking.

"Well," says Christine, "I've thought something was a bit off for a while now, and I couldn't quite put my finger on it. You know I work in cybersecurity at Busey Bank. We also do deep forensic research into companies that get flagged in our system or by the Department of Justice. If you're going to the lab to look into whatever Mitch was talking about, then I'll head over to Busey and pull up some records on Elevation's ownership. They work with us as well but have never popped up as a concern as far as I know. I can look into their operating agreement and figure out key leadership from there and even their ownership structure to see if anything seems goofy. To state the obvious, that is highly frowned upon at the bank, at best, but I do think we have a very real national security issue here."

Eric leaves the apartment with Christine and head to her SUV. "Okay, that sounds good. I'll get to work, but that seems like a stretch," says Eric as Christine gets into her SUV, and he gently shuts the door for her.

"And one more thing that you need to consider, Eric, because I do think there's more going on here than you want to consider," Christine warns through the lowered window. "I haven't mentioned a weird feeling I always get."

"What's that?" asks Eric with a puzzled look.

Christine continues, "Well, something always seemed a bit off, but if Mitch is correct about his data, then the main person who has been running your lab's analyses is Helen."

Eric immediately pauses, struck by the insinuation. "I highly doubt that, Christine. She's just a young analyst trying to find her way. I'll head to the lab to figure out what's going on, but I'm giving her the benefit of the doubt," Eric says defensively. "I'm sure there's an explanation that doesn't involve Helen."

Eric drives to his lab, still a bit miffed that Christine would even suggest Helen could be involved in international espionage. He thinks about the past two years, considering any warning signs he's missed. *She works so many hours that I guess I'm not entirely sure what she's doing when I'm not there. But there's no chance*, he thinks to himself.

"Well, that's odd." Eric is very confused as he drives up one-way Goodwin Avenue and sees Helen's Honda Odyssey speed away from the lab, clipping the curb as she takes a left-hand turn down Illinois Street. *Why is Helen here on a Sunday, and where is she going in such a hurry?* Eric pulls out his cell phone and calls Helen, but it immediately goes to voicemail.

Eric pulls into the Chemical and Life Sciences Laboratory parking lot across the street from the main lab. The lab is just off the heart of the University of Illinois campus in the School of Molecular and Cellular Biology building, but it's buried among many other laboratories on the Chemical and Biomolecular Engineering campus. Since it's Sunday, Eric has no problem finding a parking space. This is not the norm during the school week when he has to dodge students walking aimlessly or shooting across the parking lot on skateboards without a care in the world.

Eric gets out of his pickup, locks the door, and continues into the office building. Upon entering his office in the back of the lab, he turns on his Mac and gets situated to do a deep-dive data analysis for the first time in a couple of years. He cut his teeth in biochemistry in this lab and others like it, but since his promotion, he's been much more involved with the supervision of the lab. So much time is spent on the administration requirements of the university and the federal grants needed to fund this agricultural lab, as it is one of the most technologically advanced in the country, if not the world.

Eric goes to his closet and pulls out his lab coat, glasses, and lab gloves. He lays them out by the computer and lab equipment needed for his analysis, basic items like a microscope and vortex stirrer, but also items that are much newer to the industry—and this lab—such as a light and electron microscope.

Eric readies the seed samples, stalk samples, and MSDS sheets for the seed treatments from the various companies and opens the database on his computer to study the most recent lab results from Helen. Nothing seems out of the ordinary in the slightest, so he runs his own tests in the methodical fashion that he learned many years ago and executed so many times prior to his promotion to director.

After a few hours of work, Christine calls. "Eric, I'm back from the bank and downstairs. You're not going to believe what I found out. Can you let me up?"

"Same thing here," says a weary Eric, "I'll be right down."

Eric opens the main entrance door and looks around the parking lot. "Come on in. We have some chatting to do."

"Seems that way," says Christine. "There's a lot more going on here than we figured."

Eric walks with Christine toward the elevator and presses the up button. She says, "Let's wait to chat until we're inside the lab. I'm not even sure what's going on right now."

Eric and Christine enter the elevator and go up to the third floor in silence, as they are both still trying to make sense of their past few hours. Eric pulls out his badge and lets Christine into the lab for the first time.

"Are you sure I'm supposed to be in here?" asks Christine.

"You're not, but I do want to show you some things from my own analysis today. Mitch's analysis and Helen's analysis are not stacking up at all," says Eric.

"Okay, you go first, then I'll tell you what I found as well. I'm not supposed to tell you about the information I saw. So, we're in this together, it seems," says Christine.

"You know what? On second thought, why don't you go first," Eric offers as he studies Christine's somber and concerning reaction. "By the look on your face, it seems like you have some information that you didn't expect to find as well."

"I do, Eric. Mitch is right about a lot of weird things regarding Elevation Seeds, and it's much bigger than what I suspected," Christine says, sitting down and taking out a binder of documents. "I made these copies for you, but we'll have to destroy them after we're done looking them over. If I get caught doing this, I'll surely be fired, and that would be the best-case scenario. These are operating agreements and internal bank requests that seem to show a very troubling paper trail."

"Okay," Eric says softly as he sits down next to Christine at the lab table. "What do you have? And remember, I'm a lab nerd, so use crayons and short words, please."

"Crayons it is. From a higher level, in order to have a business banking relationship with Busey, you have to submit your operating agreement and some other items, like your employer identification number. The operating agreement, or OA, has the 'rules' of the company, but we are more interested in the decision-makers. For Elevation Seeds, there are two main directors, or decision-makers: Thao Te and, wait for it, Walter Herzog."

"Okay, I met Thao before, and she's the current CEO of Elevation Seeds, so that seems to make sense to me," says Eric, very confused.

"Yes, that does make sense," says Christine. "But Walter Herzog is the chairman of WH Group. WH Group owns several other companies, including Elevation Seeds. So, with some Google research and searching our internal databases, I found that WH Group also owns CO Daniels, where Thao is also CEO. And CO Daniels owns

Shafer Chemicals. And guess who the CEO of that company is, based on the OA we have on file?"

"Um . . . Thao Te?" replies Eric. "What's the big deal here, though? I'm not following."

"I'm getting there, I promise." She motions for Eric to give her a second to explain, and Eric apologizes and asks her to continue.

Christine tips her head with wide eyes in a sarcastic thanks, then continues. "So, WH Group is run by Walter Herzog. I called a friend of mine, Rebecca Groshek, at the Department of Justice to get more information on Walter. Turns out he's been heavily tied to the Chinese Communist Party, and the DOJ has been looking into him for years. Very similar arrangement to a few of the board members of Gotion, which Anna brought up the other day. Ultimately, they believe that Walter is connected to senior CCP leadership and is doing their bidding here in the United States. If that is true, then these companies are collaborating, as Thao manages them, but are also taking instructions directly from the CCP. WH Group has given millions to the University of Illinois through grants for various labs over the years, including your lab. They have also provided dozens of scholarships that focus on Chinese students," Christine continues.

"Okay, I'm following a bit more," says Eric, looking a little less confused. "What does this prove?"

"Sorry, not done yet." Christine shrugs.

"CO Daniels also buys land. And guess where they own some?" asks Christine.

"I have no clue," says Eric.

"From the public records I searched, CO Daniels owns the land that is right next to your Aunt Lisa's farm," says Christine, waiting for Eric's "aha" moment.

"Oh my goodness," Eric starts to type on his computer. "Any chance that land is around this spot right here?"

Christine leans over to view the location on his monitor. "Yeah, that's exactly where it is. How did you know that?"

"This is the epicenter of the 'circle' that Mitch was mentioning regarding the corn yield concerns he has, and it's right next to Harms Farm. Here are the other two," Eric points out.

"Oh my goodness is right, Eric. This location is the headquarters for CO Daniels, and this location is Shafer Chemicals. They are both surrounded by cornfields." Christine points to both locations. "We need to consider that the CCP is way more involved in Central Illinois farming than anyone thought."

"This is so bad," says Eric. "Unfortunately, it all makes a lot more sense given what I found out in the past few hours too. Helen has been altering almost all lab results and falsely documenting them in our main database. She's hiding corn rot from pantaphos and nematodes in the corn stalks."

"Okay, now I'm the one who is confused," says Christine.

"It means that Mitch is right about Elevation Seeds performing better, not because it's a better seed but because the other seeds are being tampered with somehow. And Helen was concealing it all from inside this lab," says Eric.

"How could any of that happen, though?" Christine's dread is written on her face as she contemplates the scope of the infiltration. "And what does that mean?"

"Well, from my point of view, and given your concerns," Eric says somberly. "It seems like the Chinese are actively damaging our food supply, and Helen, as you said," Eric pauses and takes a deep breath, "could be an agent for the CCP."

# CHAPTER 15
# FRIEND OR FOE

"IT's almost 10 p.m. on a Sunday night, Eric. Do you really think going to that farm and confronting Helen is a good idea?" Christine pleads.

Eric and Christine briskly walk out of the Life Sciences Building and toward Eric's truck. Christine has to jog to even keep up with him. Eric is determined to rectify this situation yet is deeply embarrassed this happened under his direction. He manages his team by combining trust with protocols, allowing them to develop their careers faster, but this trust has now been violated to compromise America's food security. Now he's almost paranoid. *Surely Chris and Steve weren't involved in this?* Eric's mind wanders.

"Maybe not," Eric finally answers Christine. "But this all happened right under my nose, and if it wasn't for Mitch Osterbur, it would still be happening," Eric says with heightened tension in his voice. "The Chinese are literally damaging America's food supply—and that's what we know right now. Even worse, they are using my lab to do it. I am employing a Chinese spy. I am truly hurting my own friends and families and their farms."

"Let's take a breath though, Eric. Why not wait until the morning and involve the police or the FBI? Let's just go back to your apartment and talk through it." Christine tries to convince Eric.

"I'm not going in with guns blazing or anything. She may not even be there, but it's well past time for me to take action." Eric will not be deterred as he hops into the driver's seat. "As the old saying goes, 'If not you, then who?' And this needs to be me right now. I'll be careful, I promise, but I need to talk directly to Helen to see what is going on. And I'm guessing she's at that farm where Danny and Jeff saw her. She was heading away from campus and not toward her apartment."

"Call me if there are any issues at all," pleads Christine. "I know you're concerned, but literally take a breath and keep some perspective. You just found out about this."

"It'll be fine. I'll go see the police tomorrow morning with the evidence I have. I'm not sure how that would play out either since she can easily claim it was an innocent mistake. Plus the cops will have no clue what's even involved with this case." Eric fires up his truck, shuts the door, and barely waves goodbye to Christine.

Eric leaves campus and heads east, jumps on Interstate 74 from University Avenue, then takes the St. Joseph exit to head north. As he heads north on US Route 12, the lights of St. Joseph fade, and he quickly ends up in the middle of fields: corn, soybeans, and government acres. He knows from growing up in this area that deer aren't overly prevalent, but he needs to drive carefully in case any jump out onto the road. The moon is almost full, and the upcoming beautiful harvest moon is only about a week away.

Eric slows at the stop sign at Hull's corner, about five miles from St. Joe. He's less than a mile from the presumed CCP farm. Then he takes a sharp left to search for the entrance to Hans Pein's old farm. The moon lights up the road rather well, so he slows down to about twenty miles per hour and turns off his lights. He sees a culvert and tracks down the drainage ditch running along the road, which locals call Royal Road as it takes you directly into Royal. A culvert almost always means a driveway around here, and he sees the driveway for Pein's old farm.

Eric slowly pulls onto the winding path to the main house and notices more lights than he would expect on a Sunday night. Typically, farms are extremely quiet at 10:30 p.m. on a Sunday, except for maybe some coyotes howling at the moon and chasing a rabbit or a squirrel in the middle of the night. Tonight, there isn't much bustling, but Eric sees there is some odd activity as he slowly works his way up the driveway, which is wide and made of a deep road base to be more like a private road.

Eric nears the farmhouse and sees Helen's Odyssey parked by a large red barn. This kind of barn typically houses the farm equipment needed to plant and harvest crops. A huge bay door is on the left side of the barn, and the white roof of the structure is lit by the moonlight. A large man is standing in the shadows. The man seems to see Eric and scampers back inside. Eric cannot make out who he saw but continues to move toward the barn. The road base and gravel crunch below Eric's tires as four semis and box trailers further behind the barn come into view.

Eric catches a fleeting glimpse of a forklift. The man guiding the forklift and the driver escape into a smaller bay door that Eric had not initially seen. Now all signs of life cease to exist. Other than the slow grinding of his tires rolling over the gravel, nothing is moving.

Eric sees Helen rush out of the white front door of the barn and walk toward him. Eric stops the truck and looks around for any signs of an ambush or pending danger. He does not see any, so he gets out of his truck and walks toward Helen.

"Eric, my goodness. What are you doing here?!" Helen says in a high-pitched tone, terror on her face.

"I was afraid I'd see you out here, Helen," says Eric with measured emotion. "I was at the lab late this afternoon and saw you leaving. I decided to run my own tests based on some rumors, or what I thought were rumors."

Helen pleads, "Eric, I can explain."

"I'm sure you can. We've worked together for almost two years now, and you were manipulating our tests the whole time?" pushes Eric.

"Eric, can we please talk about this at the lab tomorrow?" Helen is petrified. "It's really a bad idea for you to be here and for us to be talking together."

"I'm aware of who you are working for, Helen. The Chinese Communist Party," Eric accentuates with a scowl and demonstrative arm movements. "How is that even possible? First thing in the morning, I'm going to revoke your privileges, regardless. I just can't believe that you would be involved with this."

"Eric, you need to leave for your own safety, but it's complicated. My uncle is a very high-ranking officer in the CCP, and he has been clear with me my whole life that my allegiance to the Communist Party is a legal requirement. It is a 'nonnegotiable,' as you say over here. And if I do not fully obey direct orders, I won't just get fired from my job. Dreadful things will happen to me and my family. We don't have the luxury of freedom you have here." Helen looks around the farm with grave concern.

Eric glances over Helen's shoulder as a large Chinese man walks out of the barn and menacingly stands at attention, glaring at Eric with arms crossed. The burly man wears a generic warehouse uniform with blue overalls and a blue undershirt. Helen notices Eric intensely staring over her shoulder, and she turns and sees the guard. Helen frantically pushes Eric back toward his truck, choking back tears.

"Eric, they know who you are, and you need to leave now. Please. This isn't safe. For either of us." Tears begin to roll down Helen's cheeks.

"This is still America, Helen. Let's not forget that, okay?" scolds Eric.

"Maybe for you, Eric, but not for me. I have been blessed to have worked for you for the past two years. I promise that you have opened my eyes to how kind, gracious, and generous Americans can be. You have taken me in as a colleague and a friend. I will be forever grateful, and I have even rethought my 'duties,'" Helen says passionately, "to my country, my party, and even to myself. But right now, inside that shed are extremely dangerous and armed spies who have not questioned and never will question their allegiance to the party. They will stop at nothing to accomplish the goals they have been assigned and will not listen to anything you have to say. Please, I beg you, leave now, and we can talk later."

Eric stares at Helen, thinking about his options. Thinking about what Christine would want him to do. He is clearly on the cusp of a gunfight and doesn't even have a knife. He looks at the guard with his hand on his hip standing fifty yards away by the white entrance door to the barn. The guard takes a few small steps toward Helen and Eric. The coarse grind of the man's shoes in the gravel is oddly loud. The guard looks at Helen as she frantically waves at him to stay away, and he complies.

"You haven't seen the last of me, buddy!" Eric shouts at the guard. "I'll leave now, Helen, but I promise you I'm not going to just let communists infiltrate this country without a fight." Eric's face is now almost a shade of purple. "And you can let these guys know that, too."

"Thank you, Eric. Thank you," Helen says softly as Eric throws his truck in reverse and tears down the driveway, slinging gravel as the bed of the truck drifts to the side.

Eric calls Mitch as he pulls back onto Royal Road and says emphatically, "Mitch, unfortunately, you were 100 percent right with your suspicions. Helen was tampering with all sorts of lab results, and the companies that seemed suspicious all have ties to the CCP. I just left Hans Pein's old farm, where the Chinese appear to be running their main operation. But they also seem to have operations at Elevation Seeds and Shafer Chemicals. I still have no clue why circles are showing up around these locations, though; it makes no sense to me."

"Yeah," Mitch says calmly, "I figured once you started digging that some tough information would pop up. How did you find out about the companies, though?"

"Again, Mitch, this can't be shared at all," explains Eric. "Christine always had a bad feeling about Helen, and things just felt odd to her. You can't tell anyone this, but she went to Busey Bank to do some digging into the backgrounds of those companies and explained it all to me. I was at the lab repeating Helen's tests and realized she's manipulated almost all of them to conceal results regarding the corn seeds and even the stalks, all of which you found out on your own using some sort of old farmer wizardry. Super impressive, old man."

Mitch, still rather somber, says, "I do wish I was wrong here, Eric, but we need additional help. And we have no idea what else is going on with the CCP. What are the next steps?"

"Honestly, I'm really struggling. This is all new territory for us, but we have to do something. I don't know if that's going to the media, the police, or the FBI. I'm not sure where to start," Eric says as he pulls back onto I-74, heading back to his apartment. "University security is slightly more helpful than a bag of hair, so I'm going to lock Helen out of the lab tomorrow morning when security arrives, but that will take a minute, too. I should go to the police, at least, and see if they can be of any help."

"That's a great start, but contacting the *News-Gazette* and *Daily Illini* newspapers probably won't do much. They don't like to touch foreign relations conflicts. The news stations are just the same these days," Mitch affirms. "I'm way out of my league on this but can quietly ask some friends."

"Okay, I'll call Christine to let her know I'm okay. She's not going to like this update," Eric laments. "We need more help here, but right now, we're the ones that need to keep pulling on this thread."

"As we say, buddy," Mitch says quietly, "If not you, then who?"

## CHAPTER 16
# THE RED LINE

"WHAT in the world was that?!" David shouts in Mandarin at Helen, running out of the barn after Eric peels away from the Union.

David watched the altercation through the small rectangular window in the barn's front door. He aggressively motions for the guard, Wang, to go back inside. He needs more information from her but considers snapping her neck as he walks to her. *I need to know what she knows before we kill her,* David thinks to himself.

"That is a real problem for us, Mr. Lee." Helen says in an oddly calm voice, but David is aware that calling him "Mr. Lee" is also hiding her fear of what he's capable of doing to her.

"This is a huge problem!" David screams as he gets inches away from Helen's face. "How did he know you were here?"

"I don't know, Uncle. But I am concerned he's reviewed my work in the lab and may have found my tampering of the results," says Helen, fighting back tears. "It was only a matter of time until someone else double-checked my lab results, but I don't know what he plans to do with this information either."

"Where is he going right now?" demands David.

"I have no idea, but he's going to lock me out of the lab tomorrow morning. He'll need security to be on site to do that." Helen is visibly shaking. "We need to be prepared for other people to show up."

David is livid. "What do you mean 'other people?' Like police?"

Helen seems to be confused. "I don't know, but he's obviously very angry. I didn't expect him to come here to find me."

"Can you get to the lab right now and get everything out of there?" David says as he waves Wang over since he got a good look at Eric outside the barn.

"My badge worked earlier today, and I highly doubt he can pull my clearance on a Sunday night," replies Helen.

Wang walks up to David, glaring at Helen. "Sir?"

"Wang, go with Helen to the Illinois lab and make sure all of her items are removed. But mainly, if that guy, Eric Buchanan, shows up at the lab, you need to take him out and leave no trace behind," David directs.

Helen shudders.

"Do you have any issues with that?" David questions, seeing her hesitation.

"Well, I . . . it just seems like . . ." Helen stammers. "Why do we need to murder anyone?"

"What other ideas do you have, Helen? Our entire operation is at risk," David says, now seeing from Helen's face that she is trying to find a way to protect, or even save, Eric.

"Maybe we just move to another location and disappear," offers Helen.

"Helen. Let me be clear here: we will not fail in any of our missions. We will do what it takes to succeed. I will remind you what Sun Tzu said in *The Art of War*: 'He will win who, prepared himself, waits to take the enemy unprepared,' and that is what we will continue to do. We need to kill Eric when he least expects it."

"David, I understand our goals and the value we are providing to the party. I also understand the sacrifices that we and our enemy need to make. But I believe that killing Eric will turn into an endeavor that will ultimately hurt our objectives. It brings us attention that we do not desire," pleads a trembling Helen.

David will hear none of it. "Go to the lab, Helen. Gather all of your belongings and do not leave a trace of us. Do you understand?" he says, staring into her soul without blinking.

"Yes, sir." Helen walks to her minivan, trying to stop the tears from running down her face.

"Wang," says David.

"Sir," the guard says gruffly.

"Go with Helen and make sure she follows the directions. Head straight to the lab and come directly back. I'll work with the others to create a plan for Eric. If needed, take care of Helen if she even slightly wavers," instructs David as he points to Wang's .45-caliber Glock 21 in his waistband. "We need to wrap up our loose ends immediately, and Helen is beyond a liability. When you return, put her in the shed's lab and keep a close eye on her."

"Yes, sir. Understood," says Wang as he walks over to Helen's minivan and gets into the passenger seat. David can see Wang direct Helen to start driving. He quickly looks back at David and salutes as they head down the gravel driveway.

David walks back into the barn, dismayed at Helen's treason. He picks up his phone and texts Wang: "On second thought, take care of Helen after cleaning the lab, then we'll burn the minivan when it's convenient."

Wang replies: "Done."

David continues into the barn and opens the door. Inside the fifteen thousand-square-foot barn is normal farming equipment—two large tractors, one tractor with a mower attached to the back of it, one combine, and some trailers. It's about the amount of farm equipment that you would expect to farm about five hundred acres, which is not a substantial operation. But in addition to the equipment, there is a computer lab with encrypted connections to Beijing, a conference room with soundproof glass, and stairs that lead up to a high-tech lab on the second floor.

There are five offices along the far wall from the entrance. David, Z, Chinaloa, and Tom each have one. The fifth office is for the three guards: Wang, Chen, and Davuth. The barn smells more like crops and mud than a normal laboratory or office setting, even with a forty-foot-tall sliding door separating the two sections. There is a kitchen to the left of the front door. A safe room made of industrial-grade steel with no windows is next to the kitchen and is where the weapons are stored. Back in the far-right corner is a storage area, which holds their chemicals, mainly pantaphos, Mustargen, and reactive agents.

Z, Chinaloa, and Tom, along with Chen and Davuth, are standing by the conference room, planning the details of moving from this location.

"Thank you, Chen and Davuth. Keep a close eye on the property, make frequent rounds, and watch the security feed when you're not patrolling. If that guy comes back, do not hesitate to shoot him," directs David. "We're going to meet about our next steps, but you need to keep this compound on lockdown."

"Yes, sir," say the men as they huddle up to assign their duties. David walks into the conference room.

"Okay. We have been discovered, and our work has been compromised. I'll call General Houbin after we create a plan for our next steps. Eric has run his own lab tests and realized that Helen has been manipulating the results for some time. I do not know how he found out that Helen was here, and now he's seen Wang standing by the front door. Thankfully, it was in the dark, but I'm sure he's aware this isn't a normal farm. We have a few options that I'd like to discuss," explains David.

"Go ahead," says Chinaloa. "But we can't let this project's issues jeopardize our nuclear and water infrastructure projects. We need to be ready to leave here immediately without a trace. I told you that Helen was too inexperienced and weak to handle that project, and now we're all at risk."

"Watch your tone," David scolds Chinaloa. She puts her head down and looks back to her computer, avoiding eye contact.

David narrows his eyes and turns back to the group. "We need to be ready to leave here—and quickly—and move to the Mahomet location that sits over the aquifer. Start with the current inventory of chemicals in the semis. Save the drones and the mustard gas for last in case we need to fly them over a public location if the FBI gets involved and we need a bargaining chip. We'll start with dismantling and moving the lab to the Mahomet warehouse."

"Yes, sir," the team confirms in unison.

"Z," David continues, "contact Diego and let him know that construction needs to begin immediately on the Mahomet warehouse for our labs, safe room, farm equipment, and offices. Same setup as this location, but the chemical storage area needs to be larger."

Z nods to confirm the directive.

David turns back to Chinaloa. "We will be pumping about two hundred gallons a day of perfluorooctanoic acid, or C8, into the aquifer. We'll need four weeks of chemicals on hand, so about six thousand gallons, in between replenishments from Illinois's chemical department. Chinaloa, that is a lot of chemicals that need to be available. Make sure you are still on top of the program."

"Yes, sir," says Chinaloa, still uneasy about their last interaction. "A normal tank truck holds about six thousand gallons, and I've procured one for our aquifer operations. Shafer Chemicals has access to C8 under the guise of providing firefighting foam to local municipalities, so we are covered for pumping a sufficient amount of PFASs into the aquifer. The testing facilities, if they ever actually test for these PFASs, will never suspect we're the cause."

"Very good, Chinaloa. What's the deadline, David?" asks Tom as he takes copious notes, knowing how high the stakes are to get this executed correctly.

David turns to Tom. "I want these chemicals, except for two fifty-five-gallon drums of Mustargen, to be at that warehouse by midnight Tuesday. There's no way that Eric has enough information to get the FBI involved, but let's keep ourselves moving and prepared for the worst."

Tom continues to write down David's instructions.

"Tom, you'll move the tech lab to Mahomet as well. That will take you off the Clinton nuclear reactor's network for some time, but we also need you to move," says David. "Work with Wang when he returns this evening and use Helen's minivan to move your computers and network."

"Understood, but won't Helen need her minivan?" asks Tom.

David stares at Tom. "She will not."

The room goes silent as the group understands what David is telling them.

"Sir . . ." Chinaloa says quietly.

"Yes?" David says as he slowly looks in her direction.

"I don't see another option, but will Eric need to be killed as well?" asks Chinaloa.

"It would appear so," David says as ideas churn in his head on how to kill Eric with as little trouble as possible.

"Okay, but Helen is the only one who really knows Eric, and he will be on high alert," Chinaloa reasons. "We need her knowledge of Eric's patterns and habits to make a successful assassination attempt. We barely know anything about the guy, so this won't happen overnight."

David exhales and considers her comments. "Does anyone know where he lives? I have had almost no discussions about him with Helen."

The group shakes their heads as Tom suggests, "Maybe we have her come back here and see if she's willing to help kill Eric. Perhaps she's a good asset after all. Or she won't help, and then we know we can send her back to China immediately. It would be cleaner and easier to get rid of her there. I wouldn't mind making Eric's death look like an accident either."

David is disappointed that he didn't think through this better when he told Wang to kill Helen, but there is still time. "Cancel the last directive," David texts Wang.

"Confirmed," Wang texts back immediately to David. "20m. Returning to the Union. Nothing is compromised."

"Okay, Helen is returning with Wang. We need to create a plan with her to take care of Eric. Then we will send her back to China," David says calmly. "Z, what are you thinking?"

Z leans forward, resting his elbows on the table and putting his hands on his cheeks. "Well, if we have Wang or one of the guards just assassinate Eric, it will be obvious to people he has already told about our operations. We must assume there are people he has spoken to, and we'll get real heat put on us. I'm curious if Diego can also help us here?" Z asks quizzically.

"Interesting. We could have one of Diego's Mexican hit men take out Eric to make it look local, and we can send Wang to discretely point him out in a public setting. Then it doesn't look like we are behind it. That wouldn't put extra attention on us, which General Houbin would prefer as well. The less attention on us, the better," David concurs.

"Z, call Diego and add that to the agenda. You have a good relationship with him, but we will be asking for more of a favor here, which will cost us a lot of money," says David.

"Yes, sir," says Z. He dials Diego from his burner phone.

"Diego. Buenos noches. Yes, can we meet tomorrow, 2 p.m., at the usual spot?" Z nods to David in confirmation. "We have some activity over here and need your professional help in a couple of areas. Construction and demolition. Great. See you tomorrow."

"Demolition. I like that," David scoffs.

"It's set up, sir. I'll go alone," says Z.

Chinaloa and Tom have their heads buried in their laptops, working hard to protect their projects and quickly move them to the Mahomet countryside about thirty miles away. They look up briefly, nod in agreement at both Eric and Helen's fate, then put their heads back down.

Minutes later, Wang and Helen enter through the front barn door. Wang firmly holds Helen's arm to forcefully keep her moving into the conference room.

David asks, "Helen, is everything clear at the lab? No traces of you physically? Did you delete what you could from the databases?"

"Yes, Uncle," Helen says meekly. David can see that she knows her life is in the balance.

David eyes Wang, who confirms with a slight nod.

"Okay, come into the conference room with the group. We need to create a plan," says David. "Wang, please work with the other guards to load up the trucks. Let's get this shed cleaned out within seventy-two hours."

"Yes, sir," says Wang, letting go of Helen as she walks into the conference room.

"Have a seat, Helen." David points to a chair. "Your friend Eric has created a very real dilemma for us. It is not ideal for us to handle issues such as these inside the United States. However, we are out of options. Our cartel friends are going to help us, but we need to know more about Eric to create a successful plan. Within the next few days or weeks, where will Eric be that puts him in public and makes him vulnerable?"

"Public?" asks a weary Helen.

"Yes. We can only assume that he has told several people about his concerns and now his new findings. If we murder him . . ."

David pauses as Helen shudders, then tries her hardest to hide her attachment to Eric.

"If we murder him," David reiterates, "in private, say his apartment, then people will suspect our involvement. But if it's in public and by a cartel member, then it's much more likely to be declared a theft gone wrong and will keep the police, and the FBI more specifically, from looking at us." David pauses again to read Helen, who is now visibly shaking. "Would you like some water?"

"Yes, please," says Helen. David grabs a bottle of water from the corner refrigerator and hands it to her, still not happy with what he is seeing from her.

"Okay, let's walk through this. Any ideas?" asks David as the others mostly keep their heads down, looking at their laptops and peeking up occasionally to see Helen's reactions.

"David, I have no idea. I'm an analyst, not an assassin. How would I know what to do here?" Helen finds a stronger voice.

"We just need the opportunity," David says calmly. "But I don't need to remind you of your legal requirements to serve the party. That includes right now," David says more sternly.

"I am aware. And I want to help in any way that I can," Helen tries to say convincingly, but fails.

"Very good. In the near future, you will be returning to Beijing and, frankly, your fate there depends heavily on what you do right now," David says menacingly.

Helen pulls out her phone and looks at her calendar. "I have an idea."

"What is it?" asks David as the others focus their attention on Helen.

"Eric invited me to something called a 'tailgate' this Saturday. I didn't know what it was, but he explained it to me. The university's football team plays in Champaign on Saturday against some team that I guess nobody likes, so that makes the fans show up in greater numbers. He invited me to join him and his friends before the game. Tens of thousands of people will be there cooking and playing games in the parking lot before the game starts. He was incredibly excited, and he mentioned Gang Grove or something to me," Helen says, forcing herself to look into David's eyes.

Helen pulls out her phone again. "Here it is. Grange Grove. That's where they will be next Saturday if he decides to attend. These threats are new to him, as he's used to working in a lab, but he may assume it's safer for him in public. The game starts at 2:30 p.m., and they are trying to get there around 10 a.m. to set up for the party."

"Very good. Z, you have what you need?" asks David.

"I can see the tailgating map here." Z points at his laptop. "And I have a picture of Eric from the lab personnel page too. What is his home address, Helen?" asks Z.

"The apartments above Bub's restaurant," replies Helen with clear reluctance. "I don't know the address, but it's on Green and Third, and he's in unit 352."

"Okay, Eric trying to stay in public may help us with our assassination plan, but we'll see how he plays this," says Z as he finishes writing down the address. "I'll take it from here with Diego and keep working on transitioning my projects to Mahomet. Need anything else, sir?" Z looks at David.

"We are okay for now and just need to make this go smoothly," says David as he walks to the conference room door and opens it aggressively.

David says sternly, looking directly at Helen, "Wang, please go to Helen's apartment and bring all her items here immediately and clean up all evidence. Ms. Chan is not going to be leaving our sight for some time."

# CHAPTER 17
# NO HELP

**A**FTER tossing and turning in bed at his apartment for a few hours, Eric gives up and gets ready to go to the lab on Monday morning. Last night, Eric called Christine to let her know he was fine, and she took the news remarkably well, especially given he had the good sense to leave and not get killed. Although Eric usually has a standard eggs and bacon breakfast, he skips it this morning and heads to the lab around 7 a.m., expecting security to be able to help him at 8 a.m.

Eric gets into his truck and checks his phone, hoping to see his texts have been read. *She's not getting these messages*, he thinks as he calls her again.

"Hi, this is Helen. Please leave a message" plays on his phone for the fifth time.

"This isn't good," Eric murmurs to himself.

Eric pulls into the parking lot. The same spot he was in last night is still open. He quickly parks and walks into the office building. He skips the wait for the elevator and bounds up the stairs to the third floor. He pulls out his badge to unlock the glass door to the lab. Instead of going to his office, he goes straight to Helen's workstation and sees what he was concerned about all night: all of Helen's items are gone.

Eric goes to his office and rummages through his desk. Items were seemingly moved, but nothing is missing. *Glad I took my laptop home with me.* He goes into the computer system and sees that all of Helen's data files have been deleted. *She had to know we have copies on the server. So odd.*

Eric picks up the phone and calls University of Illinois Campus Security.

"Hello?" the woman on the other side of the phone says after what seems like a two-minute pause.

Eric knows it's a long shot to get any real help from the university's band of Barney Fife guards. "Yes, hi. This is Eric Buchanan, the director of the biochemistry lab here at the University of Illinois."

"Yes?" says the heavily disinterested voice.

"I have had sort of a break-in here at the lab," Eric stammers out, although he didn't technically have a break-in.

"Okay, how much damage is there, and when did this happen?" asks the lady.

"Well, there is no damage per se. I have an analyst who is expected not to show up today, and she snuck into the lab in the middle of the night because she knew I would fire her," says Eric, quickly realizing this isn't going to go the way he had hoped.

"Sir, unless there's any actual breaking and entering, I can't even take a report for you," says the lady dryly, and Eric presses his hand to his forehead in frustration.

Eric tries one last attempt. "Ma'am, this is probably a matter of national security."

"Sir, I'm sorry to hear that, but this sounds like a human resources issue or maybe something for the Champaign Police. I cannot help you," the lady says as Eric hears her take another sip of coffee. "Do you need any more help from me?"

"No, ma'am. Thank you. And don't burn yourself on that coffee," Eric says sarcastically.

The lady picks up on the sarcasm. "Have a nice day, sir," she says and hangs up.

Eric begins to document everything he can regarding what is missing, what was deleted, and the specific tests that were manipulated. He completes his task about three hours later and stands up to leave.

"So, where's Helen?" asks Chris.

"She's not coming back in, Chris, but I need to go," replies Eric.

"Is she okay? What happened?" Chris looks for any guidance.

"I'm not sure yet, but let me know if anyone other than our analysts comes into the office today. I need to go see some people," says Eric.

Eric makes the quick drive to the Champaign Police Department about five minutes away and asks the police officer at the front desk if he can see a detective. The station is not very big, and Eric finds it a bit surprising that he can see only a few officers milling around behind the swinging gate that separates the front desk from the public entrance area.

"Please fill this out," says the man at the desk.

"Okay, but I need to talk to a detective," says Eric as he looks into the back of the room for a familiar face. Then he finally sees his buddy, Brian, heading toward the coffee pot.

"Brian!" shouts Eric.

"Sir, you need to complete this form," says the man.

Brian comes over and says to the man, "It's okay, officer. I'll meet with him. He's an old friend. Then we'll do what we need to do. I promise."

As Brian loves his time at Freeman's, he is not an overly imposing figure by any means but takes his job seriously and fully looks the part of a middle-aged police officer. He has a short haircut and the standard police mustache and is wearing a bulletproof vest, a sidearm with extra magazines, and a taser strapped to his belt. Brian even has the "office pose" down pat with his hands on his belt buckle as he stands there ready to listen with a grin on his face.

"Can we jump into a room, Brian? I've got a story for you that you're probably not going to believe, but I'm trying to find some help," says Eric.

"Sure, buddy, what's up?" Brian shows Eric into a remarkably small conference room.

"First, I don't see you looking this seriously very often. You look legit. But let's start with the short version, then go from there." Eric points toward the direction of the university. "I run a biochemistry lab at the university."

"Yeah, I knew that." Brian nods his head.

"I have—had" Eric corrects himself, "an analyst for almost two years, and she was excellent. One of the best I have seen, probably. We do all sorts of testing, but she ran almost all the experiments, tracked the results, and then was also in charge of reporting against those results." Eric's hands act like they are dictating notes to show tracking and reporting results.

"I'm with you." Brian leans in a bit more.

"Well, this is a bit messed up, but I'm fairly confident that she has been manipulating our lab results and is literally a spy for the Chinese Communist Party." Eric leans back in his chair and opens up his arms, throwing them to the sides as if to say, "There it is, believe me or not."

Brian laughs a bit. "Okay, that is a story, but we've known each other for a while. It would be hard for me not to believe you unless you and your brothers are playing a joke on me."

"I promise we're not." Eric leans forward again. "I was out at Hans Pein's old farm because Jeff and Danny told me they saw her over there a while back. Mitch Osterbur told me—" Eric gets cut off.

"Mitch? Why would Mitch have anything to do with the Chinese?" asks Brian.

"Well, turns out Mitch has had a bad suspicion about a seed company around here, and you know how he can nerd out on data when he gets stuck on something?" Eric pretends to play on a calculator.

"I guess, but not really. I don't know that I'm following anymore," Brian pulls out a notepad. "Mind if I take some notes?"

"Not at all, but it'll get more complicated soon," says Eric. "So, Mitch does some research regarding this corn seed company and corn yields and tracks them in a database. He figures out some really atypical results that point to reduced yields, especially around a few locations: the seed company, which is called Elevation Seeds, a chemical company called Shafer Chemicals, and a farm by Harms Farm, which is behind Hans's old greenhouse andwhere Danny and Jeff saw my analyst, Helen Chan. And Elevation's yields are higher than average."

"Okay, I'm with you, 'ish,' right now." Brian leans back in. "These companies are somehow changing corn yields to make Elevation's yields *better* than the others. You're much better at this than I am, but is that even possible?"

"For now, all I know is that Mitch had some serious suspicions. I reran results yesterday afternoon for many corn seed providers, and my results showed two things that were weird but could explain Mitch's concerns." Eric pulls out his laptop.

"I know this isn't going to make a ton of sense, but I do want you to see that there's data. Then we can try to figure out who to talk to next." Eric turns the laptop toward him. "These are the yields for Elevation." Eric highlights the first chart. "And then this other chart tracks Elevation's competitors: Beck's, Wyffels, and Pioneer. Elevation is higher than their competitors overall. However, look at the data mapped by GPS coordinates that Mitch created. You can see what looks like circles around these three distinct locations. So, I pulled seeds from those areas and found they have a higher proportion of pantaphos."

"Okay, what in the world is that?" asks Brian.

"Think of it as a virus that makes the corn tired and not yield as much but is also hard to determine. You know how you get sick from time to time and just call it a cold? You never have a clue what virus you have, you just know it's dragging you down. You need to rest, it passes, and you move on." Eric pulls up another chart on his laptop.

Eric turns the laptop around again for Brian to see. "Same here. The corn crop just got a little rot, which isn't uncommon, but it reduces the yield. Farmers just assume it was bad luck, and the yield will be better next year.

"But in reality, that corn rot will continue year over year over year with the non-Elevation corn seed unless we can figure out what is going on here." Eric shows a new graph. "And here, this is what is essentially a worm that infects the corn stalk to cause issues, too, but is also extremely hard to track. The main thing is that I went out to that farm last night and surprised the analyst, Helen Chan. There would be absolutely no reason for her to be there unless she was involved in something else."

"No chance she's just doing more research?" asks Brian.

"Not really. She's dedicated, but she's more of a lab rat. Not one to go three hundred yards into a cornfield in the dark to pull some corn husks off a stalk. But—and this was super weird too," Eric pauses, "there was a Chinese guy who looked like a guard standing in front of their machine shed." Eric rounds out his hands to show the size of the guard. "Helen was very clear that I needed to leave and was in real danger."

"And here's the part that makes it sort of all come together. This girl I'm seeing, and this has to stay between us for now because she was doing me a huge favor, pulled some information on the seed and chemical companies. She found the paper trail that shows they are owned by a holding company that is owned by a company based in Hong Kong," explains Eric.

"Like Hong Kong, Hong Kong?" says a surprised Brian.

"Yes, these aren't local companies at all but work really hard to look like they are. It's all a screen with local salespeople and local Chinese leadership. In reality, they are all connected to the CCP," explains Eric. "They even buy farmland all over the country, and that's hidden, too. It's so hard to figure out who owns what through their shell companies. I can promise you they aren't buying the land at these prices because it's a profitable business model," says Eric.

"I'm still not sure I'm completely following, but let me talk to the sheriff. He's not the most tech-savvy person either but may have some guidance for us." Brian stands up and walks out the door.

About fifteen minutes later, Brian comes back into the room. "Sorry about that. Took longer than I had thought," says Brian.

"It's okay. I'm texting Christine and Mitch and trying to piece things together, too," says Eric.

"Who's Christine again?" asks Brian. "She's your girlfriend?"

"Yes," says Eric. "You'd really like her."

"Is she cute?" Brian puts on a big smile.

"She is. Now, back to the sheriff?" Eric is getting annoyed as he is in no mood for small talk.

"He'll join us here soon, but he wanted to make a call first." Brian sits back down. "I highly doubt we can do anything at this point since we really do need more proof before shaking down a farm. Here he comes."

"Eric, this is Champaign's finest, William P. Shrewsbury. He's been our sheriff for about twenty years after what I understand to be a litany of other careers. I've told him what you told me. What else do we need to know?" Brian sits down as the sheriff does the same.

"Nice to meet you, sir." Eric sits back down after shaking Sheriff Shrewsbury's hand.

"Nice to meet you too, Eric." Sheriff Shrewsbury settles back into his chair and briefly looks Eric up and down.

"I believe Brian caught you up to speed, but here's the other part that I really don't want to run too far with and make assumptions about. There's more to this case than what I'm seeing, but did the breakdown in yields make any sense to you?" Eric asks, looking intently at the sheriff.

"A bit. I have to admit I lived on some land outside of St. Joseph, in Mayview, but didn't farm much. I was an architect and a professor at the University of Illinois for many years but don't know that much about corn yields," Sheriff Shrewsbury says matter-of-factly.

"Here's something to consider that is pure speculation. If we know the Chinese own the seed and chemical companies that are involved at the epicenter of the yield loss, and we also know the third epicenter is their operating farm, then it stands to reason that those locations are involved in the root cause of the yield loss. But I have no idea what that could be." Eric slumps back into his chair.

The sheriff leans back in his chair and calmly says, "Eric, Brian speaks very highly of you, and I'm sure you are telling the truth. Our mission here is to protect and serve the Champaign-Urbana area. Ultimately, that means that we're limited in our capabilities, which range from murder to drunk college kids and everything in between, but this really sounds like an espionage case. It will be a fit for the FBI when you have more evidence connecting the Chinese to the supposed yield loss. But as of now, it looks like we're not going to be of much help. If what you are saying is true in the slightest, then you need to be very careful." Sheriff Shrewsbury leans toward Eric and looks him directly in the eye. "Over the years, I have personally seen more middle-aged Chinese men and known Mexican cartel men meeting in odd places. I highly doubt they are talking about high school football. Those cartels started coming down from Chicago about twenty years ago, and they are bad news. If they aren't directly involved in the trouble, they are distracting us so other bad people can get away with something else. It's incredibly dangerous to anyone who messes with them. That much I know for sure. I wish you the best of luck." Sheriff Shrewsbury groans a bit as he gets up from his chair. He reaches out to shake Eric's hand, then walks out the door.

Brian walks Eric out. "I'm so sorry, buddy. Keep working at it. I'll help any way I can. I'll try to do some digging as well, but the sheriff is correct. If this is remotely true, keep your head on a swivel and always have someone else with you. These people are extremely dangerous and won't think twice about taking you out if they feel threatened."

"I understand, Brian.. Are you going to the Michigan game and tailgate this weekend?" asks Eric.

"I would love to, but I can't. I'm working," Brian replies.

"Okay, I think I'm going just to be in public so other people are around me. I need to clear my head a bit, it seems." Eric keeps walking toward the front door.

"Probably not a bad idea to stay in public, brother. You absolutely need to be careful out there," Brian warns again. "The cartels have killed for much less, and you could easily be on their short list."

## CHAPTER 18
# HAIL TO THE CHIEF!

"Get a beer, Eric! This is a tailgate!" Cory shouts as he throws another bean bag through the cornhole. "Man, I'm good. Like really, really good!" Cory gets ready for another toss.

Attending the tailgate this Saturday morning is the first time Eric had been anywhere this week other than his apartment or work, compromising his 'stay in public' plan. He's been secluded to the lab, trying to pull together more evidence to engage the FBI or even local police. It took the equivalent of an act of Congress to have Helen's security clearance removed, and only after she didn't show up for work for three days.

Heeding Brian's warning, Eric looks around for anything sinister, but he isn't even sure what that looks like. He didn't get a good look at the guard by the barn but knows he's sizable. *Would the CCP really try to assassinate me at a football game? No way, right? Stay in the crowd and around people, and keep my head on a swivel.*

"I'm okay, Cory," says Eric as he keeps looking around the tailgating party and off into the distance to see if he spots anyone shady or watching from afar.

"Okay, bro. What's up?" asks Cory. "We're playing Michigan, but you're not hanging out at all, and you aren't even paying attention to my awesomeness at cornhole. This is all messed up."

"Well, this *is* a bit messed up," Eric turns to Cory with a sly grin and stops looking around, "but the Chinese Communist Party is trying to wage an attack on our food supply. There. I said it."

"What in Sam Hill are you talking about?" Cory rolls his eyes in disbelief, showing off his throwback lingo.

"Seriously, it seems one of my lab analysts—you know Helen—is part of the CCP, and I'm watching to make sure they don't try to kill me today." Eric knows that Cory isn't going to really care and definitely isn't going to do anything to help him.

"Alright, man. I'm going to leave you alone. I feel like you've spent too much time with Joel and his conspiracy theories," Cory says as he throws another bag. "Can you watch Cameron for a bit so I can focus on this game, please?"

"Will do." Eric walks over to his eight-year-old niece and squats down. "Hey, sweetie, how are we doing? You need anything?"

Cameron's red hair mimics so many in the Buchanan family. Almost all the kids look alike and could pass for siblings. "Want to throw the football around?" Cameron demands more than asks, jabbing the kid-sized Illini blue and orange football into Eric's stomach and running into some open space next to the tailgate.

"Go deep, Cam!" Eric gently throws it to her.

"Do all Buchanan kids look alike? It's the oddest thing I've ever seen!" Christine jokes as she sneaks up on Eric.

"Oh, hey!" Eric gives Christine a hug. "What are you doing here?"

"I was just checking in to see how you are doing." Christine takes the ball and throws it to Cameron. "I've been looking for more information for you but haven't had any luck this week."

"Same here, but I did see some discrepancies in some chemical inventories in some of Helen's emails I was reading." Eric gives a 'hold on' sign to Cameron so he can talk to Christine.

"What did you find there?" Christine asks, shielding her eyes from the bright sun.

"I'm not sure because it's not my department. It almost seemed like she and another analyst in a different lab who is working on cancer research were communicating quite a bit. Again, I really don't know what that means yet, but it may be something. I still can't figure out why yields were so different around Elevation, Shafer, and that farm either, but I'll keep digging," says Eric.

"Okay, but it really seems like you need to be careful. Are you concerned?" Christine's pale face shows her deep concern.

"I'll be okay; nothing to worry about," Eric lies, trying to keep his eyes from giving him away. "I'm just a lab guy and far from James Bond."

"You know you're a terrible liar, right?" Christine stares at him even harder. "This Chinese espionage program is not cheap; it's heavily involved, and we don't even know how big it is. That's a total recipe for a dangerous situation."

Eric knows she's right and works to take her out of the situation. "I hear you, but I'll be fine. Maybe you can go back to the bank and try to find some more connections? Or maybe you have some new ideas?"

"I know you are trying to get rid of me, but I'll make it easy on you this time because we have an emergency at the bank. I also want to talk to my friend at the DOJ, Rebecca, again to see if she has any thoughts that can help." Christine gives Eric a hug. "But you have to promise to be careful."

"I promise." Eric gives Christine a hug and a smile. "I'll be fine! Cam, throw Uncle Eric the ball again!"

"Here you go, Uncle Eric!" Cameron throws the ball as the University of Illinois Marching Band starts up in the distance.

"The band is coming for Illini Walk. You need to make a run for it if you want to miss a real crowd!" Eric points to the sound off in the distance.

"Okay, see you later then." Christine walks quickly away from the noise of the band.

"Guys, we going to watch the Illini Walk?" Eric asks.

"Kicked your butt again," Cory says to Johnny, the host of the tailgate. "Grab a roadie and let's roll!"

Cory, Johnny, and the others grab beers for the walk to see the band.

Eric is walking ahead of the rest of the gang to get a look for anything suspicious.

"Slow down, Eric. Goodness," Cory complains.

"My bad," says Eric as he slows down just a bit and lines up along the walking path where the band and Illini football players will be walking soon. "Is Bobbi already inside?" Eric asks about Cory's wife, who works closely with the athletic department.

"She is." Cory slyly grins. "Working hard so I don't have to! I am the arm candy though."

"Sounds about right. Well done," Eric laughs.

"Hail to the Orange," the Illini fight song, continues to get louder. Eric can see the football players start to file through the band as they line up along the walking path. The fans follow suit and create their own tunnel all the way to the main entrance for Memorial Stadium, where the Fighting Illini will play the Michigan Wolverines.

As the players parade along the walking path, something, or more like someone, catches Eric's eye.

"Cory, you see that dude there?" Eric points into the line of players across the path.

Cory looks where Eric is pointing. "I don't know what you are looking at, bro."

"There's a Chinese dude who's staring at us right over there behind the band. He's on those steps now." Eric forcefully points at the man, who turns and quickly walks away.

"Nothing, brother. You sure you're okay?" Cory almost seems genuinely concerned.

"He's gone." Eric stops and points. The Chinese man doesn't look familiar, and he knows he isn't Helen's cousin David. Maybe he is starting to lose it.

"Not sure what's going on here, but, well, you are concerning me." Cory looks Eric in the eyes. "You and Christine okay?"

"Yeah, we're fine. She's helping me to figure this out with her banking connections. If you would like to help, I'm trying to figure out some potential chemical inventory issues inside our labs. Can you get information or even get me access?" Eric asks desperately.

Cory shakes his head. "I run facilities for the University of Illinois Foundation. I don't have access to any of that. I'm sorry, man, but you seriously need to stop working so much or something."

"I'll figure it out," Eric says as the band wraps up and the crowd starts to disperse. "Let's head back to Johnny's tailgate for a bit and try to get a win today."

"Sounds good to me," Cory says, and they walk back to the tailgate and put the food into coolers.

"Game time!" Cory says after a few minutes, pointing to the stadium. "Let's roll!"

Eric, Cory, Cameron, and a few other friends all stroll into the stadium but then break up into their various seating sections. Cory, Cameron, and Eric go to the club-level seats. Bobbi typically moves in and out of the Colonnades section during the game. As an assistant director of the athletic department, she will be in the box seats shaking hands with donors and making sure they have everything they need to enjoy the game.

The game is incredibly tight with both sides trading field goals, but as expected, a rowdy Michigan fan is getting on people's nerves.

"Seriously, there's always one of these jerks at every Michigan game. It's really amazing!" Cory shouts directly at the fan, but in theory, it is meant for Eric. "Maybe sit in your own section!" Cory screams at the fan, who is a few feet away.

Eric laughs at Cory's classic anger issues during Illini sporting events. "Not sure he heard you there. You think he's aware he's sitting in the Illini section?"

"These guys are terrible! Come on, Michigan, blow them out!" screams the fan to their lower left. His super embarrassed wife next to him is not even wearing Michigan colors.

"The funny thing, Cory, is that you and that dude aren't too different." Eric points to the fan. Cory's face says all the expletive words he wants to say.

"He and you are lucky that Cam is here," says an ever-angrier Cory. "Can we please stop the run, run, pass, punt play-calling?! Please!"

Finally, halftime arrives, and Illinois is winning fourteen to ten. The Michigan man is still talking smack at nobody in particular.

"Best part of Illini sports, brother? Chief Illiniwek," says Eric, pointing to the tunnel where the Chief will emerge with a glorious dance to the full support of the marching band and a raucous crowd that gets goosebumps every time the Chief steps onto the field.

"Bum, bum, bummmmm, bum, bum, bum, bum, bum" is known by anyone who has attended an Illini sporting event. As the Chief completes the dance at midfield, all fans begin to put their arms around each other.

"Michigan still sucks," Cory says loud enough for the Michigan man to hear as he and Eric put their arms around each other, with Cameron in the middle.

Eric laughs at Cory, then catches a glimpse of the Chinese man again. It appears he's pointing Eric out to a menacing Mexican man. The man's tattoos, covering his arms and even a bit of his face, distract Eric. Then he notices the man is laser-focused on Eric's torso.

"Cory! There's that dude again, but he brought a friend." Eric tries to turn Cory to his upper right so he can see the men, but Cory shakes him off.

"Dude! Stop! CHIEEEEEEFFFFFFF!" Cory screams the chant with the rest of Memorial Stadium's tens of thousands of fans.

Eric sees the man pull out what appears to be a gun and train

# HAIL TO THE CHIEF!

it on his chest. "GUN!!" shouts Eric as he pulls Cory and Cameron away from the gun's aim at Eric's chest, and they fall back into the people behind them.

Eric is almost certain he heard a gun go off but is not sure.

"Are you okay?!" Eric screams at Cory while checking to make sure Cameron is okay.

"I'm fine. What was that for?!" shouts Cory, holding a crying Cameron.

Then Eric regains his footing and sees that he was correct.

"Cory, the Michigan dude is hurt and on the ground!"

Eric works his way forward to the fan's wife, who is holding him and screaming, "He's been shot! Call 9-1-1! Get help!!" Eric leans forward to look at the Michigan man and sees blood all over him. He knows that bullet was meant for him.

"I'm going after them, Cory. You stay here." Eric jumps over other fans to get to the entrance tunnel where the men were standing.

"What are you even talking about?!" Cory gets out of Eric's way.

Eric runs through the tunnel, looking for the men, but there are many places to run, and they have at least a minute head start. He turns to a man nearby. "Sir! Did you see two men come sprinting out of this hallway with a gun?"

"A gun?! I've been here in line for concessions for about three minutes, and I haven't seen anything at all," the confused man says to Eric.

"They must be gone. Dang it!" Eric rushes back to the stands.

"Cory, how is he?" Eric works his way toward the man.

"I think he's dead, Eric. And I think I believe you now," Cory says, still holding a crying Cameron. "But I need to get her out of here."

"Well, we need to get help because I'm assuming the man with the gun is a cartel member, given how many tattoos he had. The Chinese man probably works for the CCP and was making sure it went as planned. But I'm sure they saw I wasn't shot. I can't believe that Helen and her people are trying to kill me now." Eric looks around for any other signs of danger.

Eric, Cory, and Cameron try to leave, but the paramedics are now arriving along with security and police.

"I'm sorry, everyone. You need to stay in this area until we are done questioning everyone. The stadium is on lockdown as well," says a heavyset university police officer as he cordons off the area and the other officers create a boundary.

After about an hour, the rest of the stadium has been emptied by the police as they make sure the suspects aren't hiding among the crowd. The fans in the section of seats that were around the shooting incident, including Cory and Eric, are still waiting to be released.

"I'm glad Bobbi was able to come and get Cameron. This isn't going fast at all." Eric looks at the police tape.

"They need to talk to you first, but it seems like they are well outside their element," says Cory, pointing to the police still taking people's statements.

"Now we really don't stand a chance of finding who did this." Eric spots Brian Eiskamp coming toward them. "You believe me now, Brian?"

"Sorry it took me so long to get here, but I had no idea you two were involved," says Brian, pulling out his notepad. "Tell me what happened."

Eric scowls at Brian. "Brian, this is what I was telling you. We're getting close on this CCP thing. They tried to murder me. Even Cory almost believes it now."

"It's true, Eiskamp. He kept saying he was seeing things, and I didn't believe him." Cory shrugs. "And we almost lost Cam because I didn't listen."

"I'll take your statements here, guys, but nobody else is going to believe this was anything other than some crazy dude who wanted to inflict some damage in a crowded stadium. Since they were hidden inside the exit tunnel back by the concession area, nobody else even got a look at what happened. They were all watching the Chief. Did you see anything?" Brian gets ready to take more notes.

"Yes. That's what I've been trying to tell you." Eric tries to keep himself calm. "There was a Chinese man and a Mexican man. The Chinese guy was about average build, with a blue top and black pants. The Mexican guy wore black pants and a tight black T-shirt. I could see a lot of tattoos on the Mexican. That's also what I've been saying: the Chinese and the Mexican cartels are connected." Eric highlights the locations of the tattoos.

"Okay, we'll look at all the video footage of everyone coming and going and try to work it down to specific subjects. I'll need you to review it later, Eric. Cory, you didn't see anything at all?" pushes Brian.

"Nope. I was watching the Chief, then Eric shoves me backward between our row and the row behind us. Bruised my ribs too," says Cory with a sly grin.

"Here we go, Eric. Cory is going to complain about how he's missing a lung from his cancer ten years ago again. Take a seat and get comfy," jokes Brian.

"He does it to you too, huh? Figures." Eric slaps Cory on the side. "But seriously, Brian, we need to get the police out to that farm immediately before they make a run for it. Once they leave, I highly doubt we'll be able to find them any time soon."

"Look, Eric. I believe you, but we need more proof before we raid a farm. If this is remotely true, we'd need a search warrant and probably mobilize the SWAT unit." Brian closes his notepad.

"Brian, are you good if I go find my family?" asks Cory.

"Sure, buddy. You have my number if you come up with anything else, but it sounds like you didn't see much anyway." Brian holds up the yellow crime scene tape for Cory to pass under.

"Brian. Seriously. I'm going to head out there and try to get more information," Eric persists. "I was keeping it light for Cory, and I've been telling Christine that everything is fine here as well. I'm struggling to have concrete proof, and I get that's an issue, but I know the CCP is behind all of this, and we have much larger issues at play." Eric starts to walk under the crime scene tape.

"Look, man. I can't make that happen, and I'm sure you understand that. We just don't have any real evidence. I'll wrap this up in about an hour, then I can just go out there with you as a friend. You still live at Bub's Apartments and have a friend you can take along in case it gets hairy?" Brian asks as he taps his holstered gun.

"Yes. Ok, sounds good. I'll see you in the parking lot in about an hour. I'll bring my friend along with me, too." Eric taps his side, confirming he'll come armed, then walks toward the exit.

# CHAPTER 19
# HIDE THE EVIDENCE

"Fuel, oxygen, a tight space, and an ignition source are all we need to blow up this grain silo and make it look like an accident," David tells Wang, pointing to the fifty-foot-tall metal cylinder next to the barn. Wang has returned to the Union after the failed assassination attempt. "Let's just get Eric in there and keep moving operations to Mahomet."

Wang and his direct reports, Chen and Davuth, work on executing their plan to booby-trap the grain silo and ultimately murder Eric in the explosion. Grain bin explosions are not common, but they're not unheard of either. They are shockingly large when they do occur. It would be a great plan to cover up their operations and dead bodies alike. They have also strategically placed other accelerants in the vicinity to create a destructive chain reaction throughout the Union.

"Yes, sir. I'll set the charges. The auger will look like a faulty electrical connection that causes the detonating spark." Wang waves to Chen and Davuth to come over to help him sabotage the auger's electrical system and also install on a rudimentary timer that will be the real catalyst.

"Yes, that seems like the easiest way to create a spark and to reduce any suspicions. But we need to be far away when that explosion goes off. Grain dust explosions are massive and powerful, and this explosion needs to look like one, too," David says to the guards. "You'll need to subdue Eric if and when he shows up, but we should expect him inside the hour. Tie him up inside the grain bin and put the explosives close to his body."

"Yes, sir. The C4 is charged and ready to go," explains Wang. "We're on high alert looking for any signs of Eric. We've almost completed loading up the trailers, and we can roll out of here in about an hour."

"Very good. I'll update Z, Chinaloa, and Tom. Put the rest of the weapons in that semi where I'll be riding, but keep enough for you to handle Eric if needed." David points to the last of four semis that are being loaded. "You, Davuth, Chen, and Z will drive them."

"Yes, sir." Wang points to the red semi cab and dirty white trailer and says to Chen and Davuth, "Load up the rest of the weapons into that semi immediately."

Chen and Davuth hustle away as Wang walks over to the grain silo to finish setting up the explosives.

David hears the loud and throaty growl of a motorcycle. Diego has arrived as he has asked and pulls his blacked-out Harley Davidson close to the front door of the barn to get away from the forklift traffic and men working. David waves for Diego to join him inside and turns to walk into the conference room.

"Another favor, Diego." David and Diego sit down.

"What do you need, David? Seems like you have your hands full right now." Diego leans forward.

"I suspect Eric will show up at some point since your guy didn't kill him." David doesn't try to hide the disappointment. "The police are involved, but I'm not sure they can trace this back to me at all. Regardless, we're going to end this operation here and move to another location in Mahomet."

"Okay. That sucks, man, and I am sorry my guy hit the wrong dude. My guy and your guy, Wang, I think, both got away without an issue. I've confirmed that with our informants inside the police. What do you need from me?" Diego offers his help.

"Yes, Wang said that Eric moved at the last second and they killed another guy. It happens. I don't want any police to see us leaving here or being able to track our trucks. I also don't want any police to pull us over and see what we're carrying inside the trailers. Can you create a distraction in Champaign so we can roll over to Mahomet without any issues?" asks David.

"We can do that, hermano, but that's going to end with some of our guys in jail and a lot of damage. We do this from time to time when large drug shipments are coming down from Chicago or biker gangs are going to fight it out and need a distraction. What time are you wanting?"

"We're going to need them staged immediately. We're looking to roll in about an hour." David points to his watch to show the urgency.

"Okay, I'll have my guys go to the Cowboy Monkey in Champaign and wait in that area until you give me the go-ahead. This is going to be very pricey for you, too, David. I'm guessing two to three hundred thousand dollars. That's on top of the assassination attempt. You're okay with that?" Diego picks up his phone, ready to send the directive.

"Yeah, that's fine. We have way too much wrapped up in this operation to get caught moving it. I'll wire it to you when we're settled in," says David, leaning back in his chair with a look of exasperation.

"Okay, amigo. This must mean a lot to you." Diego shakes his head. "Cowboy Monkey is close to the police department, so the cops will respond quickly and prevent anyone from getting overly hurt. Mainly, I just don't want my guys in jail for seven to ten because they accidentally kill some dude. We'll drag it out to make sure we draw in the cops that are around Interstate 74 where you'll be rolling the semis." Diego begins texting the instructions to his crew.

"Agreed. We are close to wrapping up here. Thanks again. I'll text you when to start the fighting at Cowboy Monkey."

David and Diego stand up to leave the conference room and exit the barn from the front door.

"Hasta luego," Diego says as he jumps onto his Harley and slowly heads down the driveway.

"Wang! Show me what you have done so far," David yells at Wang. "Have you seen any signs of Eric?"

"None, sir," Wang says as he directs Chen to maneuver the forklift to load the final drums of chemicals. "Davuth is on lookout, and we're watching closely too."

"Okay, how much longer until we're ready to roll?" asks David.

"An hour at the most, sir, but I'd like to have some of the trucks leave when they are ready," Wang says.

"Negative, Wang. We'll all roll together," David explains. "Diego is going to start a bar brawl in Champaign to distract the police, and then we should have no problem getting to Mahomet without any cops seeing us."

"Understood, boss. Very good idea. We'll finish loading up, but let me show you inside the bin. Chen, Davuth, and I will be able to easily take Eric when he shows up, and we're armed as well, worst case." David and Wang duck down and step inside the small four-foot hatch to enter the grain bin. David sees a wooden chair, duct tape, and zip ties standing alone. Next to that chair is Helen, bound and gagged. She's flailing her body as much as it will move, but it's no use.

"Again, Helen, I do apologize for this, and your uncle Houbin will ultimately understand, but we need to find a way to get Eric into this grain bin, and you're the best bait we have." David walks over to her. "As the old saying goes, this isn't personal; it's just business. But the reality is you lost your way and your dedication to the party. There is always a consequence for that, as we all know. We all must make sacrifices for our duty to the CCP. Please know that the story will be that you were murdered by Eric before he was overtaken by our guards and that you were a true hero. Your uncle and your family will be very proud of you in the end."

David turns to Wang, pointing to the auger behind the chair. "Okay, where's the explosion, and how will that work?"

"We'll turn on that auger as we're leaving and set the C4 to blow in five minutes to allow us to get down the road but still be close enough to make sure it detonates," Wang says as he shows David the exposed bent metal of the auger. "This auger needs to be running to show a drain on the electricity, and the poor wiring is exposed to help sell the faulty wiring story. Due to the size of this grain bin, we need about ten pounds of C4 to make sure the barn is destroyed. The C4 is molded to explode in that direction as well. We left a fifty-five-gallon drum of diesel fuel inside the shed to help it fully burn to the ground. That combine we're leaving behind is also full of fuel. The fire department will have no issue believing it was an accident. And even better, the Royal Fire Department is all volunteers, so they will need to get out of bed and go to the fire department to get the trucks and come here. They can't even get here inside thirty minutes since we're eight miles away from the town. Plenty of time for things to get extremely hot and difficult to extinguish," Wang explains, grinning. "I've heard their motto is 'we'll save the land.'"

"Understood. Very good. Where could Eric arrive when he gets here? *If* he gets here, I guess. I would have expected him already, but maybe he thought better about dying after we almost killed him today." David steps through the hatch to get out of the bin.

"There's no other way to get onto this farm other than the front driveway, so we're looking for any signs of a truck or anyone even walking and sneaking up to the farm." Wang points to Davuth, who is now watching the driveway.

"Okay, very good all around, Wang. Let's wrap up the trailers and get ready to go." David walks back into the barn.

"Davuth! He's going to come from that direction, so use your air horn if you see anything at all!" Wang shouts.

"Nothing so far at all, sir! I doubt he's coming. I guess that guy didn't like getting shot at," Davuth replies, turning back to look down the driveway.

## CHAPTER 20
# DUTY TO COUNTRY

"Eric, you're aware that we could easily die, right?" asks Brian as they very quietly drive his pickup with the lights off into Harms Farm around 10 p.m. on Saturday night.

Eric is aware that this is well above Brian's pay grade—and even skill set—and Eric's ROTC training many years ago will need to come back to him quickly. He's banking on surprise and both of them being good shots to pull off this plan. Both Brian and Eric do spend time at the gun range in St. Joe, so he feels very comfortable handling his weapon.

The reality is that his guilt for allowing this to happen has made his decision-making suspect and, now, utterly dangerous. He didn't tell Christine what he and Brian were planning. She thinks he's back at the lab to run more analyses and document the evidence so the FBI will take up the case. If they get killed, then at least he won't have to explain that part to her.

"I'm aware, Brian. Very aware. But these Chinese guys are literally trying to kill a lot of Americans. We have no choice," Eric says with as much conviction as he can muster. He guides Brian to follow the gravel driveway behind the livestock shed. The truck will be hidden from all roads and Aunt Lisa's curious eyes from the house. No dogs are barking, so they must be in the garage for the night. *I bet Ricky Bobby wouldn't mind going on this adventure*, Eric oddly thinks to himself.

"We can easily sneak up on them. So, the main question is how many are there?" Eric quietly shuts the passenger door of Brian's Ram pickup and opens the back door to get another handgun. "I've got my double-stack Glock 9 and will take this nine-millimeter Springfield. I've got two extra magazines as well."

"Okay, I've got my Glock 40 and a sawed-off shotgun with double ought loaded. If we need more than this, then we're probably having a really bad day." Brian smiles as he softly closes the back driver-side door. "You know this path well?"

"Close enough, but we need to use the GPS on our phones too. I have a pin dropped for the main barn at their farm." Eric points in the direction of the Union. "We can walk along and through the rows of corn to sneak up from the back. Outflank them, I'm guessing is what you learned in the academy?" Eric walks over to the Harms's cattle fence and carefully ducks through the barbed wire as Brian separates the wires to create space.

"You're clear." It's Brian's turn now to get through the barbed fencing as Eric separates the wires.

"Stay low and crouch down to keep the corn husks and leaves from making too much noise as you brush past them." Eric points to his right. "We'll head west for about a quarter mile right here because this direction will be the loudest going against the planting rows. Then we can head straight south, parallel to the rows, and should be able to stay rather quiet. It's about another mile and a half to get to their farm."

"It's a super cloudy night too, Eric, so we should be able to get close without being seen. I'll just follow you slowly and stay as quiet as possible. Let's stop talking for now. Our voices and sounds can really travel out here," Brian whispers to Eric, who responds with a thumbs up.

The two men slide between the corn stalks for about a quarter mile. It takes about fifteen minutes as they try not to make any noise, which is nearly impossible.

Eric whispers, "That light out there is the farm's main pole light. We'll head to that. This is the corn row we need to take. If we go against the rows close to their farm, they'll hear us, so be careful."

Brian gives an "okay" sign, and they continue down the corn row toward the light pole.

As the farm comes into clear view at the end of the corn row, Eric and Brian get onto the ground. The cold and wet dirt beneath them presses through their jeans. About 150 yards to the south, the trucks are almost loaded. Two trucks are almost ready to head out, with drivers standing on the side waiting for the green light to leave.

"Guard there . . . and there," Brian whispers and points to a guard by the grain silo and another guard in the distance watching the driveway. "I can't see what weapons they have. Must only be handguns. Let's move behind that grain bin, then take out that guard."

Eric nods in agreement, and both army crawl behind the grain bin. They duck behind the motor for the auger that pulls the corn out of the bin and, typically, into a wagon.

"I'll go first." Brian pulls out his gun and mimics hitting the guard over the head with the gun.

"Okay," Eric mouths. Then he puts up his hand for Brian to pause. He whispers, pointing to his ear, "Do you hear that?"

Brian pauses, then cups his ear and whispers, "I do. What is that?"

Eric listens a bit longer. "It's muffled screaming." Eric shrugs then whispers, "Is it inside this bin?"

"Maybe," Brian whispers. "Let's go, then we'll peek inside." He starts to slowly move around the circular bin to sneak up on the guard.

Eric sees the guard take a step to his right to get a better look and verify the trucks are ready. Brian takes the opportunity. With all his strength, he brings the .45-caliber Glock down onto the guard's head. The guard is instantly dazed, stumbling, then starts profusely bleeding from his head. Yet, he's still conscious.

"I've got him," Eric whispers as he jumps behind the guard. He puts him into a chokehold and gently guides him to the ground. Brian pivots to keep watch for anyone who may hear the struggle. Leveraging his time as a wrestler in high school, Eric keeps squeezing until the guard passes out. The guard struggles and swings his arms, then goes limp on the ground.

Brian drags the guard's body back toward the cornfield as Eric opens the hatch door into the grain bin and peeks inside. "Oh my goodness! Helen!" Eric squats down and gets through the tight hatch, then runs to Helen. Tears stream from her wide-open eyes as she tries to speak. Eric removes the duct tape from her mouth, then drops to his knees, pulling out his Leatherman to remove the duct tape from her ankles.

"They are going to blow us up, Eric. We need to get out of here!" screams Helen.

"Eric, get cover now! Two guys are running over here with guns!" Brian screams at Eric as he leaps into the grain bin, shuts the hatch door, and jumps behind the grain auger with Eric. The guards talk briefly in Mandarin, then go silent.

"As soon as they open that door, shoot them!" says Brian.

"What about Helen?" Eric gets a better angle to shoot anyone who enters the hatch door, but the duct tape around Helen's torso still has her stuck in the chair.

The door slightly opens, and Eric sees a small grenade-like device roll onto the ground.

"Get down!" Brian screams.

The concussion from the smoke grenade pierces Eric's ears. Eric searches in the smoke for Brian and Helen through the violent ringing in his ears. He feels for Brian in the fog. Brian squeezes his arm to let him know he's okay. As Eric turns to find Helen, the hatch door opens, making a strained metallic sound. The gunfire from the hatch forces Eric and Brian to find cover behind the grain auger once again.

*Click*. Eric hears the guard run out of bullets. The smoke has risen in the bin a few feet, but he is having trouble seeing. Eric sees a silhouette in the smoke, springs over the auger, and tackles the man into the side of the grain bin. Brian moves toward the hatch door in case another shooter tries to take potshots. A handgun barrel peeks through the hatch and takes aim at Brian. The bullet releases from its chamber and finds Brian's midsection. He crumples to the ground.

Eric's nemesis punches him in the nose, breaking it. Blood spews everywhere. Dazed, Eric stumbles backward, then hears the man say, "That guy is dead. I'll handle this guy. Diego is starting the fight at Cowboy Monkey. Let's get those trucks rolling! Start the auger and set the detonator for ten minutes. I'll be done with this loser in about thirty seconds."

"Yes, sir."

The auger starts to whirl with a loud metal-on-metal grinding.

Eric gets jacked in the nose again and tackled to the ground next to Helen's chair. The man jumps on top of Eric and starts wailing on him. It's David.

Eric covers his head to protect himself, and the man moves on to body blows. Eric can barely breathe and knows he's in a lot of trouble. He looks to the left for any weapon and doesn't see anything. He can't get to the gun on his hip. He looks to the right for anything he can use to knock David off, and he sees her.

Helen is still taped to her chair but is knocked over and lying sideways on the ground. From her lifeless eyes and the blood coming from her mouth, Eric knows she is dead. The blood from the gunshot wound continues to paint her white blouse. When the men entered the grain bin and opened fire, they hit her squarely in the chest.

Eric takes another blow from David to the side of his head, which reminds him that his life is about to end as well. Eric uses his left hand to protect his head and lands a punch on David's temple, stunning him. David returns a head shot, forcing Eric to protect himself again.

"I knew you and Helen would be a problem at some point. Fittingly, you'll both die in this grain bin together," says David as he lays down another blow on Eric's head.

Eric flashes back to his wrestling days as he is losing consciousness and prepares for the next hit to his head. David rears back for another blow that could knock him out and starts to lean forward. Eric drops his hands to the ground, exposing his face. Confused that Eric is giving up, David pauses. Eric drives his hands and feet into the ground, launching his hips into the air. David flies over Eric's head, and a blood-curdling shrieking overwhelms the grinding of the auger. Eric slowly rolls over to see David battling to pull his arm out of the auger and fighting to keep from being pulled in alive.

Eric, concussed and barely lucid, laughs to himself, *"Those things always scared the hell out of me."* He catches a glimpse of another man pulling David from the auger and dragging him out of the grain bin, blood spewing everywhere from the edges of David's torn shirt.

*We have to get out of here before this explodes,* Eric thinks.

Brian is lying on the bin's concrete floor but rolling around in pain. They need to call for help, but there's no cell coverage inside the grain bin.

Eric struggles through the hatch on his hands and knees. His ears are still ringing, and his bloody nose is starting to clot. The guards and David run toward the semis with David screaming in pain and anger. One guard takes off his flannel shirt and creates a tourniquet on David's arm as he struggles to get into the last semi with his mangled arm. The caravan's diesel engines roar as the drivers quickly shift through the gears. With blood covering the side of David's semi, they accelerate down the gravel driveway with no lights and disappear into the night.

Eric pulls out his phone to call for help but then notices a clock ticking next to the hatch door. "What is that?!" he shouts.

"Eric!!" Brian is still inside the bin, his breathing labored.

"I'm coming, buddy!" Eric hunches down and climbs back into the grain bin.

"Gut shot, just below my vest," says Brian. "Get me out of here!"

"Looks like we have a bomb outside this door, and I don't know how much longer we have." Eric begins to drag Brian to the hatch door as Brian groans in pain. Blood trails behind him.

"I can get out, then pull you through." Eric pauses.

"Just pull me close to the hatch. I don't know how much time we have," says Brian.

Eric pulls Brian up by his shoulders and lays him over the bottom of the hatch door as he steps out to the outside. Brian pulls his feet toward his waist, then uses them to push himself through the door and back onto the ground outside. "Man, that hurt."

Eric reaches over to the timing device and simply hits "stop timer" with forty-five seconds left. *No kidding. It's that easy, huh?* Eric thinks to himself, then screams, "Brian, it's off. I'm going to get you help!"

Eric pulls out his cell phone to call 9-1-1. The phone has been on silent to avoid alerting the Chinese, but Eric notices fifty-three missed text messages and twelve missed phone calls. *"No time for that right now,"* he says to himself.

"Hello! Yes! I have an emergency! A man has been shot and is in very bad shape. He's a Champaign County police officer, too. Please send an ambulance now! We're about a mile west of Huls' Corner on Royal Road."

"Sir, I need an address," replies the dispatcher.

"I have no idea. Can you track my cell phone's location?" asks Eric.

"Yes, I can see that. Is this currently a dangerous situation?" the operator asks.

SOWING DISCORD

"Not anymore. The men who did this are in multiple semis and are very dangerous. I don't know which direction they went. Please send everyone you have to try to find them. They are Chinese spies and heavily armed," pleads Eric.

"Sir, we will send paramedics from St. Joseph, but all officers are currently on site or on their way to a large bar fight in Champaign right next to the police department. What is the name of the downed officer?" the dispatcher asks calmly.

"Brian Eiskamp." Eric looks back at Brian.

"Okay, I will get someone there as soon as possible, but the ambulance will be en route very soon."

"Ma'am, this is extremely serious. We need to catch these people. Send the police." Eric stresses to no avail.

"I am very sorry, sir, but we do not have any units available," the dispatcher repeats.

"Ridiculous," says Eric and hangs up the phone.

"Brian, an ambulance is on their way, but no help from the PD," Eric says.

"I heard, buddy. I'll bet my pension the cartel created a distraction for the Chinese. Those trucks will escape without having to worry about police following them or pulling them over and inspecting their trailers." Brian rolls over and doubles up in pain. "I don't think he hit anything vital."

"How do you know that? You're a doctor now?" Eric adds some levity.

"No, I just know I'd be dead by now, and this hurts like a son of a gun." Brian grimaces again. "And that first bullet stopped by my Kevlar vest feels like a horse kicked me in the chest."

Eric hears tires coming up the driveway and immediately looks down the path and pulls out his Glock.

"Brian, I think they came back." Eric pulls out Brian's gun and puts it into his hand. "Do what you can. I'll do what I can in front of you."

Eric sees headlights, then flashing blue and red lights. "Wow, the police finally did come, but they're way too late to catch that convoy."

Brian shakes his head. "No way our PD was that fast, Eric. I have no clue who that would be."

Still on high alert with his gun pointed at the car and his left hand putting pressure on Brian's wound, Eric jokes, "As they say, brother, when seconds matter, the police are minutes away."

# CHAPTER 21
# IGNORANCE IS BLISS

"Go ahead and put that down, partner. We're friendly," Eric hears a man say with a thick Boston accent. "I'm Special Agent Matthew Harmon with the Federal Bureau of Investigation."

Eric is confident he has a concussion from the whipping he just took from David. *Did I just hear FBI? Am I still alive?* Eric shakes his head to gain some clarity, but it just causes blood to come out of his nose. Helen is dead—he's fairly confident of that at least. That poor girl didn't deserve that, and his guilt for allowing this to happen returns.

"Really, Eric, it's okay. It's just us." Eric hears his cousin Danny's familiar voice. "The Freeman's bartender is actually an FBI agent."

Eric shouts to Danny, "I called 9-1-1, guys. Brian is shot and is bleeding badly. Who else is there? Can we turn off those headlights?" Eric puts his Glock back into his side holster, then returns both hands to put pressure on Brian's wound.

With the gun down, Danny and Jeff now run toward Eric. A large man is running with them. That must be the guy with the accent he heard at first.

The boys and Special Agent Harmon stand next to Eric and Brian. Agent Harmon says in his thick accent, "I'll take it from here, Eric. I'm medically trained, and you don't look too good either. The ambulance will be here in a few minutes."

"Chad? What are you doing here? What are any of you doing here?"

Agent Harmon waves to turn the car off and summons someone to come over.

Eric is beyond confused at this point and looks at the car. "And who turned off the car?"

Christine gets out of the car and sprints toward Eric.

"I'm in so much trouble," Eric says to Brian, who nods in strained agreement through his pain.

"Eric, I am truly Special Agent Matt Harmon with the FBI," Matt says calmly while taking Brian's pulse. "I have been undercover while providing reconnaissance on these Chinese operations for almost two years and have been posing as Chad Goldenstein at Freeman's Tavern. I knew you were getting closer to the CCP's operations here and starting to figure things out from eavesdropping on you and Mitch. About two months ago, I put a tracker on your truck at your apartment. That's how I knew you were here and in grave danger. Your cousins came into Freeman's looking for you after the shooting at the Illini game. I tracked you here when they told me you were involved in the shooting, but obviously, I was too late. I'm so sorry. We've known that Helen was an undercover spy planted by David Lee's organization for some time. Did everyone get away? Did you see where they went?"

Speaking to Agent Harmon and Christine, Eric breathlessly says, "Well, Brian saved my life, then got shot, and I almost died too. David kicked my butt, but I hip-bucked him into an auger. He lost most of his right arm from what I could see. Everyone got away, except for Helen." Eric stares into the dark night.

"What happened to her?" asks Christine.

"We were in that grain bin right there, and David had her tied up. He was going to blow up the whole operation with that bomb next to that hatch door. Brian and I were working to free her when David and one of his guys came in shooting, and Helen was killed. She's still inside the grain bin," Eric says as Christine bends over to hold him. "She was so brave in the end. It's terrible."

"Everyone, we need to get back behind our cars right now, please," Agent Harmon says forcefully.

"Why do we need to do that?" Jeff points to Brian. "He can't be moved right now."

"I hate to say this, guys, but the FBI does not want this information to get out into the public and cause a panic. I'm going to rearm that detonator timer, and we're going to let this blow up to look like a grain dust explosion to cover up this scene. The FBI will compensate you all greatly for your efforts and your discretion." Agent Harmon works to nudge the group backward.

"Hell no! We're not going to do that," Christine says adamantly. "You knew something was going on here the whole time and didn't do anything! You almost got Brian and Eric killed, and a guy was killed at the Illini game. Not to mention Helen was murdered tonight too."

Danny turns to Jeff and whispers, "Well, he was a Michigan fan." Jeff tells him to keep it down.

Eric rips into Agent Harmon. "I have no idea what you're even saying.. The CCP has infiltrated our food supply, modified chemicals for our corn productivity, and definitely has many other projects in the works. All of these projects will kill more Americans. And you're going to cover that up?"

"I am fully aware of your frustrations, Eric, but the FBI has limited resources," Agent Harmon says calmly, trying to pacify Eric. "We, and the other agencies, don't have the resources to track, study, monitor, and then infiltrate all the projects the CCP, the cartels, and other local criminals plan and execute. We need to be vigilant and concerned about full acts of war, like bringing down our entire water infrastructure or even hacking into and seizing our airline system for simple dispatches and communications. The CCP is currently working to disable our air traffic control GPS navigation system, which is what all airlines use today for routes, tracking, and coordination in major airspaces. This is simply an issue of reducing corn yields."

"You are a liar, Agent Harmon." Eric's face is flushed with anger as his veins pop from his neck. "I know, and you know too, that there are chemicals that are missing from the U of I that could create enough mustard gas to kill most of the people during an Illini football game. Or all the fans at Duval Field for a St. Joe football game. Or a Fourth of July parade."

"How do you know that?" Matt stiffens as they all perk up, hearing the ambulance well off in the distance.

"I couldn't figure out how the yields were being reduced around the three main hubs: this farm, Elevation Seeds, and Shafer Chemicals," Eric coyly explains. "I also discovered the inventory levels for Mustargen had been manipulated in our systems, which is what our colleagues use for cancer research to create chemotherapy drugs. In addition, we've had wildly fluctuating inventory levels of pantaphos in the system, so I assumed it was being stolen. I couldn't figure out what was happening."

Eric forcefully points down the driveway. "But when the last truck was rolling off out of here, one of the guards put David into the semi while he was bleeding all over the side of the truck. The guard then swung back around to shut the back door on the trailer. Guess what was inside?"

"Drones," Agent Harmon says meekly.

"That's right, and you knew it, didn't you?" Eric shouts at the FBI agent.

"We did," says Agent Harmon.

Jeff looks at the rest of the group, "I have no idea what you are saying, Eric. What's the big deal about drones?"

"Hey, guys, that ambulance coming any time soon?" Brian asks, opening his eyes for the first time in a while.

"They are almost here, buddy, but Agent Harmon here wants to blow this up in order to cover up their mess and buy us off to keep our mouths shut." Eric points to the special agent. "The big deal is that those drones were running in the middle of the night spraying fields that don't have Elevation Seeds in them and causing corn rot from increased levels of pantaphos. Isn't that right, agent?"

"That's correct." Agent Harmon averts Eric's glare.

"And that's not the worst part. That Mustargen that has been stolen can be easily converted into lethal mustard gas. Those drones are fully capable of being loaded with mustard gas, flying over thousands of people, and spraying the gas directly on them. Isn't that right, agent?"

"We have a plan for that, Eric. We would jam them if we thought that was a real risk." Agent Harmon stares at Eric. "I'm sorry, buddy, but this one got away from us."

"There is no way you could jam them without fully knowing where and when. That's just a crapshoot, and your main plan was hope. You just hoped that they would keep doing smaller things that wouldn't trigger a full-scale war. Then you could just do damage control like you're trying to do now. No way that we're covering this up for you."

The ambulance lights are getting close.

"No chance," says Danny.

"No way, Goldie, Agent Harmon, whatever," says Jeff.

"Matt, I've been around this community long enough, and you have too." Christine is really angry and letting Agent Harmon have it. "These people around here not only deserve the truth, but they are your first line of defense. If they are aware that something weird is going on, they will be the ones to keep bad things from happening. Look at what Eric and Brian did tonight, and the FBI is nowhere to be found. It's disgusting. A very sweet girl was murdered because of it. No chance you're blowing this up and trying to pretend like it was just a freak dust explosion. No way! And I promise you that you're not going to shut any of us up. Elevation Seeds, Shafer Chemicals, CO Daniels, and WH Group are all going down because of this. I guarantee it."

Eric hears the full wail of the ambulance and motions for Danny to guide the paramedics over to Brian.

"Over here!" Danny waves emphatically.

The ambulance pulls up, and Eric points to where Brian lies on the ground.

"We'll take it from here, but you look like crap, buddy. Do you need the hospital, too?" One of the paramedics asks Eric.

"If you can just give me an ice pack and a rag to clean myself up, I'll be fine," says Eric, starting to remember he got a bit pummeled. He looks down at the blood on his shirt.

The paramedics put Brian on a stretcher, secure him, and start to roll him into the back of the ambulance. "We'll see you at Carle Hospital, buddy!" Danny says as Brian gives a very weak wave of his hand and disappears into the back of the ambulance.

Eric turns to Christine. "How did all of you make it here, again?"

Danny says, "Jeff and I went to Freeman's looking for you because you weren't answering your phone, and we were worried about you after the shooting."

Christine nods. "I did the same thing. I called and texted so many times, and you weren't responding. I texted Danny, and he told me they were going to see if you were at Freeman's because they hadn't heard from you. I drove over there as well. Agent Matt here didn't know you were involved in that shooting at all because the news claimed it was a random shooting and nobody else was at risk. Then he heard that you were there, and I guess it was time for him to come clean." Christine is so mad that her face is bright red, and she has a blood vessel that looks like it could burst at any moment. "He told us he is with the FBI and that you were in real trouble. He pulled up the tracker for your truck and saw that it was parked in the back of the farm. We drove over there to find you. We woke up Aunt Lisa, and she hadn't seen you. Then we heard gunshots off in the distance and assumed you were in real trouble over here at this farm. Both Agent Harmon and I knew this was where the Chinese were located, so we hurried here. We were still too late to help at all or even see where they went. I'm so sorry, Eric, but you should never have come over here with just Brian."

"Goodness. That's a lot, but I knew this would be dangerous. I didn't want to risk getting you hurt, Christine." Eric turns to Agent Harmon. "If you could track me, can we track those trucks? Did you put a tracker on them too?" Eric asks with bewilderment.

"We tried a few times, but they aren't stupid by any means. They run sweeps on all their vehicles every day and every time a vehicle moves off this farm. They know we are here watching them. Again, they stay well within the boundaries of our gray zone war with them. They are very careful not to push any of this into a direct conflict. The CIA does the same thing to the CCP in China, Hong Kong, and even Taiwan."

Christine shakes her head again. "You guys really need to get better at your jobs, Matt. This is ridiculous!"

"I agree, and we need more great people in order to do that, Christine," says Agent Harmon. "This may be too soon, but it's something to consider, Eric. I talked to my superiors about a month ago and mentioned that we could really use someone who has your level of biochemical engineering background and courage. That's a tough combination to find, as you can imagine. You figured all of this out well before we did, and the FBI has been aware of this program for about three years."

"Our lab analysis shows this program has been in place for seven years or more with plenty of CCP analysts. You're not even close." Eric shakes his head. "Now I know what our old friend Mark from Tumble Inn was saying about operation Volt Typhoon. The FBI is a day late and a dollar short on all these threats, which makes Christine's point even more important. You need to be so much more transparent about the risks to our country. Stop playing politics with our safety and our children's safety. You have to know the CCP is playing the long game. The only people who don't know that we're at war with the Chinese are the US citizens. We need to get our heads out of our butts before we fully crumble from within."

Agent Harmon extends his hand. "I do understand what you are saying. I have been around these parts for almost two years, and the people are wonderful, genuine, and true patriots. I would like to say it's that simple, but it's just not. When I discuss these exact points with my superiors, they quickly pivot to 'global economic interdependence,'" Agent Harmon flashes air quotes. "Many of them buy into the notion that if China and the US are both dependent on each other economically, then we will never get to a full-scale war. That's beyond naïve and short-sighted to me, but I am just doing my job here the best I can. Now, we have five people here. Would you like a ride back to your truck, Eric? I can't fit everyone, so I can't get you guys back to Freeman's. Can you find a way?"

"I'll take them to Freeman's and their cars, no problem," says Eric. His face continues to throb from David pounding on it; however, the ice is helping to numb the pain. "Agent Harmon, what about Helen, though? Her family needs to have closure."

"I'll take it from here with the local police as well," says Agent Harmon. "You all need to get home and get some rest. Christine, please watch Eric tonight for signs of a concussion."

"Shove it," Christine snaps. "And you're not driving anywhere, Eric."

"Right . . ." Agent Harmon avoids Christine's glare again.

Christine drops the boys off at their homes in the country, as they decide to get their cars in the morning from Freeman's. It has been a long day already, so Christine takes Eric home. He heads straight for the shower to wash the blood out of his hair and run hot water over his aching body. As he heads to bed, he dumps his bloody clothes into the trash and quickly passes out under the sheets.

The next morning, Eric wakes up to a very lively Christine, who has breakfast made. His iPad is sitting on the table. Christine sets down the breakfast and says, "Here you go. I hope you're feeling better. Take a look at today's *News-Gazette* on the iPad."

Eric reads the headline out loud, shaking his head, "'Royal Dust Explosion Destroys Farm.' I really don't like Agent Harmon."

"I really, really don't like him," Christine agrees, then begins to blush immediately. "Oh, and sorry about sort of flipping my lid last night. My emotions were really raw, and I, well, thought I had lost you."

# CHAPTER 22
# MORE DISCORD

"Where is my niece's body, David?" General Houbin asks David sternly. They are inside a drab top-secret conference room in the Ministry of State Security in Yidongyuan compound in Beijing, China.

General Houbin has summoned David and his team to his headquarters to personally express his disappointment in their operations falling apart. The compound is nestled deep inside Beijing's city limits, just blocks from the Central Party School of the Communist Party of China. David and his team know this area very well from their time rising through the ranks for decades before they became senior enough for international espionage.

"The FBI triggered the C4 detonation, sir. I believe that Helen's body was eliminated in that explosion," David says confidently. "The lead researcher's police officer friend inadvertently shot and killed her while we were escaping from the farm. I believe the FBI put her body inside the grain bin, then detonated the C4 to hide all evidence of our operations and evidence of our outsmarting them."

"Understood. My sister will be devastated, but we know the price of war. I will handle that," Houbin states firmly.

"Yes, sir," David says, sitting at attention next to his humble, or more like humiliated, team leaders, Z, Tom, and Chinaloa.

"Thao, are you still on the line?" asks Houbin, leaning into the speakerphone.

"Yes, sir," Thao snaps from the other end of the encrypted call.

"What is the plan for Elevation and Shafer now that they are compromised?" General Houbin sits back in his seat to listen.

"Sir," Thao speaks softly, and the group leans in to hear better. "The local people, especially the farmers, have been told by Eric Buchanan and Mitch Osterbur that the explosion was not an accident and that it was a Chinese operation that went bad. The reality is Buchanan and Osterbur did figure out all aspects of our espionage and yield reduction program, including the drones and the mustard gas. Both of them and their friends have been very public about it."

Chinaloa turns around and looks through the plate glass window behind her. General Houbin isn't paying a ton of attention again. He is staring past Chinaloa and through the window behind her because he likes to see the activity of Kunming Lake. David smirks a bit, seeing Chinaloa realize the general is not just blankly staring at her, then thinks to himself, *Stay long enough with the military, and he, too, can be just short of worthless but absolutely feared.*

Thao finishes her status update: "We created a counter-story through our connections inside the *Chicago Tribune*, but it is not working effectively. Sales for Elevation Seeds to farmers and sales for Shafer Chemicals to other seed companies have plummeted. I do not see us being able to recover, and we need to sell those companies immediately or just shutter them."

David, rather wide-eyed, now looks at his team with disappointment and a little fear. They are hoping this is just a verbal thrashing and nothing more sinister. All are still jet-lagged from General Houbin forcing them to drive back to Jacumba Hot Springs, cross the border, and even fly commercial from Tijuana to Beijing in disgrace. Chinaloa looks like she's aged five years from the trip alone.

Thao mutters something over the phone. David says, "Thao, please lean forward into the speakerphone while you're talking. We can't understand you."

"Sorry," Thao says, although David can almost hear her roll her eyes. "We have changed the name of our holding company, CO Daniels, to Kimber Alcott Murphy and Siems, since a few people did connect the dots. That new entity will continue to be our general partner for our land acquisitions, and we have hired more lawyers to make our front company look like a law firm. In addition, we can use some more friendly lawyers to help us navigate the legal system here as well. The reality is also that our land acquisitions over the past ten years have been wonderful investments for us, so we do need to properly maintain those and keep them legal in all aspects of US law. If we do need to refinance them for additional funds, that is an option, sir."

"Unacceptable!" Houbin pounds the table and looks to his direct left at David. "All of this work, money, and time, and it's all shut down. Very disappointing, David."

"General Houbin, I am very sorry," David apologizes again and quickly bows his head. "But please remember we caused significant disruptions over the past seven years, and we have learned so much about how to infiltrate US systems and colleges and install dormant spies into key positions. We were able to collect extremely significant information about US technology, chemical storage, and inventory management practices and install backdoor access into their primary infrastructure systems. In addition, I believe the seed technology that we stole has garnered extremely rewarding gains that reduce our our food supply risks in the mainland."

"I do agree with that, David." The general calms down and sits back in his chair. "Now, what is the status of the nuclear and aquifer projects and Thousand Talents Plan?"

"Those are still all going very well, general," David continues. "Z is still leading our food supply espionage, even after our setback with Elevation Seeds. He has recruited a higher-level agent from Fayetteville, Arkansas. He is a graduate of the University of Arkansas and has a PhD in Poultry Science. Again, we will leverage a lot of what we learned from the University of Illinois activities and apply it to countless future projects. His recruit has been installed at Tyson Foods in Springdale, Arkansas, in their distribution department."

"Very good. How did you find this recruit? Was it through the Thousand Talents Plan?" asks the general with piqued interest in his pet project.

"Of course, sir." David finds a bit more courage. "As you know, we are sending thousands of students abroad, mostly to the United States, to become experts in many areas of industry and science. The program, still called Qiming, has been a huge success for us in finding, recruiting, and installing top-level students into sensitive positions throughout the world. I am in contact weekly with the Ministry of Industry and Information Technology to make sure we are heavily focused on the success of this program."

"Very good, David. What about infrastructure?" General Houbin continues to be intrigued.

"That too is progressing well, sir, but will take a little longer than expected. Tom," David points across the table as Tom sits up straighter, "leads our infrastructure projects and is focused on penetrating the Clinton nuclear facility's controls. He has spent years studying Stuxnet's successes, failures, and project approach."

"What did you learn from Stuxnet? I'm somewhat aware of that project." The general turns to the right to listen to Tom.

Tom looks directly into the general's eyes to maintain his attention. "When the Americans and Israelis created that computer virus, or worm, back in the early 2000s, they were very smart and realistic about the capabilities of the Iranian nuclear facility they were targeting. Ultimately, this computer worm had many more uses, like most of the malware we create. The project engineers realized that attacking the most advanced systems and software was a lot riskier than figuring out the backend network, which is the gatekeeper to those systems. In this case, the Siemens Step7 software was the main target. So, they built their virus to target

Microsoft Windows operating systems. Then, the virus would seek out the Step7 software. That software was not capable of identifying viruses at the time, so the virus ultimately landed on the SCADA, supervisory control and data acquisition, systems of the Iranian nuclear facility control panels." Tom finishes, wipes the sweat off his brow, and grabs a glass of water.

"That's right. Do I remember correctly that Stuxnet would modify the code of the control panels but return no error messages to the panel when the feedback loop was complete?" the general queries Tom.

"Yes, sir. The programmable logic controllers, the PLCs, were compromised at that point by the virus, and ultimately, that worm infected over two hundred thousand computers. It literally destroyed over a thousand nuclear centrifuges and took almost 20 percent of the Iranian nuclear capabilities out over the course of a few months. It was a huge success and one that I studied in great detail. That is the blueprint for what we are doing at the Clinton nuclear plant."

General Houbin rubs his chin, thinking, then says, "Again, if I remember correctly, the irony of that project was that Iran had gained access to those Siemens programs illegally around an embargo, so they imported their own destruction. Let's learn from that lesson as well as we continue to provide hardware and software to American companies. We'll keep allowing them to import their own destruction from our companies. It pays to know your history."

"Yes, general. That is the plan. But ultimately, the Volt Typhoon operation was shut down by the FBI. The viruses that were left behind are still dormant and will be very destructive in the near future," Tom confirms.

"Tom, how long until we can prove out and use our capabilities?" The general seems genuinely interested. "We currently have economic leverage over the United States to keep them working with us openly, but we continue to prepare for an invasion of Taiwan. We need to keep their military at bay and relatively dormant for another year or two. Especially as we continue to build out our artificial intelligence infrastructure."

"Within a year, sir." Tom relaxes and speaks a bit slower as well. "We will be able to degrade a limited number of centrifuges. You can gently let your contacts in the CIA know that we have that capability. They need to continue to allow us to proceed with our projects, or we can shut down a number of water treatment plants and the cellular infrastructure. They have left us alone nicely with our money laundering for the cartels, though, so thank you for that. Those funds are being put to great use to fund these projects and compensate our embedded agents."

"Agreed, Tom." David works to keep the meeting moving. "Those CIA agents looking the other way with minimal disturbances have been critical. It's still surprising to me they can't see that they are the frog in the pot that is boiling. Maybe they do see it, though."

David moves the discussion to the water infrastructure programs. "We also have the water supply project that is led by Chinaloa. She's been excellent as usual, and Thao facilitated a two-thousand-acre land acquisition just west of Mahomet and south of Mansfield via our new holding company, KAMS. It is in the middle of forests and cornfields, but we confirmed it sits over a deep part of the Mahomet Aquifer that is rarely tested by their mobile testing units. The farmland, which is of limited use to us above the ground, is heavily wooded and provides our operations with great cover. We will inject a large amount of arsenic into the aquifer for a year or two before the levels get too high and contaminate the EPA testing sections. Even inside a year, the section of water that we're poisoning will be enough to trigger the closing of that aquifer for further testing. We'll just report it to the EPA anonymously. General Houbin, you can then use that information as further leverage. The

EPA will have no way of knowing if this is the only aquifer we have contaminated."

The general nods, an actual grin on his face now. "Very good, David. That project could yield some incredible results for us. We still have a healthy source of potent inorganic arsenic here in China and will begin to smuggle it to you via the cargo ships we're sending to New Orleans. You can pick it up from there and take it to the new property."

"That works fine, sir. We'll use the C8 as well in the meantime. Thank you," David says.

"Fair enough." The general acquiesces and seems content with the grilling of his fellow MSS associates, along with a well needed ego boost. "This group knows this, but we are playing a *very* long game here and need to be determined as we continue setting up the pieces on the chessboard in our favor. The next generation—or even the generation after that—will be the one that ultimately takes the king. Remember your humility, remember your country, and always remember your party. Now, get back to America."

# CHAPTER 23
# DUTY TO FAMILY

"I TOLD you I was hearing something. If you had listened to me in the first place, none of this would have happened!" Lisa carries the mashed potatoes over to the dining room table. "Now sit down and eat!"

The week after the explosion was a long one for the Buchanan and Harms families. The cousins were persistent in countering the FBI's planted story of a grain explosion at every turn, and Mitch crisscrossed Central Illinois to visit any group that would let him explain the details. The swelling in Eric's broken nose is barely noticeable now, and his three broken ribs are healing nicely. Broken ribs, it turns out, are remarkably painful and difficult to heal, with the breathing and all.

"She's not wrong," says Eric to Anna and Tina, trying to poke the bear. "You girls should really listen to her more often."

"Oh, please, Eric. That is about the last thing we needed." Anna points to the wall. "Her Euchre girlfriends already made her a satin cape that says 'Drone Commander: I Hear Things.' How did they even make that?"

"It's very nice to be listened to again. Thanks, Eric." Aunt Lisa turns to leave the table where her kids are sitting with the Buchanan boys, with Christine and Eric at the end.

"Cheers, gang," says Joel, who came in from Franklin, Tennessee, with his family to celebrate everyone being alive. The full group toasts each other with their Sunday red wine.

"I'm really glad everyone is still alive. That's really neat," Joel says, cracking up. "So, can you catch me up on what has happened over the past few weeks since y'all blew up a farm?"

Danny leans in. "Let's not forget that a very nice girl was also killed."

"Good point, Danny, but let's try to keep this a bit lighter today, okay?" Jeff grabs some more ham from the middle of the table.

"I gotcha." Danny looks at Christine. "Rumor has it you had a change of plans?"

"Looks that way, Danny." Christine glances at Eric. "I was ready to ship off to San Francisco for an artificial intelligence job with Nvidia, but now I've decided to stay around here with this guy to see what else he has up his sleeve for fun and adventure. I would highly prefer to keep it to Illini football and basketball games, if possible," Christine jokes.

"That seems fair and probably a good idea. We'll just see how that plays out in real life," Cousin Tina says to Christine. "He's been getting into trouble pretty much his whole life, and he almost seems to like it."

Eric leans in, pausing to emphasize his joke. "Or . . . we could move down to Frisco, Texas, have a couple of boys, and live in the suburbs!" Eric bursts out laughing.

"No chance!" Christine says, laughing with Eric. "Maybe when I'm old and ready to be bored to tears!" Christine turns back to Tina.

"But, Tina, you may be right," Christine agrees. "Eric says he may want to try to track down that David dude and see what he has planned now."

"Eric! You are *not* allowed to do that!" Eric's mom quickly emerges from nowhere. "You almost got killed last time. I will not allow it!"

"I was just a bit unprepared the first time, Mom. I'll be fine." Eric smiles at his mom as she shakes her head, knowing that he won't listen anyway. She goes back around the corner into the laundry room, defeated. "I've been taking tactical gun training and even started some Muay Thai classes. I'm also thinking of becoming a pilot. I'll be fine, Mom!"

"Where did she even come from?" Eric asks the table.

"Sheila is part mom, part eavesdropping ninja, Eric," Anna says. Everyone else nods in agreement, but the rest are too afraid of Sheila to say as much. "She may be five feet, two inches tall, but I will not be messing with her. You're on your own, buddy."

"Fair enough," says Eric. "Danny, is Eiskamp swinging by today? How's he feeling?"

"He's doing well overall," Danny updates the group. "His belly is healing up where he got shot, and he's walking around just fine as far as I can tell. He says he's going to be back to work full-time in another couple of weeks. I told him we're all over here, so he'll be swinging by any minute. He misses Goldie at Freeman Tavern, though. Oddly, so do I. You just can't replace that funny accent of his. Have you heard from him, Eric?"

"He did call me about a week ago to check in. He was still hinting around to see if I could help the FBI out a bit on some cases. I guess I'm considering it, but I really just want to hang out for a few weeks." Eric looks over at Christine. "And I probably need to convince more than just Mom of what I want to do now. We're still having a lot of fun at the lab doing incredible research, and we have a great team. I can tell you, though, I'm vetting my team and analysts very, very thoroughly now."

Aunt Lisa, in her happy place, is doing dishes and watching the cars roll up and down the country road right outside her window. She calmly says, "Mitch is here," and goes back to work.

"Nice," says Jeff. "You guys aren't going to believe what he's been up to."

"What's he been doing?" asks Christine.

Danny chimes in, "Just give it a minute. He'll need to be the one who tells you."

"Mitch!" the table echoes as he walks into the kitchen with Marsha.

"And Marsha!" Joel adds on.

"I get it. I get it. Mitch is the hero, and I'm just his side action," Marsha says, laughing and using her hands to highlight herself from the neck down while dipping down on one knee.

"What are we hearing about something special?" asks Cory.

"Who, me?" Mitch grins. "Well, I'm still mad that the Chinese were able to get this far into our country's ag industry, and I really prefer it doesn't happen again. So, I started a new organization. I have our state senator's backing, as well as several other legislators. We're working to create and pass, key word there, legislation surrounding ownership of our farmland, background checks on foreign companies, and making sure that we're not handing our food supply over to bad actors. Currently, we're working to ban China, Russia, Iran, Iraq, and Venezuela from owning any land inside the United States. We'll start with some easier progress, such as farmland and land around military installations."

"Nice, Mitch!" Joel golf claps. "Very nice job. So far, so good?"

"It's early, Joel, but as more people find out and understand the full extent of the risks that are not going to stop out here—until we stop them, that is—the more likely it will be to turn into common sense in the near future. The main initiative is called 'Farmland is Our Land.'"

Danny chimes in, "That's not bad at all, Mitch. Who came up with that for you? That's probably the important stuff, but tell us what else you have." Danny starts to crack up a bit. "You going to be a big movie star now too?"

"Yeah, yeah. I've been chatting with Mike Rowe's team about a new show. Mike heard about what was going on out here in Central Illinois, and it really got his attention. He said he's been very concerned about this for probably twenty years. He wants to shoot a show, but just one season for now to see how it goes. He wants to call it *Farmers for America II*, which builds off his first show..." Mitch's voice trails off as he blushes from the attention.

"It's very cool, you guys. Mitch has been incredible." Marsha jumps in as Mitch starts to clam up. "He's been walking them through the data he gathered and gave to Eric that broke this whole thing open. They love it and want to keep supporting him as well. Mitch is going to be heading up to Chicago next week to try to work out some more details with them."

"Ya don't say," says Jeff as he stands up and shakes Mitch's hand. "I thought you were royalty because of where you lived, but now you're going to be a Hollywood star?"

"Easy, easy, guys. The main thing for me is that we protect our land, our food, and our families. Do me a favor and don't forget the lessons we have all learned from this. Do not sell your land to bad actors, and you better know who you are selling it to." Mitch is getting a bit agitated.

Aunt Lisa turns around and says in her unmistakable, coarse voice, "Brian Eiskamp is here. Joel, text your dad that he's arrived. He wanted me to tell you." She goes back to doing dishes with a wry smile on her face, like she knows something that no one else does.

"Yeah, where is your dad, Joel? I haven't seen him for a minute," asks Mitch.

"You'll see," says Joel. "You know what? Brian is hurting a bit right now. Let's go meet him outside. Cory, you have your stuff?"

"On it," replies Cory, getting up and walking toward the garage.

"All of us need to go?" Anna looks at everyone walking away. "What's going on here?"

"Just head outside, Anna. Come on now," says Joel as he shepherds the others out of the kitchen, through the garage, and into the driveway.

Brian gets out of his truck. "Well, hey, guys! You didn't need to come out here like this. I can make it inside. I'm good."

"Hey, Brian, how are you feeling?" Eric asks. "Yeah, not sure what's going on here. Joel seems to have some plan."

"That's shocking," Brian says. "What's the plan?"

"Oh my goodness!" Tina shrieks in excitement, and everyone turns toward the driveway.

Eric's dad is slowly driving a beautiful baby blue antique convertible that is almost twenty feet long. The 1963 Pontiac Bonneville has spinner wheels with whitewall tires and extended fender skirts on the back of the car.

"I can't believe it." Brian starts to walk toward the car.

Les slowly pulls up, and the group gathers around. Eric explains to his confused girlfriend, "Christine, this is exactly like my Grandpa Buchanan's old convertible that I've mentioned before. It was his pride and joy. He would drive it around town whenever the weather would allow it, but I'm not sure he ever made it over forty-five miles per hour."

"But we did!" Cory jumps in, holding a case of Coors Light.

Les gets out of the car and flips the keys to Brian. "Here you go, buddy. I've spent the past few weeks finding a Bonneville that was just like my dad's. I think we got close. I know how much he meant to you and the time that you spent with him in his convertible. We wanted to let you know how much it meant to us that you risked your life to go with Eric and ultimately saved his. This is yours."

"Mr. Buchanan, this is incredible, but what do you mean by 'yours?'" Brian gets choked up.

Cory strolls up and slaps Brian on the back. "It's yours, buddy. Now let's go look at some crops!" Cory lifts the case of beer.

Brian looks at Eric with a furrowed brow and arms open trying to understand.

"Don't look at me, Brian. I had no idea, but that's so cool! I still really appreciate you saving my life." Eric smiles and gives Brian a hug.

"I'm still not sure how we're counting that as saving your life, but I'll take the credit." Brian shakes his head. "Saving a life does

## DUTY TO FAMILY

look better on my file than 'got shot and pulled out of an exploding grain bin.'"

Brian takes the keys from Eric's dad and slides into the driver's seat. "Like riding a bike! I do miss riding around in this classic. Les, your dad would always ask me to help him move a folding table or something. He really just wanted to drink a beer with me."

Anna notices Aunt Lisa starting to pace and strain to keep her eyes dry.

"What's going on there, Mom?" Anna snickers. "After all these years in the country, now you have allergies?"

"Leave it alone, Anna!" Aunt Lisa wipes her eyes. "I brought you into this world, and I can take you out of it. I can't believe Dad's Bonneville is back. I haven't seen that in thirty years."

"Whatever you say, Mom." Anna turns and giggles to Tina.

Cory opens the passenger-side door. "Danny, Jeff, Joel! Let's go! It's time to country cruise!"

"You guys be careful now!" Sheila chimes in.

"We'll be fine, Mom! We'll be fine!" Joel says as they all pull out a beer.

Christine tries to grasp the situation.

"It's okay," Eric reassures her. "Country cruising was started generations ago. That car may not get over twenty-five miles per hour."

"I have no clue what they are even saying." Christine turns to Eric. "There aren't even any crops in the fields. It's after harvest."

"Just an old joke. Grandpa Buchanan used to call it 'checking out the crops.' Cory calls it 'country cruising.' The main thing is that the guys just go drive around the countryside slowly and safely, then have a few cold beers and swap lies."

"Okay, but you're not going with them," says Christine.

"Yeah! You're not going with them! You have a girlfriend here!" Sheila says.

"Where did you even come from, Mom?" Eric laughs as Sheila gives him her best scolding stare.

Danny slides into the front seat. Jeff and Cory are already in the back. Danny turns to Eric. "Looks like you're not going to be able to make it. What are you guys going to do now?"

"Nope. Looks like we're not making it, but no problem. We've got plans," Eric says with some excitement.

"What are you guys doing?" Cory asks with a shocking hint of interest in his voice.

"Well, we're heading to Champaign to take the train up to Chicago, stay at the Drake Hotel, and catch a Cubbies game tomorrow. About seven rows back from home plate!"

Christine grabs Eric's hand. "It's okay, Sheila. I'll make sure he stays out of trouble."

Eric smiles back at Christine. "If not you, then who?!"

## ACKNOWLEDGMENTS

As the old saying goes, it takes a village to raise a child. Well, my village was Royal, Illinois, and this book is dedicated to all those who helped raise me into the very average person I am today. I often wish they had tried harder, but here we are.

To my parents and extended family, I hope this book brings back many wonderful memories of our collective childhoods in Central Illinois, from our cozy and safe town to throwing rocks at passing trains to beautiful sunsets and harvest moons. We truly have a special family, and this book is definitely a salute to the ones that came before us.

To my wonderful wife, Christine, and incredible boys, Blake and Grant, I hope you get a little better understanding of small-town living. The love and support you feel from your many "second moms and dads" can't be replaced and will stay with you for the rest of your life.

To the group that helped me get this book across the finish line, Mom, Cory, Christine, Teri, Smitty, Thao, and Stacey, thank you so much for the hours you spent reading and improving the book. If people like it, then I'll take the credit. If not, then you guys should have tried harder as well, but I'm so grateful regardless, as I know your effort came from a place of love.

And finally, thank you to Ashley Mansour and her Brands Through Books team for getting this idea from my head and onto shelves in such an efficient manner. I'm very grateful for the process, the soul-searching, and the final result of your incredible program.

## ABOUT THE AUTHOR

JASON BUSBOOM WAS BORN AND RAISED IN THE SMALL TOWN OF Royal, Illinois. After being worked like a rented mule by his parents and extended family in exchange for Dairy Queen and the occasional cheeseburger, he earned a degree in Supply Chain Management from the University of Illinois Urbana-Champaign.

Jason began his career as a strategy consultant in Chicago, serving clients across the country before completing a master's degree in real estate and construction management at the University of Denver. After being saved from being a ski bum in Colorado by his wife, he is now based in Texas, where he owns and operates apartments in the Dallas-Fort Worth area. He's also very proud of his two sons, Blake and Grant, who never listen to him, which they get from the family dog, Ricky Bobby.

But back to the book. Having grown up in a farming community and being intimately familiar with real estate and property ownership, Jason is deeply concerned about the rising influence of foreign investments in America's agricultural, water, and energy resources. With the growing threat of espionage and the covert efforts of foreign actors, particularly the Chinese Communist Party, he advocates for greater vigilance and dialogue within the agricultural community to safeguard the nation's critical infrastructure and food supply.

His debut novel, *Sowing Discord*, is a thought-provoking call to action for American readers who are not only seeking to be entertained by a gripping espionage thriller but to learn valuable insights into the state of their country's most precious infrastructure. Blending his family's rich history in Central Illinois with pressing modern concerns, Jason challenges stakeholders to recognize their responsibility in protecting America's heartland before adversaries, whether foreign or domestic, exploit its vulnerabilities—a process that, he warns, is already underway.

Made in the USA
Columbia, SC
16 July 2025